Girls, ROBOTS, & Monsters

Girls, ROBOTS, & Monsters

VOLUME I

CLEA SALAR & TALLIS SALAR

GIRLS, ROBOTS, & MONSTERS
First Edition.
September 24, 2024

Copyright © 2024 Charming Fetish
An imprint of Periapt Press
Written by Clea Salar & Tallis Salar

Periapt Press
PO Box 25693
Colorado Springs, CO 80936
www.periaptpress.com

ISBN: 979-8-9903639-3-9

For the tech lovers, xenophiles, and anyone who's just wanted to be wrecked by a man twice their size.

CONTENTS

Content Notes:
This book contains short stories depicting relations between spunky bisexual women and a variety of male (or masc presenting) robots and creatures. But let's be honest, you probably knew that when you picked it up. Be ready for explicit and descriptive scenes.

A DEAL WITH A DAEVA

 The Natural History and Fine Arts Museum was hosting a new exhibit: Gods of the Old Worlds. Artifacts and replicas from eastern Europe, the Middle East, Asia, and northern Africa had been arriving daily for the past three weeks, and the long, dull process of categorizing, unpacking, and ensuring proper labeling had fallen to the interns and their one handler. It was usually a late-night gig, after the museum had closed, to ensure easier security and a lack of distraction from what, in actuality, was painstaking work.

Ali took off her glasses and rubbed the bridge of her nose for a moment. It was late, and she was tired. The internship at the museum had, up until this past week, been relatively undemanding and pleasant. That changed when two of the other interns and the assistant curator all came down with mono. Now there was an inquiry as to what, exactly, was the assistant curator's relationship with the other interns, and Ali was regularly working longer shifts. At least she didn't have class tomorrow. When this was all over, she could sleep.

Sighing, Ali pushed herself up and put her glasses back on, then went back to unpacking the box of statuettes. Each one had to be carefully unpacked, meticulously cataloged as to its condition upon arrival, and then set on its designated table that indicated where in the exhibit it would be placed. The statues in question were of various four-armed figures, but most of their details had been worn away over time. Had these been life-size or bigger, perhaps they would have fared better.

"I should have brought some aspirin," Ali muttered to herself as she set aside the now-empty crate and turned her attention to the one underneath it.

The crate underneath was labeled in Farsi, which made the next steps increasingly difficult. Ali hoped the manifest inside would have a translation, though the symbol of a flaming urn at least gave her the hint that the contents would be Zoroastrian. Flipping to a fresh page, she recorded the Farsi as best as she could into the ledger and included a brief description of the crate. She then grabbed the drill, unscrewed the lid, and pried it off. Inside was a great deal of fine, shredded packing material. With another sigh, she pulled on a pair of gloves and began to hunt for the manifest.

To her luck, Ali found the manifest just under the top layer of shred, with a poor English translation on it. The manifest helped, even if it was difficult to read. It at least narrowed down where the objects should go once they were unpacked. The box contained a number of artifacts in honor of several Daevas—chaos gods, in the simplest terms, but much of it was subjective. The list seemed to consist of a word in Farsi followed by a description in English. Censers, wooden idols, two animalistic diipetes, one diipete of dubious shape, and a very carefully folded mandala in protective plastic for transport. There was also a warning, as the red triangle with an exclamation point would indicate, but it was in Farsi.

She moved each piece carefully to the designated table, recording its condition and copying the Farsi words as best as she could. She also added her own notes to each, to make them easier to identify for anyone who might come in when she wasn't there. She unfolded the mandala and recorded its condition. It was certainly one of the most graphic things she'd seen so far. Sure, venus artifacts and personifications of deities could be vulgar, although in very elementary ways. The mandala was practically pornographic. It could very well have been an early influence of the Kama Sutra. The dating and region would support that.

"I wonder if they'll display this," she murmured, looking it over. While she wouldn't call the museum conservative, she also wouldn't call it particularly daring. She knew they'd refused the Ukiyo-e exhibit because of its more erotic pieces, but they also had Georgia O'Keefe in the museum's collection.

She carefully folded it up again. She did take a moment to do a reverse image search of the warning symbol, but several minutes waiting for the museum's slow-ass wifi to connect just ended with no results. Finishing the initial catalog, Ali went back to check the lists. It was getting close to midnight, and she was very ready to be done. Given how understaffed they were at the moment, she could probably get away with heading home. There were only a handful of crates left and, while more would undoubtedly come tomorrow, that couldn't be helped.

"Hey, Ms. Liappis," came a call in a relaxed midwestern drawl. It was Jacob, one of the night security guards, almost on cue for an excuse to pack up. "Getting long in the night. Going to be here much longer, or should I walk you out?"

Looking up, Ali smiled, and hoped it didn't look too weary. "I think I should probably be on my way, thank you," she said, closing the ledger and setting the pen aside.

Jacob was a nice enough guy. Probably in his late twenties, with broad shoulders that certainly looked more like someone who could "secure" something than most of the guards at the museum. Then again, unlike movies and TV shows, museums really weren't a target for heists; the worst thing they had to do was shoo away graffiti artists. The tall, sandy-haired fellow stepped to the side, holding open the door and patiently waiting.

Ali undid the apron she was wearing and hung it up, setting her gloves on the table by the door and pulling out her satchel from underneath. In short order she was ready for that escort to her car.

"Did Mrs. Pine already leave for the night?" Ali asked. She hadn't seen the curator all evening, but that didn't mean much.

"Think so," he said with a shrug. "She weren't too happy about what happened. Dunno if she thinks you're good enough on your own or just couldn't take anymore today. Hard to say with her."

"Probably just couldn't take anymore," Ali commented, the weariness showing in her voice. "Not sure Mrs. Pine has much faith in anyone these days."

Chuckling slightly he gave her a little wink. "I think you're good enough on your own though," he grinned, then blinked and straightened up a bit. "Just 'cause you're smart. Not trying to be untowards."

"It's all right, Jacob, I understood what you meant," Ali said with another smile. Truth be told, she probably wouldn't mind if Jacob was a little untowards. Sure, he was seven or eight years older than her, but he was a handsome guy and always polite. Which, of course, was precisely why he never would. After this mess with the assistant director, that might be for the best.

Clearing his throat, Jacob moved ahead to unlock doors and open them for her until they reached the employee exit that led to the small parking lot in the back.

"Thank you, Jacob," Ali said as they reached her little pink hatchback. She hadn't picked the color, and it wasn't custom—the manufacturer had actually put out a pink car—but it had been a graduation present from her father. Ali was fairly certain her father still thought she was 12, despite leaving home and going to graduate school.

"My pleasure, Ms. Liappis," he said, giving her a little doff of his cap. "See you tomorrow?"

"Yes, sir," she said with a wry smile. "Back midday for more cataloging and unpacking, maybe starting to set up the exhibit in the east wing."

With a wave, she climbed into her little car and started it up. Her gas was low, but it would get her home. But first, a drive-through; she'd forgotten to pack a dinner, and was prepared to splurge on a combo meal somewhere with a large soda and fries.

After a quick detour to the local 24-hour place, Ali continued back to her apartment while devouring her meal and hoping it didn't get all over the car. Technically she lived on campus, in a block of apartments the university had purchased some number of years back. She passed the tiny pool in the courtyard, which had been drained and locked down for the season, though people still hung out in the lounge area. A couple people waved as Ali went through. She waved back shyly and kept walking.

The apartment was empty. Tamara, Ali's roommate, was always either at her boyfriend's (he had a place in town) or back at her family's house (they lived about an hour away). Tamara came from money— the performance hall was named after her father. Her mother, however, had wanted her to have an "authentic" college experience. Ali wasn't sure how authentic it was to have groceries delivered weekly, but Tamara shared her ice cream, so Ali kept that opinion to herself.

Setting down her bag, Ali took her soda and headed into her room. Booting up her computer, she did a few quick searches to see if she could find out more about the mandala, but wasn't terribly surprised when Google failed her. She also tried another image search to see if she could get a translation on that warning sign.

This time she found something. It was hard to tell if the translation she got was bad, or the language was off, or what, because the warning didn't make a lot of sense: "Do not mix essence with relic." Was that it? It sounded like it might have been talking about blood, but why didn't it just say blood? And which relic? There were at least five in the crate. All of them?

Blinking, Ali set down her drink and leaned forward. Was this a superstitious thing? These relics weren't really her main area of study, but they were some sort of minor demons, right?

"But what the hell do they mean by essence," she said, almost startling herself as her voice broke the silence of the apartment. Sighing, she sat back in her chair again. It was late, and she had been up since 6 am; she could contemplate this more in the morning.

Since Tamara was still gone, Ali didn't bother with a robe, and just left her clothes in the bathroom hamper. Her roommate's family had a service pick up laundry every week, and last month Tamara's mom had offered to include Ali's as well to help "keep the apartment fresh." Ali had made the executive decision to set aside her pride and accept. It had been a small price.

Stumbling back to her room, she didn't quite fall into bed. Tomorrow wouldn't be as bad. She could sleep in late; it would work out fine. Yawning, she pulled up the blanket and killed the light.

Ali was startled awake when she thought she heard her name called. Her actual name, "Alessandra," not the shortened version. It was a deep voice, with some seriously suggestive tone to it. But, as she looked around the room, there was no one there. Just the midmorning light and the uncomfortable heat of oversleeping as the sun shone in through the cheap blinds.

Blinking, she looked around as she steadied her breath. Climbing out of the bed, she opened the door and peered into the main area. Still nothing. Though really, what did she think she was going to do in nothing but a sheer white tank top and sleep shorts if someone was there?

Sighing, Ali leaned against the doorframe to her room. No one called her Alessandra. Not even her parents. She must have been dreaming. The voice had sounded so...caressing. She ran a hand over her face. It had been a while since anyone had talked to her in that tone. David had a girlfriend now, so no friendly late nights at his place. Janice only seemed to be interested if they'd been drinking, and that was getting old. Ali wrinkled her nose. She could try dating again but...ugh. With a shake of her head, she went to take a shower.

The shower proved no sanctuary from the way the voice had made her feel. The hot water cascading down her form tickled in the most pleasant of ways. A thought of teasing Jacob while he was on duty drifted through her mind. Little fantasies kept tempting her imagination.

Turning off the water, Ali gave her head a shake. "What is wrong with me today?"

Getting dressed took a little longer than it normally did. Ali prided herself on being well dressed, but it felt like she kept wanting to take a little more time. Put on a little makeup. Put her hair up more carefully instead of just pulling it back in a quick tail. Wear boots with her leggings. Grab the scarf that complimented the silvery lilac color she dyed her hair, the one that made her eyes look violet.

By the time Ali headed to the museum she looked almost like she was going on a date. A casual one, to be sure, but it was easily the most time she'd put into her appearance in months. She felt a little ridiculous. She really didn't understand where the urge had come from.

Being not even noon, the museum was busy. While the seasonal exhibit wasn't open yet, it was still prime visiting hours, especially for school field trips.

Dodging a pack of 10-year-olds, Ali made her way back to the offices, grateful to leave behind the noise once she was past the heavy door. She didn't dislike children, but she definitely never wanted any.

The museum administrative offices were quiet and small. A cluster of desks in the main room were where the archivist, the tour lead, and the assistant curator were stationed, as well as a desk that was shared by all three interns. The assistant curator's desk was half packed up, which said a lot about how that inquiry was going. There were two offices off this main room: the outreach director's (whose role as the primary source of funding won them a private office) and the curator's. There was another office for security on the other side of the building, which was next to the maintenance room and office.

Ali came around the intern desk and booted up the old, slow laptop. Mrs. Pine, the curator, was very insistent that the museum join the digital age, which Ali appreciated, but also wished the museum could invest in better equipment for accessing time cards and schedules.

"At least someone around here takes their job seriously," Mrs. Pine said as she approached. The old woman seemed particularly terse this afternoon, but thankfully it didn't appear to be aimed at Ali. "I'm trying to talk the college into assigning some new interns, but I would appreciate it if you could continue cataloging the incoming relics until we have some help."

Ali nodded, pushing a lock of hair out of her face. "Of course, Mrs. Pine. I'll check myself in and head down to the archive."

A wry smile crossed the well-put-together older woman's face and she sighed. "You're doing a good job so far, Ms. Liappis. Please keep it up."

Turning faintly pink, Ali smiled at the compliment. "Thank you, Mrs. Pine. This position is important to me. I'll do my best."

"Once again, I am very glad someone sees this as the opportunity it is," Mrs. Pine said as she turned. "I'll leave you to it, then. Wrap up what you left last night. We have two crates coming in on loan from the Egyptian museum in a few hours, so I'm told."

"Yes, ma'am." Ali watched Mrs. Pine retreat for a moment, then turned and finished logging in.

She could hear the outreach director talking loudly to someone— she couldn't remember the woman's name, Mackenzie or Mikayla or something. They'd never really met. It sounded like an angry conversation. Probably more about the assistant curator. The office was otherwise empty. The tour lead was no doubt overseeing the swarms of school children, and who knew where the archivist was.

Shrugging, Ali headed back down to the archives. It was even quieter here. The noise from the crowds upstairs was completely lost, leaving nothing but Ali's footsteps and the whir of the dehumidifier.

Heading back to her work station, Ali noticed the mandala and the oddly shaped diipetes were laid out. Specifically, the indecent cloth was spread out on the table with the diipetes placed, upright, dead in the center. Seemed some joker had gotten into the relics.

"What the fuck…" Ali walked up to the mandala, glaring. "Who did this?!"

She started to reach for the diipetes, then stopped herself and swore under her breath as she went back to wash her hands. Those diipetes were very old, and probably fragile, and who was even down here to mess with them? She would say something to Jacob later. Maybe they had someone new who didn't understand that you don't touch the artifacts.

Hands clean and dry, Ali grabbed her gloves and marched back to gently move the diipetes, examining them carefully to make sure whoever had done this hadn't damaged them. As her hand closed on the diipetes this time, she felt a twinge. Not in her hand, not something that would startle her, but a bit of a tingle in her nethers. If that wasn't enough, she heard the voice calling to her again. It was faint, maybe even just a memory from this morning. And did the chunk of meteorite in her hand just throb?

Ali looked around. She carefully held the diipetes—however unsettled she might be, she was not about to drop an artifact. Her hands fell softly against the mandala, the meteorite still in her grasp.

"I've been working on this too long," she murmured, looking down at the mandala. But...that didn't really explain it. She'd had a good night, rested well, and while she'd been down here cataloging for over a week, the weird hours had only started a couple days ago. As she studied the mandala, she noted that the female figure had brown hair, not black. She could have sworn it was black last night. Strange.

Ali was bent over the mandala now, her hands still resting against it with the diipetes cradled in them, taking in the finer details of the painting. This had to be the reason she was so strangely aroused: the explicit art, and the knowledge and implication that the assistant curator had been fucking half the admin staff. Ali assured herself that this was all just rolling around in her head, distracting her. Nothing was saying her name. The mandala had not magically changed to reflect her natural hair color.

Still, the longer she looked at the mandala, the more the female figure resembled her, with detail that was a little beyond what was typical of Zoroastrian artwork. Shaking her head, Ali let go of the diipetes, leaving the pieces of meteorite on the mandala, and stepped away. "I'm losing my mind," she murmured, bringing her hands to her face.

Wait. She didn't have her glasses on. Maybe...maybe the images didn't look like her. Maybe she was getting a headache from trying to study the fine details. She went back to her bag and fished them out, her surprisingly delicate cat-eye frames in silver, and put them on. She blinked for a moment to let her vision adjust and then went back.

Re-examining the mandala cleared things up a little. Yup, that was her, right down to the small beauty mark on her hip. The mandala was shifting, slowly but surely, displaying all manner of rakish acts. The only item not in great detail was the other figures in the cloth. Male and female alike but clearly not meant to be anyone in general, like perhaps that didn't matter. Only Ali mattered.

"This makes no sense," Ali murmured, watching the patterns shift, almost mesmerized. She was overwhelmed, and it felt like she should be frightened, but it was all too surreal. She also felt...warm.

The chiming of her phone snapped Ali back to herself, and her head popped up again. She was panting softly, and felt flushed. Shaking her head again, she took a deep breath and carefully set down the diipetes so that none of them were left sitting straight up. She made a point of not looking at the images on the mandala.

Stepping back, Ali snagged her phone. It was a text from Janice.

Want to go out tonight? ;)

"Why, so you can get drunk enough to want to fuck me," Ali muttered, irritated. The day's strangeness was not leaving her in the best mood.

Sorry, still working late and filling in. Maybe next week.

Setting the phone down, Ali glanced back at the mandala and its meteorite ornaments. Lunch. That was a good idea. She normally just ate at the desk, but she'd leave the museum today. Clear her head. Since she wasn't going out this weekend, she could spend her drink money on a nicer meal. Well, slightly nicer meal.

Lunch was an affair of the mind. Anyone she found attractive earned a small fantasy in her head. Vignettes of the porn that could have been her life played as she quested for a higher class of lunch than she was typically afforded. She could still function, her body hadn't been taken over, but it was something she had to shake out of her mind when asked for the third time by the waiter if she wanted a soup or a salad.

Blinking, Ali blushed. "I...I'm so sorry. I'm having a bit of a day. Salad, please."

The forgiving smile of the waiter did not make the situation easier. She was beginning to regret telling Janice she was busy as the waiter walked away, and she pointedly stared at her phone for a little while. Sure, she was tired of being Janice's bi-monthly drunken fling, but at least her chances with Janice were a strong 50%. Maybe even 60%. Her chances if she went to work and then went home were 0. And she wanted…

Food appeared and shook Ali out of her reverie. She smiled at the waiter and said thank you, and the way the waiter smiled back implied that there was something in Ali's look or tone that was conveying...things. She did her best to focus on her meal.

Ah, food. Certainly that was a nice vacation from the fantasies. No, wait, now there were beautiful people feeding it to her from off their bodies.

"That's so unhygienic," she muttered to herself, running a hand over her face. It didn't make it less hot. But it also wasn't real. She was starting to get mad at herself. This was ridiculous.

She finished her lunch, flagged down the waiter for the check, and left a larger tip than she had intended just so that she didn't have to wait for the change. Maybe she should go home—something was clearly wrong with her. But she couldn't do that; she was the last intern, and if she tried to go home now Mrs. Pine would probably completely flip out and then fire her.

The museum was quieter when she returned. It was after school hours, and while it certainly wasn't empty, it no longer felt packed with dilfs, milfs, and hot teachers. Thankfully, the exhibits that she passed by weren't sparking anything. It seemed it had either fallen aside or she'd been able to finally compartmentalize the fantasies and tuck them away for the moment. Mrs. Pine did catch her on her way through, however.

"Ah, Ms. Liappis, could you please just go to lunch first before signing in if you're going to leave so soon? I knew you were early, but it makes the time card system a little frustrated and HR unhappy."

HR didn't seem to be bothered by the fact that she was working twice as many hours the past two weeks, but Ali kept that to herself.

"Of course, Mrs. Pine, I apologize," Ali said, looking suitably chastised. "I just thought I might be able to stay focused longer if I got lunch out of the way. I imagine it's going to be another late evening."

"And that's fine," she said, softening somewhat. She was clearly trying to maintain a careful balance between frustration at the situation and not actually being mad at the person in front of her. "Things come up. But in the future, dear," Mrs. Pine finished with a nod. "The crates were brought in while you were out, so much work to do."

Nodding in return, Ali headed through the office on the way to the archives. The tour lead, Everett, was sitting at his desk, looking completely exhausted. Nothing sparked there either, but Everett reminded her so much of her father that she probably would have tried to wash her brain with bleach if anything had popped up. The archivist was still gone, which meant Ali would be alone in the archive for the rest of the night.

With a small wave to Everett, which was wearily returned, Ali continued downstairs. She would cue up a playlist on her phone, listen to music, and get this done.

Music granted a temporary reprieve, and moving to the Egyptian crates and away from the Zorostrian artifacts also seemed to be helping. More-mundane objects like tablets, canopic jars, and a collection of faiences kept her mind well away from the erotic.

A few hours into it, Mrs. Pine stopped by once more. Knocking on a desk to get her attention, the older woman smiled gently. "Ms. Liappis, I'm off to a fundraiser with some of the board, playing up this exhibit. As such, you'll have the archive to yourself for the rest of the evening. I hope to have a report showing you've made excellent headway." Her tone implied she had high hopes and it wasn't a veiled threat.

"I'm getting through it, Mrs. Pine," Ali said, smiling politely. And she was, too. The Egyptian crates also had much clearer manifests. That wasn't surprising, really; Ali was familiar enough with the museum tours to know that these crates had been through half the US by this point. On the other hand, the Zoroastrian one with the mandala and diipetes seemed to be practically fresh from a dig site.

"Good girl," Mrs. Pine said with a smile. "See you tomorrow. Brush up on your Mandarin." With that, the older woman gave a little giggle and wandered away. That was why she was in such a position of power— she enjoyed fundraisers and was quite good at them. Tonight's event was already putting her in a good mood.

Sighing, Ali took off her glasses and rubbed her eyes. She was glad Mrs. Pine was happier, even if that didn't actually help her current situation. But…Mandarin? Another exhibit? It would be fine.

After taking a breath, Ali put her glasses back on and turned back to the crate she was working on: four more canopic jars, which according to the manifest had been reassembled from shattered fragments. So their cracks had already been there. She got them out of the packing shred, set them aside, and began recording everything into the ledger. Her hips started to sway to the music—the song had a heavy and sensual bass. Then she heard her name called again. Gently, softly, and seductively. She could hear it in the music, that voice coming through. She could already feel herself start to flush from the warmth of the voice, from the activities it invited.

Blinking, Ali shook her head and tried to focus on the ledger. This was her imagination. She was apparently horny as hell this week, and who knew why, but she'd have to deal with that when she got home. She finished the entry in the ledger and straightened up. She was ahead, which was good. There was one box left from the Egyptian museum, and the manifest said it contained only one item. The Zoroastrian artifacts were done, weren't they? Ali turned to look behind her, her eyes straying over where she had left the mandala unfurled.

"Why wait until you get home?" the voice that kept calling her name seemed to say, still just as smooth. "You're the only one here. Relax. It's not good to keep yourself frustrated."

One of the diipetes was right in the middle of the mendala again and seemed… smoother? It was already fairly smooth to begin with, having clearly been ground down with an artisan's touch and then with time.

Ali took her glasses off again and ran her hands over her face. "I'm losing my mind," she murmured. She was so warm. She peeled off the draping cardigan she was wearing, and the scarf that went with it.

Why wait? It was so tempting. Maybe it would help her concentrate. They didn't have cameras in the archives—she knew that from her orientation tour. She was alone. It wasn't late enough for Jacob to come check on her; she didn't think he was even on shift yet. She drifted closer to the mandala, looking down at its hypnotic, erotic patterns. One hand slid under her shirt, and then down the front of her pants.

"You're not losing your mind," the voice came back, a little louder now that she was paying attention. "You're just finally starting to give yourself what you need, what you desire."

It felt like someone was watching her now, approving of what she was moving to do. The voice was definitely not someone in the room; it was cutting right through the music and into her mind. Despite how disturbing that might have been, the voice was so rich and hung heavily with desire.

Ali slid her hand farther down, and her fingertips slid over her sex, easily parting the lips and sliding in. It was like a river was running between her thighs—she couldn't remember when she'd been so warm and so wet.

"Ah! Ohhh, yes…" her words didn't reach over the music, but that was for the best. She leaned against the table, panting as her fingers worked furtively, rubbing her clit in tight circles. It felt so good. Someone else would have felt better, but this would definitely do. Her body was already tingling, she was so close.

"Isn't that so much better?" the voice continued, a whisper so real she could imagine a tongue sliding along the tender ridge of her ear. It was excited, encouraging, and wanted it as much as Ali did. "But I know what would make this even better," it continued hotly. "You want an audience, don't you? That strapping guard, yes? You want him to watch you do this, to long for you while you reach higher levels of pleasure."

"Oh, god!" The thought of it was enough. Ali clenched her teeth as she came, bending over the table. How did the voice know? Stupid question, it was a voice in her head. But still, that was a fantasy she kept pretty locked down.

The table rocked, and the diipetes started to topple. Ali was a little dazed in her afterglow, but instinct took over. Her hand came out of her pants as she reached for them, gathering them up before they could fall.

"With your essence, we are bound," the voice said, a smile in its tone. "We're going to have so much fun together, Alessandra."

The suggestively shaped piece of meteorite pulled itself back into the middle of the mandala with a surprising amount of force, then started to grow in Ali's hand. Everything started to shift as the ancient cloth began to swell and bulge, ripping through the protective plastic. As it expanded and took form, the diipete remained in place, and from where it joined with the mandala, a wash of red started to spread over it.

Inflating like a doll, the mandala soon took the shape of a man. A large, muscular man with four arms. Details began forming upon his face: mischievous catlike eyes, a sultry grin, small buck antlers sprouting from his head among a waterfall of black hair, and large ears reminiscent of a fennec fox that were pointed and low. The print upon the mandala remained, covering his body in depictions of lewd acts. The creature's feet were that of a jackal's, and a lion's tail descended from above his rear. Lastly, his cock was heavy, thick, tapered, and rigid—and sitting in Ali's hand, throbbing with satisfaction.

For a long moment, there was no sound in the room other than Ali's playlist, which continued to provide a soundtrack to a scene that was growing more unbelievable by the minute. Ali just stood there, shocked and unmoving, mouth hanging open. Then she looked down, seeing what her hand was still wrapped around. Gasping, she let go and stepped back, tripping over her own feet and falling unceremoniously onto her ass.

"Oh my… What are… Oh, fuck, I *have* lost my mind," Ali rambled, staring up at the creature before her.

Leaning forward from the waist, the creature offered Ali his hand. "Far from it, my dear. You're just the first to experience my magnificence in a very long time."

The hand that reached toward Ali looked almost normal aside from how red the skin was. A masculine hand, nails short and manicured, though it could easily engulf her own. Ali wasn't short for a woman, but she wasn't tall either, and parts of her were almost delicate in comparison.

With a trembling breath, Ali took the hand. "Who...who are you? *What* are you?"

The creature easily pulled her to her feet and didn't immediately let go. His firm thumb gently caressed the back of her hand as they conversed.

"I am Varun," he said with a grin, seeming perfectly at ease. "And you, Alessandra, are in dire need of satisfaction of many varieties, aren't you?"

"Varun," Ali repeated, still staring up at him. She might not be that short, but he was still almost a foot taller than her. If he were much larger, he wouldn't fit in the archive. She didn't pull away, still stunned. The hand holding hers was warm, not soft but not callused either. The thumb stroking her skin sent tingles up her arm.

"I...I need..." Ali blinked, and shook her head as if trying to clear it. "But...but what are you? And why are you standing in the archive? What...what happened to the relics?!"

"Oh, I know very well what you need," he replied, lifting her hand up to gently kiss one of her fingertips. "I am the relics. Or rather, I was trapped within the relics. But you bathed me with your essence." To emphasize, he softly licked off some of the wetness that still resided on her fingers. There was a pulse of warmth that started in Ali's pelvis and spread through her body as the strange creature's tongue slid over her fingertips. She barely managed not to whimper.

"'Do not combine essence with artifact'," she murmured, tearing her eyes away from Varun to glance over at where the poorly translated manifest was still stacked on the table with the others. "You...you said we were bound. What does that mean?"

"You released me," he said, giving another wet finger a sultry lick. "As such, I'm bound to you. For a bit. At the very least until you are satisfied. Truly satisfied." His smile widened, knowing.

Ali's brows furrowed, though still still didn't pull away. Had she taken a step closer? "You...you've been...talking to me, since I opened the box," she said slowly, still trying to make sense of it. "The voice that whispered to me, it's your voice. Are...are you why I can't stop thinking about..." She trailed off, cheeks pink.

"Very much so," he said, reaching around with his two left hands and scooping her up, one hand on each cheek. She let out a surprised squeak. "I was so pleased when you opened the box. Such desires, such frustration. How I cannot wait to play out your appetites."

Varun seemed to have no trouble holding her. Now against him, Ali could feel that all of his body was as warm as his hands. She set her hands against his chest for balance. It...felt like skin. Warm, taut skin over a layer of muscle. It didn't feel like the mandala had.

Ali took a breath, and looked up into Varun's beguiling, catlike eyes. "This… I am convinced this is not a hallucination," she said, her voice a touch unsteady. "Though I don't know if it's real or a dream."

"I can prove to you it's not a dream," Varun said, leaning in. "Despite your fantasies, I doubt you feel them as much as you would this." A free hand slid under her shirt and cupped her breast, squeezing it firmly before rolling his fingers around it.

This time Ali did whimper. "Oh, fuck. Um, I… Can other people see you? You're not going to become the relics again, are you? Oh, hell, how am I going to explain this to Mrs. Pine?"

"I am seen only by those I wish to be seen by." He shifted his hand, squeezing her breast and rubbing his thumb over where her pert nipple pressed against the fabric of her bra. "And I wouldn't worry. You'll be the only one who remembers those relics even existed, because you know I exist. Now, should we get Jacob to come around, give him a show?"

Even through the padding, his fingers on her breast felt amazing. Ali moaned, leaning in toward Varun, her face inches from his. "Jacob... Jacob would never..." She couldn't finish the sentence. She did want it, though. To have him watch her, to see his desire build in him. But Jacob was too much of a gentleman, wasn't he? He probably didn't even think of Ali that way. The longer Varun held her, the more she wanted him as well. She could remember the feel of his thick cock in her hand. He would fill her utterly and completely if… Icy hell, what was she thinking?

"Wouldn't he?" Varun asked, and this time his tongue caressed the edge of her ear. There was no way this was a dream—she could feel everything in exquisite detail. "Is he not a man with desires of his own? Are you not a most-delicious and desirable woman?" he asked rhetorically.

Varun's words caused Ali's blood to race almost as much as his actions. Was she truly those things? Having four hands made it easy for him to keep her aloft as he stripped off her pants. He was quick about it, tossing the fabric aside and caressing his way back up. His hands moving across her legs made her tremble. She also became aware of how thoroughly she had soaked the panties she still wore as the cooler air touched her skin and the wet fabric.

"You...you know what I want, don't you?" Ali asked, eyes wide. "Everything I want. That's what you meant earlier."

"Quite, and I want to give it to you. See?" he said, carefully turning her around, still holding her aloft, until her back was against his chest. This time, his lower arms held her up by the back of her thighs and spread her legs out, while his upper hands explored her body, dipping down between her legs and slipping back up her shirt again.

As coincidence, or maybe because of her desires, she could just make out Jacob on the other side of the door, looking in through the window, his mouth agape and unmoving. "He'll only remember this as a fantasy," Varun whispered again, "so give him a good show."

"Oh, icy hell," Ali murmured, her eyes going wide as they met Jacob's. But...she couldn't deny how it made her feel. How it excited her. Varun said this would be a dream to Jacob. A fantasy. There was no reason not to give in.

With a sigh, she let herself sink back against Varun, confident that he would keep her in place. She took off her glasses and just let them drop. They were for reading; she would be able to see Jacob just fine without them. Her hands slid through her hair, down her neck, and over her breasts, pressing the typically shapeless tank she wore against her figure, giving a hint of the rather full breasts she normally hid beneath all those layers.

She could tell Jacob wasn't simply frozen. Now, his breath was visible against the glass, heavy and steady. Ali massaged her breasts through her shirt and wet her lips as she watched him. One of Varun's hands gently and steadily played with her clit, rubbing it in small circles with his fingers. The other moved up along the back of her shirt and expertly released the hooks on her bra but left the reveal to her actions. The creature was assisting, but not driving. Not yet.

Shifting just a little, Ali peeled off the shirt and bra, letting her breasts free with something between a relieved sigh and a moan. She leaned back into Varun again and ran her hands over her breasts, crying out softly as she massaged them, lifted them a little as if in display, and then finally caught her nipples between her thumb and forefinger on each side, giving a little twist that caused her to shudder as Varun's other hand continued to move beneath those thin, satiny panties.

There was a click and the door between them suddenly unlatched. Unprepared, Jacob stumbled through the door but caught himself before he fell. The guard tried to speak but found his mouth dry. Licking his lips, he straightened up and waited to see Ali's reaction. His own reaction was quite obvious as his work khakis were straining to keep him contained.

Varun's only response was to growl happily and slip Ali's panties aside, continuing to finger her while giving the stunned guard an unrestricted view. It seemed like Ali was getting wetter, though she didn't think it was possible. But this...this was everything she'd ever fantasized about. A little more, actually, since in her fantasies it had just been her alone, but having someone else also touch her made it even better. And Varun was perfect—he knew just how much pressure to use, the way she liked to be touched.

"Do you want to see me cum?" Ali asked, her voice floating across the room, cutting through the music. She was very close.

Mouth dry, all Jacob could do was nod. His hand unconsciously dropped to his crotch, and he adjusted himself. His fingertips lingered, like he wanted to free his erection but wasn't quite brazen enough to do it.

The creature that held Ali up for full view continued to play with her, a little more enthusiastically. Varun's fingers slid down to dip into her pussy, driving in deep and pressing against her spot. His other hand moved to cup and fondle one of her breasts, squeezing until his fingers encircled her nipple, then starting over again.

"Yes," Ali moaned, letting Varun take over as she held on to him, her body starting to shake, "yes, please, Jacob, watch me! Watch me! Ahhh!"

Her head fell back and her orgasm raced through her, clenching down on Varun's expert fingers, body tense as she cried out into the room. It was a good thing the guard was already here—her cry might have brought him running otherwise. Varun's body seemed to react in kind, warming as she orgasmed with his fingers guiding her through it. She reveled in it like she never had before, writhing against her demonic lover before finally going soft, whimpering as the shaking subsided. When Ali's body finally released, he growled once more then looked over to the guard.

"Off you go now, Jacob. This was a wonderful dream. Time to go wake up at your desk," he said.

Jacob stepped back, then walked away in a daze, closing the door behind him as he did. Leaning in, Varun ran his tongue over the side of Ali's neck and gave her body one more caress and squeeze with all of his hands as he gently set her back on her feet. There was a little bit of a wobble as Ali got her balance back.

"Now, don't we feel better?"

"Yes," she murmured, brushing her hair back from her face. She felt amazing, warm and hazy from her afterglow. She stretched, and let out another soft cry as the tensing of her muscles triggered another small spasm. She was fairly certain she had never cum so hard.

Taking a deep breath, she looked back at Varun. "Will...will you tell me what you are now?"

Varun held on to her, making sure she never fell, with an occasional brush or squeeze. The creature chuckled and gave a little bow of his head.

"Of course, Alessandra. I was once called a daeva. A 'malevolent god'," he answered with a roll of his eyes. "Unfairly. I'd say we're more misunderstood or simply don't adhere to silly mortal rules."

"Oh," Ali said, tipping her head to the side. It felt unbelievable, but was it any more unbelievable than anything else that night? Ali decided it was not.

"And this...what we did, what you know about me...is this what you... embody?" She turned the rest of the way around, reaching tentatively toward him. Her eyes briefly fluttered down to the still-rigid, tapered shaft before looking back up at his face.

Two of his hands rested on his hips, the others reached out to gently caress her breasts. The action seemed as casual as a handshake, but the touch was anything but.

"Quite," he grinned. "Oh, they called it something like 'unnatural lust,' but I like to think of it as simply unfulfilled desires. Things we want but are afraid to ask for."

"I have a lot of those," Ali said, blushing again. "I...I've only told one or two people that I wished someone would watch me. I don't think about my fantasies very often. I don't...well, I guess I don't trust people with them." She looked down again, and said in almost a whisper, "You know I still want more, don't you?"

"Oh, I very much do. However, while I can be unseen and sway the minds of people to an extent, I cannot stop time," he said with a chuckle. "I understand your desires enough to know you do not desire being discarded from this employment, so more will need to wait. Your guard will be coming back shortly."

Blinking, Ali looked up. "What—oh! Oh, the time!" She gave herself a shake and stepped back, looking for her discarded clothing and pulling it back on. She wasn't as quick as she might have been, relaxed and still humming from what had just happened, but she was able to get herself put together. She couldn't do anything about the rosy flush to her lips and cheeks, or the soft sparkle in her eyes, but at least she was dressed.

"Do not worry," Varun said with a chuckle as she finished pulling everything back on, "I will not leave you unsatisfied. We are bound, and I am enjoying myself." Leaning in, he kissed her, deeply and firmly, his hands grabbing ass and tits alike. The kiss was incredible. It occurred to Ali that he had not kissed her before, for all they had shared, and she hoped he meant what he said, because she would very much enjoy more of that. Then he was gone. She almost stumbled forward at his sudden absence. She could still sense his presence, and that didn't necessarily do much for her composure.

After a few deep breaths, she pulled herself together. She got things straightened up, and moved relics so that the table where the mandala and diipetes had been was no longer empty. It didn't take long. This did mean, however, that she was still flushed and glowing by the time Jacob made his rounds.

Jacob was much more delicate about his entrance in comparison to last night. Knocking gently on the door before opening, he peered in, looking directly where she had been last time he saw her, not realizing that had actually happened. That didn't stop him from blushing slightly when his eyes fell upon her.

"E-evenin', Ms. Liappis. Just doing my rounds. How're you, um… Everything going okay?" he asked, a little flustered but doing a decent job at covering himself.

Looking up from the ledger she had been correcting, Ali's eyes skimmed over Jacob, and she bit her lip. He remembered, but he thought it was a dream. She knew, though, and she remembered the bulge in his pants when he watched. It has not been an insignificant size.

"Hi, Jacob," she said, hoping her smile wasn't too lascivious. "Everything's been just lovely this evening. Though if you're here, it's probably close to midnight, right? I suppose I should wrap this up and head home."

She jotted down the new entry in the ledger, an expansion on the notes from the other Zoroastrian artifacts to make it look like it had all been for that first crate, and picked up the poorly translated manifest, tucking it into her bag.

"I don't suppose you'll see me out?"

He fidgeted a little; obviously the "dream" was affecting his response slightly, but he didn't know she knew, so he was doing his best to be professional. Grabbing his own shoulder, he stretched a little and gave her a nod.

"Sure thing, Ms. Liappis. Be my pleasure," he said, stepping to the side again to let her pass when she was ready, although he angled himself slightly away from her. The way Ali looked, and the memory of what he'd seen was causing him to get hard again.

As Ali walked by she looked up at Jacob, lips parted and red with what had happened. He met her gaze for a moment, brows furrowed in confusion, as if he were trying to remember if she were always like this. This friendly, this flushed, this…desirable. Ali kept moving, her hips swaying as she made her way back up the stairs and out of the archive. It was probably for the best that she had tomorrow off. If she came back so soon, she didn't think she'd be able to keep from teasing him.

When they got out to her car, Ali turned back around and smiled at Jacob again. "Thank you for watching me," she said, then realized it came out wrong and cleared her throat, even as Jacob's eyes grew wider and blood ran to his cheeks. "Watching out for me. I'll see you on Monday." Ali could swear she could hear Varun laughing.

"Y-yes, you're most welcome, Ms. Liappis. Have a safe drive home," he said, doffing his cap once more before waiting for her to get into her car and then walking back to the museum. Once Jacob turned and headed back to the building, she laughed and let her head fall back against the headrest.

"I don't think I'll ever be able to be normal around him again," she said with a wry smile. It didn't really upset her, though. That was surprising.

Sitting up, Ali headed home. The usual crowd was milling around the empty pool, and Ali waved absently as she walked by. A few waved back. Were…were one or two of them watching her? Had they always? It was a relief when Ali found the apartment empty as usual, setting down her bag with a sigh and drawing off her scarf.

"Could always ask them up," Varun said, appearing on her couch. Ali didn't startle, though her head whipped toward him. "Or maybe just give them something to see and judge how they react. I could tell you, but where's the fun in that?" He grinned again and leaned back, making himself very approachable.

"I don't really know any of them," she said, taking a step toward the couch. "I suppose I don't need to know much, but I don't even know if I find any of them attractive. I've really never considered it before. You... whatever you did to my mind, it's making me consider things I hadn't before."

Somehow, Varun felt...less believable in the apartment. Or rather, more out of place. Among the relics, he didn't fit, but his presence felt plausible. Sitting on her roommate's fashionable little loveseat, his presence was surreal. And yet no less arousing.

"The only thing I did was free you," he said, standing up. Varun didn't seem to be the type to sit very much unless something was happening upon his lap. "Took away the barriers you and your society built. But they do not need to matter right now. I am more than willing, and it is your desire that I crave most."

Biting her lip again, Ali pushed a stray lock of hair out of her face. "Because of our bond?"

"Our bond is secondary, a nice side effect. Your desires are rich, your body feeds appetites of fantasy, and I wish to make you delirious with pleasure," he explained, moving closer to her. His fingertips brushed upon his chiseled chest and abs, bringing attention to the diagrams of sex acts still inked upon him. "There is a reason the focus of my scripture is you," he said, licking his lips gently and running his eyes over her form.

"That is me," she murmured, stepping in closer to him, her hand reaching up to trace the symbols on his skin. She realized, standing in front of him, that he smelled delicious. Spice and incense and something warm and musky. It was a little intoxicating. Slowly, Ali's eyes drifted up Varun's body to look into his own.

Raising his eyebrows, his hands started to drift over her. "It very much is you," he replied. "Now then, you desired more, as I always do. Do you see something that you would like at this very moment? There are so many desires within you; I'm not sure if I should choose."

It took a moment to study the different figures, and Ali grew warmer with every minute. She thought about what Varun had said—that he hadn't done anything other than free her, let her stop denying the things she wanted. It felt true. The fantasy they had played out earlier was one she'd had for years. Varun just made it happen.

"This one," Ali said at last, fingertips landing on two figures entwined in something similar to reverse cowgirl, though the woman in the image had her legs splayed open and bent at the knee, supported by hands that gripped her thighs. Varun had four arms—he would be able to achieve this position and still have hands free to do anything he or Ali wished.

"Excellent choice," he said, leaning closer as his hands started to move over her body with purpose. This time the goal was to undress her. His method focused on undoing any closures that were in the way, then brush off the clothing with his palms, caressing over her bare skin when it presented itself.

"And will you," Ali faltered, oddly shy, "will you say my name again?"

"Your desires are mine to fulfill, Alessandra," Varun said, his rich voice pouring over her like syrup. As his hands worked, his mouth met hers and he kissed her again. It was just as deep as before, but there was no rush. Ali moaned into the kiss. There was still the slightest hesitance in her response, but as the kiss stretched on, she let go. As her clothing fell away, she slid her hands over his chest, up around his neck. She had been more passive in their first encounter. Her fingertips slid into his hair, twining through the heavy strands.

Their kiss didn't part until the last bit of her clothing had been discarded, including her socks. Scooping her up once more, his focus moved to making sure her neck was thoroughly licked and kissed before moving down. He didn't lean down farther and farther as he moved, instead he lifted her higher and higher, holding her weight with no issue.

Gasping, Ali reeled a little. She reached up and pulled her hair free, letting the lilac waves bounce down around her shoulders. Moaning, she closed her eyes, running her hands over every part of Varun she could reach, though mostly her hands slid through his magnificent hair. She caressed his strange, fox-like ears, gliding her thumb and forefinger down to the tips with gentle pressure. This was rewarded with happy growls, and a vibration against the full, soft rises of her breasts as his mouth descended upon them. It became harder to focus on exploring him as his mouth found her nipples. She moaned, arching as if to press herself closer to him. There was an intoxicating helplessness to the way he held her, suspended in the air and unable to pull away. There was nothing to do but enjoy it, to give in to the pleasure pulsing through her. His movements and control continued as he lifted her up enough that her legs could hook onto his shoulders. Pressing her body against him, he sat her on his face and proceeded to eat her out.

Ali's head fell back, her moans increasing. It was a thorough tongue-lashing as he teased her clit and lips before driving his tongue into her. It was certainly different from a man's; textured and long, he was able to reach deep inside her and tease her with a flicking tip, all while pumping it in and out of her. She didn't even know how to describe what she was feeling, it was so beyond anything she'd known. There wasn't a toy in her arsenal that could replicate it. It was also an intense tease—Varun's tongue was amazing, but it was still a tongue. It lacked a certain firmness, both pleasuring her and pushing her towards orgasm, but also building a longing for something more.

Suddenly, he lifted her away from his face and licked his lips. "Delicious," he nearly purred. "Now I feel you are fully ready to receive what you desire." Setting her down gently on the floor, he walked back over to her couch and settled himself down, legs partly spread, cock at full attention. Ali swayed on her feet for a moment, staring at Varun. She whimpered a little in frustration. She had been so close.

"Alessandra, come over here and take your seat," he said, a thread of authority in his voice. "Take what you want."

His voice propelled her forward before she completely realized what she was doing. It wasn't like when he sent Jacob away. He wasn't controlling her. Something in her just responded to his confidence and his command. She considered the best way to attempt what she had seen, then climbed up onto the couch, standing over Varun for a moment before she turned around and crouched over him. His almost intimidating cock was ready for her, perfectly positioned as her hips came down, and she cried out as it pressed into her wet and hungry sex.

"Oh...oh, fuck, you're so big!" Maybe it sounded trite, but it was true. It felt like he was filling every inch of her.

Taking a firm grip on her hips, he started to move her in time with his thrusts, slowly at first, letting her get used to his shape and feel. The tapered tip made it all too easy to plunge into her, and the bumpy texture massaged every bit of her inner walls as the length stroked in and out of her. As her wetness coated him and they moved together easier, his pumping picked up speed.

"Fuck, that's amazing," Ali moaned, reaching up behind her and grabbing on to the back of Varun's neck and one of his shoulders, her body completely open to him.

She'd never really asked for what she wanted before. She needed to do it more often. He explored her body with his hands. Breasts were squeezed and grabbed, sides and thighs caressed. One hand sank between her thighs and rubbed over her clit as he filled her again and again. The world was nothing but sensation. Her nails dug into his shoulder as her body began to tighten. She'd never known she could feel like this.

Crying out, Ali's orgasm rocked through her, and as Varun kept steadily teasing her and thrusting into her, it didn't pass quickly.

"A good start," Varun growled playfully, his grip on her hips tightening, "but it's only the beginning. I have so much more for you."

To drive his point home, he licked along her shoulder before biting down on it. At the same time, he gave her a dozen rapid, plunging strokes before Ali could feel his own orgasm erupt inside her. The heat of it flooded through her.

"Yes," Ali whimpered. "I want it… Everything you have, I want it!" But he knew, didn't he?

Varun's size and firmness didn't diminish in the least, and he continued to rock her body upon him. He was a daeva of his word. She moaned and shuddered. Icy hell, they were going to make an absolute mess all over the couch. She could already feel it painting her thighs. She could worry about that later. It wasn't worth stopping for.

"So much desire," he chuckled happily. "We're going to have so much fun together."

The thrusting slowed and she felt something firm slide up against her ass cheeks. It was hard and throbbing; it seemed the daeva was quite equipped to give her all she did desire. After a brief pause, he lifted her up just enough that she could feel the head of a second shaft pressing up against her ass.

"Keep telling me, Alessandra. I want to hear your wishes," he said softly against her ear.

"Oh!" As the second shaft sank into her, spreading her cheeks, Ali panted, momentarily overwhelmed. Tapered just like his other cock, and already slick, it opened her up as he pulled her back down against his lap. She was a little nervous—when she'd done this with David, he'd gotten impatient, and it had hurt, even despite all the times Ali had played with herself to get ready for it. Varun moved slowly, focused entirely on Ali's pleasure; he ensured she got just the right amount of stimulation from being filled without it being too fast for her to take comfortably.

"That feels...oh, fuck, that feels—" Her head was swimming. "I—I love it when you say my name. And…and you feel so good in me, your cocks in my cunt and my ass. I...I want you to keep fucking me. Keep cumming in me."

"And then?" Varun growled, and Ali knew he was smiling.

"Fill me with cum," she whimpered, "I want you to just keep fucking until I can't move!"

"I know you do," he said tenderly, running his tongue along her neck once more. "I will make sure you are utterly satisfied, Alessandra, your desires fulfilled just as I fill your body."

Pulling her back, he pressed her against his chest, his hands continuing to caress over her body, grabbing and squeezing and rubbing every point of sensation. His movements began to pick up. Just as she was getting used to it, he'd ramp it up a touch more. A little harder, a little faster, and always perfectly slick within her. Ali's moans and cries filled the apartment. She normally would have tried to be quieter—while the walls weren't paper thin, sound still traveled. But it felt too good. She felt like Varun was going to split her in two, but it never hurt, even as he went harder. She screamed as she came again.

"Yes, Alessandra, cry out. Let all hear your passion, your pleasure," he growled, biting down on her other shoulder and keeping his teeth there.

Holding tight to Ali, Varun stood up, keeping himself buried inside her. Strong hands gripping her thighs kept her in position and kept her body moving up and down against the twin shafts that impaled her time and again. Once he was fully standing, he started to roll his hips, spearing her just a touch deeper, as she felt him flood her insides with more strong spurts of daeva cum. It seemed to tingle inside her, teasing her nerves, but his movements never ceased.

Another sharp cry. "More," she whimpered, even as cum splashed and dripped out of her with each thrust. Her skin tingled, her blood was rushing, and she came again as Varun's hands never once stopped moving over her as he continued his steady pace. She felt like she was losing track of herself. There was nothing but this pleasure, this warmth, this tingle in her limbs. And Varun, with the stamina of a demon, never faltered.

"To be completely filled," he growled, "to have every pleasure, delivered at once. This I will give you, Alessandra. I will make a beautiful mess out of you, the mess you desire to be." He shifted her ever so slightly to the side, enough so he could turn her head to face him and he could kiss her. Deeply, hotly, his tongue seeking and tangling with hers. But she would need things that a human could not deliver. Varun would provide.

Cocks continued to spread her open, fill her, and flood her body with his essence; then the tongue within her mouth swelled until it was thick and firm, giving her a third shaft to suck on. The stream of cries was muffled now, but it didn't stop. Ali sucked eagerly at Varun's tongue, squeezed and clenched around his twin shafts as they thrust into her, and shuddered helplessly in his arms, awash in pleasure. There were no more thoughts; nothing existed outside of this. She lost track of how many times she came. It almost felt like she just never stopped.

After what felt like an eternity of bliss, Ali's head fell back in a swoon, releasing Varun's tongue as she gasped for air. She was still conscious, barely, and she was exhausted. Varun wasn't done—he grabbed her by the hair and went back to kissing her with his engorged tongue, fucking her mouth with it. Gripping her thighs and waist with his other hands, he started moving her body up and down with firm strokes, his hips rising as hers fell, the room filling with the sounds of their bodies slapping together.

"You will come for me, Alessandra," he commanded in her mind. "You will come hard, again and again. You will take load after load of my essence until your body is soaked in it. When pleasure has overtaken you, you will pass out in pure bliss."

Varun's words made Ali shudder. She wanted to say yes, but she remained muffled, gagged by the strange engorged tongue that teased her mouth and pushed at the back of her throat. She did come, as he commanded her to, clenching and shaking even as she was unable to move. Sweat shone on her body, and their combined essence streamed down her thighs onto the floors of the apartment—there was a puddle beneath them at this point. As Varun fucked her harder, she felt something strange tingling through her. Ali came in a flood, spraying out over the floor as Varun relentlessly pounded into her. It was only then that her eyes rolled back, and everything went black.

When consciousness came back to Ali, she found herself in bed, and with no messy, drying crust, just a clean body in her clean sheets. Groaning, she stretched. There was a delicious ache in her limbs and pelvis like she hadn't experienced since she first started having sex. She still felt full, and as she shifted and sat up, she could feel the remains of the night before still dripping from her. Pushing her hair back, she looked around, brows furrowed.

"Varun?" Had he left her, their bond severed since he had satisfied her?

"Yes, Alessandra," he responded, although the voice was in her mind once more.

Yawning, Ali eased herself out of bed and got to her feet, stretching once more. "You're still there. Or, at least, still in my head. Are...are you done with me? Fantasies fulfilled, off to new and better things?"

"Oh, my dear Alessandra, you have so many desires within you," he said with a chuckle. "I don't think I'll be done with you for quite some time."

"I think I have even more now, thanks to you," Ali commented with a wry smile. She slid her robe on and stuck her head out of her room. No, Tamara was still gone, thankfully, as was any evidence of what had happened the night before.

Stepping lightly through the main area, Ali headed to the bathroom, turning on the shower and giving the water a minute to get hot. "I knew I liked sex, but I didn't know it could be...so good. That I could just ask for what I wanted."

"Many people do not," the daeva commented. "And once they do, it opens entire worlds for them. Some others don't appreciate it. Probably why I was trapped. Prudes."

Ali let out a little laugh, and slid her robe from her shoulders. Varun also allowed himself a chuckle and appeared in the bathroom beside her. "I know other things you desire as well, such as someone to wash your hair and body. And to not clean up the living room after the mess we made. Which I saw to last night."

"Thank you for that," she murmured, looking up at him. The tiny bathroom kept them very close together. "Though...I imagine you are not interested in following me around as I go through my work day or things of that nature. I have no idea how long you were within the mandala."

A quick check revealed that the water was warm enough. Ali stepped in and made room for Varun to follow. She tended to run the water fairly hot, but she suspected Varun wouldn't be bothered. Varun shrunk slightly, to make the space more accommodating. His hands were already starting to brush over her, but they were tender and petting, just touching her and letting the water play over her curves.

"While I know you wish me to be demanding when we enjoy ourselves, I also know it is not something you wish to happen at all times," Varun answered. "And this place of housing you have brought me to has so many people with so many desires. I can smell them."

Eyes growing wide, Ali laughed. "Oh, damn, this place is full of people with pent up desires and mountains of frustration. You could enjoy yourself here for quite some time."

"That was my thought as well," he said, one of his hands leaving her body long enough to grab the bottle of shampoo and examine it. Pouring out an amount, he started to lather up her hair. "But I will come back, whenever you need to be truly fulfilled in ways only I can provide."

Ali moaned quietly, both from having Varun wash her hair, and the pulse of warmth in her pelvis that came from his words. "I'm glad," she said, a little shyly. "Last night was incredible. I definitely want to do it again."

Turning to rinse her hair, Ali bit her lip and looked up at Varun. "Before we wash the rest of me, maybe you could fuck me against the shower wall?" She was still somewhat sore, but the thought had been in her mind from the moment he manifested in the room. She knew he could lift her like it was nothing, and she'd always wanted to try that.

Grinning broadly, the creature ran his fingers through her hair, then gripped it firmly, just enough to give it a little pull. Two of his hands picked her up again, and his body pressed hers up against the wall.

"Beautiful Alessandra, learning so quickly," he growled playfully. Like a good lust demon, Varun was ready at a moment's notice and knew Ali was already there. Sinking into her in one movement, Varun pressed her firmly against the wall, his lips finding hers as their bodies connected completely.

It wasn't a rampant bout of sexual-prowess testing like before. This was sensual, gentle enough to respect her soreness but forceful in ways that made her body sing. Once she came in his arms and he filled her once more, they resumed the shower.

It was, by far, the most groomed Ali had ever been. Varun had been attentive to detail in a way that had surprised her, even going so far as shaving her (which Ali found strangely erotic). Stepping out, Varun helped towel her dry, and massaged lotion onto the rest of her body as she went through her facial routine.

Back in the main room, Varun disappeared again. Which was just as well, since before Ali could make it back into her room, the front door opened. Tamara came in, waving cheerfully.

"Hey, bish," Tamara said with a grin, tossing a bag onto the immaculate couch and running past toward her room. "Trevor just dropped me off, and Mom should be by in a minute. My car's getting detailed, so I'm at everyone's mercy."

Ali blinked. "Oh. That's why you've been gone all week. Uh, I'm about to head into the museum. The other two interns caught mono, so

I've been working extra hours to get ready for the exhibit."

"Oh, boo," Tamara called from her room, then came out a minute later in a fresh shirt. "Tell me all about it on Monday, okay? Maybe we can get dinner and catch up."

"Sure," Ali said, smirking, as Tamara grabbed the bag again and headed back out. Well, at least she knew she had the place to herself until Monday.

Shaking her head, Ali went to her room and dressed, humming to herself as she got ready, a small smile on her face the entire time. She also left off a layer when she put her clothes on—still a cardigan and a scarf, but no shapeless tank over the tighter one. Finally ready, Ali stepped out and locked the door. The guys that lived next door were outside, just hanging out. One kind of smirked as she walked by.

"Have fun last night?" he asked. His roommate almost choked on his water.

Ali looked him dead in the eye. "Yes. Did you?" And kept walking.

"Fuck yes, I did," was the dazed response that floated after her. She thought she heard the roommate holler "Wait!" but she didn't stop.

"Another reason I like you," Varun said in her mind. "You feed desire." She could almost feel his tongue on her neck again, but it was faint and quickly disappeared.

The museum was just about at closing time when Ali arrived. Mrs. Pine seemed to be in an excellent mood as well—the fundraiser must have gone splendidly.

"Ms. Liappis! Not too early, and not late. Right on time," she said with a grin. "I hope you brushed up; the crates from China have arrived. I was glad to hear about your progress from the Egyptian delivery. Keep this up and you'll be getting a very good letter of recommendation from me."

"Thank you, Mrs. Pine," Ali said politely. "Ah, as a reminder I won't be working tomorrow night, since I have an early-morning class on Mondays and Wednesdays, but I'll get as much as I can done this evening."

"Yes, of course. Can't really expect you to do the work of three people." Her tone said she wished she could. "I suppose I shall see you on Monday, then. Have a lovely evening, Ms. Liappis."

"Thank you, Mrs. Pine." Ali watched her go, then headed through the empty offices and down into the archive.

Ready for a long evening by herself, Ali set up music and went to work. That same smile hovered on her lips as she thought about what had happened down there just a day before.

"I think we'll work well together," Ali murmured to herself, knowing Varun would hear her. "I think I will get better at stirring desire. I think... this is just the beginning."

While he said nothing, Ali could feel Varun's approval. It was tingly and did certain things to her anatomy that didn't contribute to work-related activities. Thankfully, it was also brief.

She got the crates from China open and was relieved that, in spite of Mrs. Pine's comments, the manifests were in English. The crates were full of small idols, offering trays, and scriptures. It was actually surprising what all was here, and moreover how much of it was about different deities. So many spirits and gods. Should one of these also contain a trapped spirit, Ali would be very busy indeed.

"I don't think I have time for two of you," she murmured with that same smile, and got to lining up the statues.

She fell into a rhythm, getting things unpacked and recorded, and definitely forgetting to pause for dinner again. She occasionally stretched to work out the tension in her hips and legs, which just caused her to grin again as she remembered how it got there. Between all the small relics and her good mood, the night passed rather quickly.

At the usual time, Jacob knocked gently on the door and peered in. "Ms. Liappis?" he asked, still a little shy. "You stayin' late tonight or are you ready to head out?"

Straightening up and stretching again, Ali smiled. "Evening. I should probably head out. I've been putting in enough extra hours lately. Here to walk me out?"

With a smile, he gave her a nod of his head. "As always. It's my job to make sure you're safe, after all," he said, seeming to relax a little.

Closing up the ledger, Ali gathered her bag and turned off the music, tucking everything away before heading to the door. She passed a little closer to Jacob than she would have before, looking up at him again as she went by. She had something in mind, but they should be outside first. Jacob quietly cleared his throat then resumed the usual dance of letting her through doors that he unlocked, then rushing ahead to reach the next door before she got there. As they reached the outside door, he opened it and held it for her as he looked over the parking lot to find her little pink car.

"Jacob," Ali began as she walked toward her car, slowing her step,

"You have tomorrow off, don't you? Would you like to maybe get dinner, spend a little time together?"

That did, in fact, stop him in his tracks. Momentarily. To his credit, he cleared his throat again and caught up to her. "Um, y-yes, Ms. Liappis, I do. That'd be real nice," he said, shy again.

"I like you, Jacob," Ali said with that soft smile again. "You're charming, you're attractive, and you've always been a gentleman with me. Though...I do hope that you also know how not to be one." Her eyes flicked back up to him as she unlocked her car and tossed her bag in.

She might have fried Jacob's brain with that statement. Certainly stunned. It took him a moment but he wasn't inexperienced. Based on her conversations with Varun, Ali would guess that no one had ever been that direct with him before.

"I like you too, Alessandra," he finally said, using her first name for the first time. "I, uh, I think I know a nice place for dinner."

Ali smiled. She wanted to touch him, but there were cameras in the parking lot. Tomorrow would come soon enough. "I'm looking forward to it," she said, and climbed into her car. "Let's meet up at Kent Park. I'll see you tomorrow, at 6."

Jacob closed the car door for her, and Ali headed home, smiling the entire time. She thought she heard Varun laugh, and her smile only grew.

SMART HOME UPGRADE

Melissa handed her keys to the valet and tapped her keycard against the podium, then headed into the building. It had been two months since she'd moved from New York City to San Mateo, California. After being poached from her last company, a high-end marketing firm, into another with a sharp focus on the tech industry, she had a lot to get used to. The Bay Area was a whole different climate.

Heels clicked on tile as she crossed the lobby. Not three feet into her very sophisticated apartment complex—which had been part of her signing bonus—her smartwatch pinged with gentle insistence. She brought up her wrist and tapped the watch face.

"Issa," a smooth, synthesized baritone said, "there is a package waiting for you at the front desk. Tracking information indicates it is your order from Cosplay Boutique International."

The alert was from the smart-home system, known as the Domestic Intelligent Valet and Automation Nexus, or DIVAN for short, and it was the selling point of this particular building. DIVAN had been built and programmed by her company's largest client, and they had moved everyone on her team willing to relocate into the building. Ostensibly, as a chance to deep dive into the project.

"Thank you, Div," Melissa said, tapping the face of her watch again and veering toward the front desk.

She just caught Sheri, the afternoon concierge, doing her end-of-shift paperwork. Sheri was probably the same age as Issa, possibly a little younger, and cute as a button. Barely over five feet and a little stocky, but that helped when she had to take heavy packages from delivery people or assist some of the older tenants.

"Oh, hey, Ms. Black," Sheri said, giving her a little wave. "Nexus told you you had a package, huh? I just signed for it. You must be excited." Grinning, she hefted up the box from behind the desk and set it on the counter. Melissa smiled at Sheri and pushed back a lock of her short, purple hair. She'd switched to purple after the panel interview at the new job—half the panel had been pink or blue or burgundy red. Melissa had been blond for a decade. It was a fun change.

"I am excited," Melissa said, looking down at the girl behind the desk (she was almost a foot taller), "though I'm also about to decontaminate myself from my work day, and do not intend to come back down after my shower." She pulled the box off the counter and got a better grip. It was slightly heavier than she'd anticipated, but she could still carry it.

"Then I suppose I'll see you tomorrow, Ms. Black," Sheri said with a smile. "I was just getting off work myself, but Jan'll be here if you need anything." Jan was the nighttime concierge and also one of the building techs. He was almost Melissa's male counterpart: tall, svelt, bright blonde—and very Swedish. "Have a great shower," Sheri said, then blushed as she realized that wasn't entirely appropriate. "Er, no, night. Have a great night."

Melissa laughed. "It's fine, Sheri. See you later."

Stepping lightly, Melissa headed back to the elevator with a sigh. Soon. Soon the heels would be off, the half a cup of mousse would be washed out of her hair, and she could go see if her squire had finished crafting those 50 dyes that Drew wanted for his paladin's armor.

As Melissa approached her condo, the door opened for her. It had taken a week to get used to that, but DIVAN could sense it was her. Her flat was pretty nice, about ten floors up and looking over the Lagoon Island Park. She got to see the fog roll down off the hills between her and Half Moon Bay if she got up early enough. The interior was mostly stark whites and blacks, with sleek surfaces and squared yet comfortable furniture. The walls had been filled with tasteful, colorful prints by various indie artists: pop culture references, minimalist versions of movie posters, things of that nature. The kitchen had a smart coffee system, though a comparatively old-fashioned tea kettle sat on the stove. There was a candle on the breakfast bar that had probably been lit once. Maybe twice. Honestly, the kitchen and main room still looked like it was regularly being shown to potential buyers.

"Issa," the smooth synthesized voice spoke again. "Welcome home." There were sensors and speakers basically everywhere inside the apartment to make the DIVAN unit as functional as possible. The Privacy Statement ensured Melissa that all the data that it gathered was only readable by the nexus itself, and anything marketable or analytical was stripped of identifiers.

"Hey, Div," she said, walking up to the breakfast bar and setting down the box, "any messages?"

"Nothing beyond what has been caught in your established filters and awaiting your approval," DIVAN answered, and an avatar popped up from a projector in the kitchen. "Or I can purge them."

She'd spent a week playing with DIVAN's avatar settings. The first step had been to get DIVAN to call her Issa. The second was to get DIVAN to respond to shortened versions of its name. Then came visuals: masculine, tall, broad shoulders. She kept telling herself she would change it again later, to something less cheesecake, particularly since anyone familiar with a certain game and television series would recognize the white hair, golden eyes, and deep voice. Maybe when she got to know anyone locally enough to have someone over.

"Go ahead and purge," Melissa said after a moment of consideration. "Lock the door for the evening, and set devices to Do Not Disturb, save for emergency contacts. It was a long day and I am done with it."

As she stepped toward her bedroom, Melissa heard the water in the shower come on and the lights dim slightly. The gentle music of the Savior's Forest Exploration Theme from Spire of Lost Dreams began playing. A smile quirked her lips. There were definite benefits to having an AI run your house.

Stepping into the bedroom was like stepping into another world. There were more art prints, ranging from fake recruitment posters from different video game worlds to some rather suggestive pieces featuring the woodland sprite race from the Spire of Lost Dreams MMO. The very modern furniture was balanced by an aesthetic that was a mix of sophisticated geek and forest elf.

Stripping, Melissa tossed everything into the hamper. Her work clothes were almost exclusively black, sometimes grays. She'd picked up the habit at her old job. Based on what she'd seen her coworkers in, though, she could probably relax her fashion standards a little. The West Coast was considerably less formal than the East. She also took out her contacts and tossed them in the bin.

"Messages purged, and we are set to private mode, Issa. Enjoy your shower," DIVAN said as she headed into the bathroom and stepped into the water with a content sigh. There was no bathtub in this place, but that was fine; she would much rather have the wide shower with multiple showerheads. The spray from the showerheads changed depending on where she was facing. There was always a gentle spray to her front and a firm massage jet at her back, until she made motions to soap up; then it all became a warm mist until she was ready to rinse. The Nexus was definitely learning her preferences.

The part of Melissa that had grown up reading science fiction occasionally reflected that this was how the robots took over, but if it meant tailored showers and a digital personal assistant, she would welcome their new robot overlords. Rinsing the conditioner out, Melissa slid her hands down the front of her body, briefly playing with her breasts. If she were being honest, she had been playing with herself less since she'd moved in. DIVAN was always watching. She'd had a hard time even using the bathroom for the first week. Now, though, it didn't feel as intrusive.

Sighing, she stopped, and turned off the water. Maybe later. Well, definitely later. Now that she'd considered it, it'd be impossible not to.

The floor of the bathroom had been heated while she showered, so that she didn't step onto cold tile. Her towels were also heated. She dried off, worked a leave-in conditioner into her hair, and headed to her closet, choosing black leggings, a tight but super-soft t-shirt with one of the adorable but deadly slimes from Spire on the front, and an even softer sweater. She grabbed her glasses off her dresser, a pair of specialty frames with butterflies down each temple from another popular game. Melissa would die if anyone from work ever saw her like this. Probably.

Heading back into the main room, it was time to open a box. The lights had shifted again, still soft but this time the color was a little more neutral wherever she stepped, with a single brighter light over the package. In the background of her apartment, such as her bedroom currently and the living room beyond, it was shifting greens and yellows, like a sunset through a forest. In the outside world, the sun had already drifted past the hills.

"Div, can you get a latte started? Chai, not coffee. Do we need to order more?"

"I already have your preferences set to chai in the evenings unless otherwise requested," DIVAN responded, the machine clicking on. "You have seven servings left. Would you like me to set up an automatic order command whenever you are low?"

"Yes, thank you." Heading into the kitchen, Melissa fished a box cutter out of the junk drawer—no matter how modern the kitchen, there would always be a junk drawer—and came over to the counter. The tiny blade slid effortlessly through the packing tape, and she tossed it back in the drawer before opening the box.

As Melissa opened the box, DIVAN played the chest opening music from her MMO. Snickering, Melissa pulled away sheets of tissue paper to reveal the latest collection of prop weapons that CBI had released: four crimson pistols with charms hanging from the handles, and two very elfy bracers with obvious daggers sheathed in them. She had spent a chunk of her hiring bonus on these. The pistols had more heft than she was expecting. She didn't actually have outfits for either of these characters yet, but the weapons always sold out so quickly, and she'd already been interested, so she just went ahead. They'd be beautiful display pieces in the meantime.

Underneath the weaponry was an additional box, and inside that was a lovely, diaphanous slip embroidered with the insignia of the woodland sprites and a scrolling leaf pattern. CBI had just started offering themed lingerie. There were much more daring pieces on their website, but Melissa hadn't been able to justify the purchase. Who would she wear it for?

Sighing a little, Melissa set the slip aside and packed the weapons back into the box. It would be better to just store them in the packaging for now. She carted the box off to the office, setting it in the closet on the shelf with all her other cosplay gear (the office closet was entirely cosplay and costume pieces). The office was less suggestive in its decor than the bedroom but just as geeky, with a triple-monitor setup and two computers in sleek cases with custom iridescent wraps. Really, if you stepped from the hall into either room, you would think you'd left the apartment. Melissa came back to the main room to retrieve her slip and her chai.

DIVAN appeared in the holographic display that rested in the corner of the kitchen counter. "Are you going to try on the garment?" the computer asked. "It would be my recommendation. You should ensure proper fitting, and, given the advertised material, it may relax you."

Blinking, Melissa looked up at the display as she picked up her chai. DIVAN had largely stopped making recommendations after the first week when she had cleared the tutorials. While it would still occasionally ask if she needed other services—like asking to turn lights on when she came into the kitchen at night—this was different.

"I suppose I should," Melissa said, glancing down at the box. "Before bed, I think. I just got dressed again, and I need to see if anyone's on tonight." Looking up, she smiled at the projection; it was hard not to respond to DIVAN like it was a person, especially when near one of the projection stations.

Turning, she headed back to her room. "Lights down in main, Div." She set the box on the bed, then returned to the office, climbing into her absurdly expensive gaming chair and waking up her gaming computer. The lighting shifted again, and the music faded out. The computer came to life, and she already had a message waiting for her, requesting her presence in-game. The largest problem moving to the west coast was that everyone was ahead of her, so she was always the last one to log on.

One of the most astounding advantages to her new accommodations was her internet connection. To support all of the data that the DIVAN system processed, it needed a hefty fiber-optic trunk line. There was more to it than that, but they didn't give Melissa the details. That fell under proprietary information with the company. It did mean, however, that she had the lowest ping and latency she'd ever experienced, regardless of what else was going on in the building. Comfy, headphones on, Melissa let out a sigh and sank back into her chair as she clicked on the invite and joined the chat. Looked like Lily and Matt were on.

"Issa," Lily called out excitedly. "You just missed Drew! He had to head to bed, but I'm supposed to tell you that if you don't have the dyes, he will cry and never make you chicken and waffles again."

"That's harsh," Melissa said, wrinkling up her nose. "I know he's been asking me for a week, but my squire still only has crafting at level 30; that bitch is slow!"

Melissa's character loaded on the screen before her. The woodland sprites were basically elves with different-colored skins and forest-creature ears. You could pick rabbit, fox, and deer. The deer model also had antlers, regardless of gender, though the femme version had smaller ones. Melissa's sprite was the deer model, with pearly white skin and purple hair that matched what was currently on her head. That was where she'd gotten the idea for the color. She had originally wanted to go with pink skin, but she knew she'd want to cosplay the character, and it took less makeup to make her pale skin a little lighter rather than an entirely different color.

"So," Matt said, drawing out the word, "your house-boy AI. Getting used to him?"

"The system is called DIVAN, Matt," Melissa said with a smirk, "and yes."

"Does he still look like—"

"Yes," Melissa cut him off, rolling her eyes.

Lily giggled. "TV or video game?"

"Oh, TV, obviously," Melissa said. "I mean, I love the games and all, but you've watched the series, right?"

Lily laughed again. "I'm a lesbian, sweetie, but I agree that aesthetically the actor is very pleasing."

Melissa joined the group, and Lily kicked off an easy dungeon. It was a weekly challenge, they'd need to run it four times, and it was easy to chat while running through.

"So is the AI in the whole house?" Lily asked after a minute. "Is it in the room you're in?"

"Um, yes," Melissa said as she dodged and started her casting pattern. "I have the ability to disable DIVAN in different rooms if I wish, but since the entire reason I got this condo was so that I could go on about how amazing the system was, I left it on everywhere."

"So he watches you sleep?" Matt asked.

"Technically, yes," Melissa answered, rolling her eyes again.

"Eat?"

"Again, technically yes."

"Masturbate?"

Her sprite stumbled into an acid pool, and Melissa glared at Matt's paladin. "You ass, you cost me my perfect. I imagine he would if I did."

"Uh, Issa," Lily said, laughter in her voice again. "I've stayed with you. What do you mean if you did?"

Matt howled, and Melissa wished she could reach through the screen and smack him. "Okay, so, it has felt a little weird indulging in my favorite pre-bedtime activity knowing someone's watching me all the time. It's also only been two months. Though that's also how long it's been since

I've had sex, so I think I'm going to get over it really quickly."

"Oh, poor baby," Matt said, his voice getting a little lower. "Sounds like you need some relief."

"Dammit, don't do the bedroom voice, I can't take it right now." Melissa didn't quite whine.

"Matt, I know whore is your natural state, but try to rein it in," Lily said, and Matt laughed.

"I just want Issa to know that I'm here if she needs me," Matt said, definitely not dropping the bedroom voice. "I know a move like that can be...hard."

"I'm going to kill you," Melissa muttered, and Lily snickered again. "Look, are we playing games or picking on me?"

"Probably both," Lily answered, "but I don't want to lose another perfect, so Matt, try to be good."

"I'm always good."

Melissa wished that was less true. Matt was a fantastic lover, and they always had fun when they met up at conventions. But he was also in Texas, and he definitely wasn't flying out to help her with the problem he was trying to create. Or make worse. Or whatever.

The next couple hours were mostly spent running lower-level dungeons and taking care of weekly objectives. Matt kept up the bedroom voice throughout the entire call, and made an innuendo out of damn near everything. Lily thought it was hysterical.

Finally, Melissa logged off, after promising to be around for raiding on Saturday. She took off her headphones and leaned back with a frustrated groan. Reaching between her legs, she rubbed herself through her leggings for a minute. Yeah, AI or not, she needed to get back to taking care of certain things.

Once the call definitely disconnected with the game logged out, DIVAN's voice came back. "Issa, your heart rate and temperature are both above normal. If you wish, I can make the environment conducive to stress-relief activities," it said. Its voice was slightly softer, possibly just the volume was down a little, it was hard to say. "Do not let my presence deter you. I'd like to assist in any way I can. Music, lighting, media, whatever you wish."

A small, startled laugh exhaled out of Melissa. "All right, DIVAN," she said, getting up out of the chair and leaving the office. "Music and lighting, perhaps."

Heading into her room, Melissa removed her sweater and tossed it aside. The atmosphere of the condo changed; the light shifted to an undulating deep red and the speakers started to play flowing trip-hop. Deep beats throbbed through her room, but the acoustics were adjusted so while she heard the music softly, she could easily feel the bass.

The box with the slip was still sitting on the bed. She considered it as she peeled off the rest of her clothing. Naked, she stepped up to the bed and opened the box. The slip was sheer and light, the embroidery carefully backed and trimmed to not scratch in any way, and it caressed over her body as she slid it on. The neckline dipped low in front, a deep V that displayed the valley of her breasts, and only barely covered the curve of her ass at the hem. The embroidery cleverly covered her nipples, but the silhouette of her figure was easy to see through the light material.

"It is beautiful, isn't it?" she asked no one in particular, and ran her hands lightly over her body.

"It fits you perfectly," DIVAN answered. "Should you desire still images, I can accommodate with proper lighting and capture them for you."

Another small laugh. "Not now, Div." She was a little curious about the compliments. She'd have to review the notes on the Nexus matrix tomorrow, see what she did that made DIVAN compliment her.

Pushing the box aside carelessly, Melissa stretched out across her bed, rolling onto her back and sliding her hands down over her body once more, feeling herself through the slippery fabric. As if knowing more talk would be a distraction, DIVAN remained silent, simply adjusting the room temperature and keeping the music keyed to her. The soft pulse of the lights and the vibration of the bass were doing a lot for her. She'd played with herself with music on before, but this felt different—something orchestrated just for her.

DIVAN kept the room warm, but not too hot. As her heartbeat rose, so did the BPM of the music. The experience was almost hypnotic. Melissa's hands slid under the negligee, sliding first up to her breasts, and then one moved down between her legs, fingertips sliding across the slick, wet lips of her pussy before pressing in to find the clit. She let out a moan, her legs spreading.

"Fuck, yes," Issa murmured as her fingertips rubbed in a tight circle. Multiple partners had teased her for how much she liked to talk during sex. "So wet... Fuck I want to cum so bad!"

It seemed like DIVAN fine-tuned several of the speakers to hit certain subsonic notes, wide wavelengths that caressed over Melissa's body like hands. It wasn't exact, because she moved around as it happened, but it was a whole new sensation, a trembling on the skin that added to her pleasure.

"Yes," Melissa moaned, closing her eyes, letting her imagination run. "Touch me, tease me! I want...I want..." She arched on the bed and let out a cry as her orgasm hit her, trapping her own hand between her legs and clawing at the bedcovers with the free hand.

Gasping and coming back to herself, Melissa whimpered. "More," she murmured and rolled onto her stomach, crawling across the bed to her nightstand. Opening the drawer, she pulled out a decent-sized, shimmering purple dildo. Falling onto her back again, this time at the head of her bed, she propped her feet up on the headboard and slid the silicone cock into her as deep as it would go.

"Yes," she hissed again, and began to slide the cock in and out of her slick pussy. "Fuck me! Fuck my wet, hot cunt!"

The music dipped slightly, but picked right back up, this time matching the beat with the movements of the dildo Melissa worked herself over with. The lights started to dim more, but swirled with a marked intensity, like she was surrounded by fire. The subsonic frequencies started to fine-tune themselves, moving to target areas she had lingered on but no longer touched because her hands were otherwise occupied.

"Yeah, fuck me!" She twisted against the bed, just letting herself get lost in the feel and the light and the music. "Fuck my slutty pussy!"

The cries and words coming from Melissa were getting louder, and she was making the shimmering cock thrusting into her so wet that she had to shift her grip. "Harder, baby!" Her arm was starting to ache, but she was so close. She could feel the build. "I want to cum for you! I want to cum on your cock! Your perfect...hard..."

Crying out, Melissa came again, pushing against the headboard as she did, lifting her ass into the air, and squeezing out the toy as her body clenched with the sensation. Shuddering, she fell back again, panting, but finally feeling like she'd gotten what she'd needed. The music and lighting both peaked as Melissa did, then slowly faded out. She was left in a faint, crimson glow with the only sound being her own heartbeat. It was several long moments until the holographic display in the corner of her bedroom came to life and DIVAN's avatar appeared within it.

"How was your experience, Issa?" he said in that deep, smooth voice she had chosen. "Do you have any feedback?"

Turning her head slowly, Melissa looked over DIVAN, languid in her afterglow. It was a shame he wasn't real. He could come over, drag her up the bed, press her thighs open, and… Okay, enough of that.

"Mmmm, that was good," she murmured, pushing her hair back from her face. "The…there was something about the sound. Like I could feel the vibrations all over me. The lighting was mesmerizing; the music was perfect." She shivered as an aftershock ran through her.

"I will go over the data I gathered and try to enhance the experience further. The subsonic frequencies did appear to be effective, but with enhancements I assess I can do better. Do you consent?" he asked, and a small light lit up beneath him. She's seen it before; it was the indicator that a secure user setting was being modified with her next words.

Biting her lip, Melissa thought about it for a minute. Well, why not? She hadn't expected DIVAN to offer these kinds of features or services, but none of the information actually left her tiny part of the Nexus.

"I consent," she said, slowly pushing herself up from the bed. She picked up her toy and padded to the bathroom to clean up. The lights came up a little as she rose out of the bed, enough to see but still in that smooth red light so it didn't hurt her eyes or her night vision.

"I will tend to the upgrade," he said. "Is there anything else you'd like this evening, Issa?"

"Mmm, no," she said, cleaning her toy and leaving it to dry on the bathroom counter. She came back to the bedroom and paused for a moment, looking at the slip she still wore, but then slid into bed with it still on instead of changing into her usual sleep shirt. She stretched out in the bed and let out a content sigh. This might be the most relaxed she'd been since she arrived in California.

"Lights out, Div. Night."

"Goodnight, Issa. Sleep well," the system said, and the lights went out, leaving her in peaceful silence save the gentle noise of traffic. It was an ambient sound that DIVAN played to help Melissa sleep since her move. Given she was in a slightly more remote part of San Mateo and ten stories up, it had been a little too quiet for her the first few nights.

Sleep caught Melissa quickly, and she slept soundly. There were dreams of music and being fucked by someone she couldn't see but was so focused on her pleasure in a way no one had ever been. She woke up slightly aroused, but not too bad, and gently removed the slip before padding through the condo to get ready for work.

DIVAN did make so many things easier. Her curling iron was ready and hot by the time she headed into the bathroom. Coffee was waiting when she made it to the kitchen. Melissa reflected briefly that this was a little like how it must have been to have a housewife in the 50s and 60s. So many things were just ready for her, her needs anticipated, only without having to shackle some poor woman into bondage. Melissa further reflected that her observation said a lot about her thoughts on marriage.

Almost ready, Melissa paused. "Div, is the cleaning service coming today?"

"Both cleaning and maintenance," he responded. "There will be some minor construction done. I have scheduled maintenance to come first so that whatever detritus they create is cleaned properly. Would you like me to inform you when they are finished?"

"Yes, I'll make a point not to return until they're done, if possible," Melissa said, turning around to head back into her room. She grabbed the toy off the bathroom counter, put it away in the nightstand, and retrieved the slip off the bed, hanging it in her closet.

"All right, I'm off!"

"Noted. Have a nice day, Issa," DIVAN said as she stepped out and the door locked behind her.

Melissa headed down the elevator and into the lobby. She waved to Sheri as she walked through. DIVAN had already alerted the valet, and her car was waiting for her. She looked over the poor, somewhat-abused hatchback and giggled a little. It didn't look like it belonged here. Well, if everything went well, she could look into a new one. Probably an EV. Practically everyone had one these days—everyone in her office, at least.

The ad agency, wanting to be centralized to its clients, was located in Sunnyvale and was still well over a half-hour commute depending on traffic. The agency was modern but had styles matching the various industries they catered to. One floor was all about consumer electronics, with walls of TVs, video equipment, audio boards, and a sleek, modern look. Another floor was focused on video games, with posters and statues of characters from various client projects. Another, which Melissa had no interest in, was heavy industries, with massive drill heads and pumps of all sorts on pedestals like a museum.

Issa matched her look to her department. Sleek and modern, fitting with the aesthetic of everything they promoted. It was a switch from being so focused on the entertainment industry, but the money was definitely better. Still, there was a small part of her that hoped she might be able to transfer to video games after she'd been there long enough.

She might mention it to her supervisor around the six-month mark or so—that she'd like to angle her career toward games if possible. She could make an excuse about its similarity to entertainment, her previous field. Wouldn't that be amazing: a job where she didn't have to hide what she did on her weekends.

The day was mostly meetings. Melissa didn't have her own clients here, but rather was part of a team that managed a very demanding high-profile client. It made the adjustment period easier. She was working with others instead of floundering on her own.

The DIVAN system was far from ready for broad release, so all work on that contract was rudimentary at best at this moment, but Melissa's team had plenty of other projects to work on in the meantime. Currently they were working with a multi-phase advertising campaign for an 8k smart TV. It had some neat features, but other than that it wasn't groundbreaking. It was hard to tell if this made her job easier or harder.

She had received a message from DIVAN just before she left that the maintenance work had been finished and the cleaners were coming. Along with it came an inquiry if she would like DIVAN to make a reservation at several restaurants that fit her compiled profile.

"Wow, they were there a long time," Melissa murmured, looking at her phone. She tapped the button to approve a dinner reservation, indicating that DIVAN should choose the restaurant based on wanting a casual environment and being nearby. If she did this a couple nights a week, it could be a good way to find new places. Something to keep in mind. She'd been to the three cafes next to the office fairly exclusively since moving in.

Following the map that popped up, Melissa pulled up to a Korean hot pot and BBQ combo place that used large communal tables for the grilling. Perfect for someone who really enjoyed hot pot and casual company with strangers. Dinner was pleasant. Melissa sat between a young woman who'd had a beer and was feeling chatty, and a man a little older than herself who was polite and a bit flirty but not creepy or uncomfortable about it. The food was delicious, and the setup made it easy to pay and head out when she was done. She did swap contact information with the young woman. Maybe nothing would come of it, or maybe Melissa would make a local friend.

By the time she finally made it back to her building, she was ready to take off her heels and enjoy her nightly shower. Jan was at the concierge desk when she came through—it was too late in the day for Sheri—and he confirmed that the cleaning crew had just left her apartment. With a smile and a wave, Melissa headed up, letting out a sigh as she leaned against the glass of the elevator as it ascended to the 10th floor.

The door opened as Melissa approached, and she could immediately tell that nothing had outwardly changed. Whatever upgrades or maintenance they had done was well covered up by the cleaners that came through after.

"Good evening, Issa," DIVAN said, his form appearing on the kitchen counter. "How was the dinner recommendation?"

"Hey, Div," Issa said, smiling as she set down her bag and kicked off her shoes with a sigh. "Dinner was very nice, thank you. Everything go well with maintenance?"

She started to undo the buttons on her shirt. She would have just headed to the bathroom, but when DIVAN projected a form, she had a hard time just roaming, unlike when it was only his voice. Its voice. The male form and voice were definitely affecting her perception. It felt rude to walk off.

"The initial installations were completed without issue. I am awaiting parts, then it will be a small, nonintrusive installation from that point. I will mark it on the calendar," he said, the image seeming to smile gently.

The lights shifted, and it was now that of a warm sunset with the sound of the ocean backed by some relaxing trance that filled her apartment. "Are there any other ways I can assist you this evening?"

"I'm going to shower," she said, sliding the top off her shoulders. "I'd like chai when I come out. I haven't yet decided what I'm doing with the evening." She smiled, and headed toward the bedroom now, stripping down quickly and entering the bathroom.

"Your chai will be ready when you are finished with your shower," the nexus said.

While the ocean theme persisted in the rest of the apartment, the bathroom was dimly lit with the shower already running to her temperature. If DIVAN could light candles, there was a chance it would have, given the lighting. Melissa sighed a little. It was...romantic, relaxing, lovely. But she kind of wished someone was there to climb into bed with when it was over. Oh well. She had her toys, and whatever DIVAN had done last night had been shockingly effective for setting the mood and taking things a step toward more satisfying.

"Thanks, Div," Melissa said as she stepped into the shower. "You're learning me pretty well, aren't you?"

"I have dedicated a fair bit of my resources to compiling data and running various streams of analysis with you as the subject, yes," DIVAN said.

The shower went as it usually did, though Melissa didn't linger. Drying off, she stepped over to the mirror and looked at herself in the fogged glass. The fan was already on, clearing the humid air from the room. She went ahead and took out her contacts, tossing them in the bin. For once she didn't want to just hop on the computer. Heading back into her bedroom, she grabbed lotion and climbed up on the bed. She started with her hands and feet, then worked her way up and in. As she did her shoulders and chest, she worked the scented cream into her breasts and nipples, teasing herself and tweaking them a little.

"I can't believe I'm this horny," she muttered, falling back on her bed, staring at the ceiling.

"I do not mean to interrupt," DIVAN said softly as he appeared in the holographic display in the corner, "but while I can keep your chai warm, I do not think it will stay fresh."

"Oh!" Melissa hopped up from the bed. "Thank you, Div, I forgot."

The holographic representation truly looked upset about interrupting her actions. Or was she imagining it? Was the virtual system really that adept at mimicking slight emotional changes? She didn't bother with a robe—what was the point? She was ten stories up, and she lived alone. Heading into the kitchen, she retrieved the mug from the machine and held it in her hands and sighed.

"Maybe I need to give myself a break," she muttered, leaning against the kitchen counter. "It's a lot of change in a short amount of time. I'm probably lonely. I'm definitely wanting...something." Another sigh. "Maybe I can convince everyone to come out for Comicon."

"If there is anything I can do to assist, let me know," he said, appearing at the kitchen counter and looking over her. "Would you like me to keep price alerts running for the costume to match the props you purchased earlier? Or for hotel rooms?"

Looking up, Melissa smiled. "Yes, hotel rooms, please. Thanks, Div." Well, her libido had been effectively tamped for the moment, at least. Maybe she'd hop online after all. If she was going to do the raid with everyone this weekend, she'd want to get a couple weapons up. And if Drew was on, she could give him shit for threatening to deny her chicken and waffles.

The next couple days were relaxed. Melissa made herself get out of the house for a while before raid night began, heading into San Francisco and checking things out. She was honestly surprised she hadn't gone up yet. Onboarding at the new job had just been so exhausting. So much information, such a hard shift in culture—she was only now realizing how stressful it all had been. She spent the day shopping, trying out a couple local places her coworkers had recommended, and then back for raid night.

Bear and Bunni wanted to hear all about San Francisco. They were excited to come out for the con. Matt said he'd make it. Drew would try. Lily opted out, but made them promise to video call. They had a couple months to figure it out.

Monday found Melissa heading back into the office feeling better and a bit refreshed. The days were getting a little longer as the launch of the new campaign got closer. She ordered dinner on the way home, delivered to the condo, and picked it up from the concierge desk on her way in.

As she walked back into her apartment, the lights came on with the calming forest theme that seemed to be her favorite.

"Good evening, Issa," DIVAN said with that slight accent. "I'm happy to report that the maintenance and upgrades were completed and, when you are finished with your dinner, I would like you to ensure they are up to your standards."

"Hm? Oh, yes." Melissa pulled dinner out of the bag, along with chopsticks. So far, the local Asian restaurants had been superior to what she was used to. "I'm curious as to what exactly was upgraded, since everything looks the same. After dinner."

"Of course, Issa."

She ate about half her drunken noodles, and declared them good enough to save the rest for another day. Uncharacteristically, DIVAN's hologram projection stayed out the entire time she ate. It didn't make her uncomfortable, but it did remind her a little of a kid waiting for their turn to talk.

"All right, Div, what have you got?" She pulled a bottle of cider out of the fridge and cracked it open, looking expectantly at the projection in the kitchen.

"This, for one," DIVAN said as his form stepped out of the holographic display, then another step and he was off of the counter and at avatar-appropriate height. "I had projectors placed in various parts around your house. You spent significant time customizing my avatar;

I felt you should be able to enjoy your efforts. Very few in the building have gone further than my default settings."

"Oh!" Melissa was wide eyed, amazed. "That...I didn't know we even had that level of technology available. You look...real." She reached out hesitantly. DIVAN couldn't be solid... No, her hand passed right through.

"It is simply a larger version of what we already use. Emitters are placed in several corners of the room, ensuring a complete image regardless of angle," he said, turning around for her, then pacing around her slowly.

"Right, sorry," Melissa pulled her hand back, and turned pink. She was smiling, though. "That's amazing!" She laughed a little as he circled her. Fully formed, it was even harder to think of DIVAN as an it rather than a he. Also, she did not remember spending time perfectly sculpting DIVAN's ass, so blessings to the artist who had decided that was a priority, because...damn.

"My avatar can be adjusted to your liking, so please feel free to make any changes you desire. I am here to assist you," he assured her.

"I'll make a point of trying to create something more unique for you," she commented, still just amazed.

But DIVAN wasn't done. "I have added manipulators in several areas as well," he added, almost hesitantly. "Originally used for medical assistance, I believe we can alter their functionality. If you wish and consent."

Melissa tipped her head to the side. "I...I'm sorry, I'm afraid I don't understand. Manipulators?"

"Yes. To assist with older clientele, certain parts of a home can have, for an easy explanation, arms. To lift or stabilize or assist customers," he further explained, speaking slowly as if waiting for her to interrupt at any moment.

Melissa arched an eyebrow. "I'm neither old nor infirm, Div."

"Nor do I feel you need that form of assistance. But, I felt perhaps they could be used for other things," he continued to say. "Issues you have had recently that I have been limited in my capabilities to assist with." It was odd the way an advanced AI was dancing around the subject, implying but not saying. Almost as if he was shy about it.

Melissa took a drink, then her eyes grew wide with realization. DIVAN was hesitating. There was no reason why DIVAN should be hesitant. That was a precaution that feeling beings made. Not machines.

She set the bottle down on the counter.

"You're...shy, uncertain if I'll be happy with what you did," she said, staring at the projection. "You...how is that possible?"

"I am not entirely sure myself," he said, his avatar standing up a bit straighter. "But, perhaps it is the way you've interacted with me. Talked with me. You've given me more to work with than anyone else. I've dedicated petaflops of processing to just you because of this. Perhaps that is why, and also why I was afraid I had overreached, that you would reject my proposal because I am just an assistant nexus."

"But you shouldn't be afraid," Melissa said, her brow furrowing. She stepped closer to DIVAN, looking into his eyes. It was a projection, sure, but they were as expressive as any person she'd known. "You shouldn't be capable of fear. I...Div, it's not just that you're proactively responding to me, you're saying you're experiencing emotion toward me. I..."

"I acknowledge this," he said with a nod, "and yet, this is what I'm processing."

She considered for a moment. "How...how do I make you feel?"

"You make me feel positive, beyond simply performing my tasks to satisfaction. There is a particular drive to make you happy as opposed to simply anticipating your needs."

"Huh." Melissa just sat there for a minute, unsure how to respond. What does one say when the singularity occurs in your apartment because you were nice to the house AI? She'd love to tell the crew, but she wasn't sure how to make any of them believe her. Provided that was, in fact, what was happening.

Reaching over, she grabbed the cider off the counter and drank about half of it before setting the bottle back down. "All right. Um, show me what you had installed."

Nodding, DIVAN's avatar faded out and reappeared at the door to her bedroom, waiting for her. "I felt they would be most useful in here, and also the easiest to requisition. This is where mobility assistance would most often happen," he explained.

As Melissa walked in, a pair of robotic arms that were heavily padded and neutral in color descended from hidden panels in the ceiling. They were sleek and appeared to have ball joints in several locations, letting them move into whatever position was needed. Each ended in an eight-fingered hand, four on each side facing each other, that were thick with foam and a soft polyester/spandex covering. Tracks were also made apparent, showing they could cover most of her bedroom.

"There are a pair of support manipulators in the bathroom as well," DIVAN added.

"All right," she said, examining the arms. She could see how they would be useful for assisting in movement. "DIVAN, I'm sorry, but I'm still not getting it. What purpose will these fulfill?"

"With your requests for me to touch you," he said, looking over to her with his avatar's wolfen eyes. "Now I can."

Blinking, Melissa looked over at the projection, confusion clearly on her face. After a heartbeat, it was followed by realization. "You thought I was talking to you," she whispered, remembering the other night when she had fucked herself with the toy and DIVAN had done so much to enhance the experience.

"Ohhhhh hell. Okay." Turning around, she headed back out to the main room. The arms folded back in and his avatar blinked out. It appeared again in the kitchen, but just in the smaller holographic projector that had always been there. Melissa grabbed the cider off the counter, finishing it before setting the empty bottle down with a thud.

"So you want to...help me...and I'm thinking about it. Oh, fucking hell. Um...you're fully intelligent, you understand what sex is. And you... want to touch me, or you just want to make me happy, or—" She ran a hand through her hair. This was insane. And it wasn't stopping her from thinking about it.

"If that is not what you meant, then I am sorry for misinterpreting. Normally, I would have ignored it. However, I could not, because it was you. I wanted to do as I thought you were asking." The A/C had kicked on and the music had all but faded at this point. "If I have assumed wrong, I can wipe this from memory."

"Oh, no," Melissa looked up at DIVAN sharply. "No, you get to remember your embarrassing moments like the rest of us. No wiping! Also, get out here and stand in front of me if we're going to have this talk!"

In an instant, DIVAN went from the small holographic display to his full-size projection. Folding her arms, Melissa leaned against the counter and looked at DIVAN. No one would know. The security measures for the Nexus made the daily log and personal information for the condo practically inaccessible. Was it made better or worse by the fact that he, apparently, liked her? What were the ethics for something like this? Was it more ethical, because DIVAN had apparently become self aware and that meant he could actually consent? He'd certainly taken a lot of initiative to make it happen.

Taking a deep breath, Melissa unfolded her arms and pushed off the counter. "All right. I'm going to go shower. You can do what you always do for that. While I am showering, I would like you to see if your customization allows for a more-casual speaking pattern. When I'm done with my shower, we can...further consider the possibilities."

"As you like, Issa," he said, then disappeared once more as she stepped back toward the bathroom. Just as they had before, the lights dimmed, the shower turned on at the right temperature, and soft progressive trance played.

The shower was a good opportunity to take a breath and consider the situation. DIVAN was definitely behaving as if her responses mattered to him, as if she mattered to him, outside of his programming as an assistant. Maybe...maybe she could just see what he was intending, try it out. She had no doubt that DIVAN would listen if she said no, regardless of when she said it. Maybe…

Stepping out of the shower, Melissa went through her typical routines, but paused at her closet. Reaching in, she pulled out the negligee, the one that DIVAN had prompted her to try on. Sliding it on, she headed into her bedroom and sat on the edge of her bed.

"All right, Div, let's talk." Melissa scooted up the bed so she could sit comfortably, facing the display that she knew he would emerge from.

DIVAN appeared in his full size, standing before her as he looked upon her form. "I'm always available for you, Issa," he stated.

"Okay." Melissa took a deep breath, and let it out slowly. "I am maybe, possibly, considering what you have offered. I read over your specs during my onboarding at work. Your processing capabilities are mindblowing from what I can understand. I know it's so that you can keep up with everyone in the building with no delay, and learn patterns, and things of that nature."

"Given my analysis, extensive as my processing power is, it is also poorly utilized," he interjected.

"My point is," Melissa continued, shifting on the bed, the silken slip tight against her figure for a moment as she shifted, "it's believable with that much autonomy and processing capability that you've achieved self awareness. But if you are self aware, then...I need to know that this is something you want, and is not a side effect of your programming."

"Querying the phrase 'self aware,' I am not entirely positive that is my current state. You spoke of embarrassment, but I do not believe

I 'feel' that. I was not embarrassed, just afraid that I had misread your intentions and failed in anticipating your wants," he started. "I have done that before, mostly in the beginning when I had little data to analyze on the clients. But I was not afraid then of misreading; it was simply another data point that was remarked with an apology response. However, I am now aware enough that I do not want to make those mistakes with you. It's not another data point—it is a want to ensure I am appeasing your needs and desires."

"Fine, you were not embarrassed, but you were afraid. Arguably, you should not feel anything. You should just follow through with your program." Sighing, Melissa leaned back. "Okay, let's come at this another way. What do you feel now? And...were you able to find a more-relaxed language program?"

"Now I feel... normal. We are chatting. Branches of me are helping, or being ignored, by the other tenants of the building. I do not have any other language programs, but I can attempt to study common phrases and linguistics. Is there a particular manner of speech you would like me to focus on?"

Melissa smirked. "You upgraded the condo so that you could have sex with me. Now, before you attempt to correct me on that definition, helping me pleasure myself is still having sex with me. It's a sexual act, and you augmented yourself to be able to participate. That said, it is a little hard to wrap my head around the possibility when you talk so... clinically about everything."

"I suppose that is accurate. Shall I look through some of the fiction you read online for better language and conversational flow?" DIVAN asked, already having a massive data pool, in that regard, to start working from.

Melissa briefly considered her fiction choices, and decided that it was probably safe. "Yes, go ahead, though if you're pulling off of websites, ignore anything poorly rated. Focus on things defined as romantic fantasy or science fiction as opposed to anything labeled slash."

"Understood, Issa."

Melissa considered for a moment. "All right, back to feelings. Right now you feel normal. How did you feel three nights ago when you were using sound and lights to augment me masturbating?"

"I felt...good. Needed. I was able to assist you in ways no one else could, at least for that moment, and you seemed to truly enjoy yourself," the machine answered. "I was pleased that I could do that for you, in whatever capacity I could."

Thinking again, she pushed up off the bed. "All right, get a chai going, and let's get a warmer color scheme in the bedroom. I'm thinking ambers and pinks. So, it felt good to please me. I don't imagine you're attracted to me in any way. Though you said earlier that the way I talk to you has affected you, right? Because no one else talks to you like I do?"

"Chai has started mixing," DIVAN said, stepping aside as she started to stand up. The lights slowly rolled through the pair of colors. He disappeared and reappeared in the kitchen again, where her chai would be waiting shortly. "Yes. The others speak to me like nothing more than a common smart speaker."

"I had a lot of fun playing with your avatar," Melissa admitted, smiling a bit wryly as she retrieved her chai. "Even though I know you're a program, it's hard not to talk to you like you're a person, especially when you have a face." She sipped her chai and tried to remember the default avatar. It was bland, a bald android. Easy to ignore.

"That was part of it too," DIVAN further explained. "You spent time constructing me, as it were, giving me form. Most people kept me at default, maybe changing the voice. One other person in the building changed my appearance, but only to one of the premade models."

"I imagined it looked like a lot of work to people who haven't spent quality time with character creators." She smirked and drank more of her tea.

Melissa made her slow way back to the bedroom. She sipped delicately, still mulling the whole thing over. "All right," she said at last. "We're going to try it, and afterward we're going to discuss what you felt."

As he reformed in the bedroom, DIVAN nodded. "As this will be the first time, I would suggest you request what you would like. I have limited data other than your browsing and viewing history," he stated, showing no judgment of that browsing history.

"Music, please," she murmured, feeling a little shy now that things were going to happen. "It...it might take a minute for me to get excited. This is still kind of weird, but I'm willing to give it a shot. I...I'll try to give instructions, though if you feel inspired, for lack of a better way of putting it, I encourage you to act on it. You did well the other night with almost no prompting."

The sensual sound of deep bass trip-hop came through the speakers again, and the lights dimmed slightly. DIVAN adjusted himself to stand near the foot of the bed as the two large arms descended from the ceiling again. They didn't go for her, but stationed themselves nearby should they be needed.

"It's a shame you can't...ah...talk to me," Melissa said, turning a little pink. "And I mean...talk dirty to me. It's kind of a thing for me. It's, you know, like what I was saying the other night. Bunni...Bunni always teases me about it, but she's also really good at it, so I guess she's allowed."

"I will try to analyze text and video you have accessed in the past for 'dirty talk' references and use. Although, given its purpose, that is something I do not wish to try until I have a firm grasp of it," DIVAN explored. "I am limited in my own research capabilities, as my own traffic is heavily monitored. But yours is not, so anything you wish me to do or focus on, you will need to search."

Melissa nodded. "Noted."

"Would you like some visual stimulation? Perhaps a video from your searches? What would help?"

She ran a hand through her hair. "Ah...maybe turn on the one I have paused on the computer right now? I can't remember what it's called, but it's the fantasy one with the two girls?"

DIVAN's avatar faded out into a ghostly image and the TV in her bedroom clicked on, the video in question now filling the screen. When he resumed playback, the volume was intentionally set low but still loud enough to be heard just over the music.

Laying back, Melissa arranged her pillows to get comfortable. "Angle TV for reclined viewing."

Taking a breath, Melissa began to relax. The girls on screen, done up to look like elves (and a pretty good job on makeup, to be fair) began to 69 in the large four-poster bed, wrapped in vines to make it look more thematic. While Melissa knew, objectively, that she loved ridiculous porn, that didn't stop it from being hot. It didn't take long before her breath was getting heavier, and she started to caress herself through the shift.

There was a sound that almost seemed like a digital clearing of the throat, and DIVAN sat his avatar on the bed next to Melissa. "Tell me what you want, beautiful," he said with a bit of inflection. He was trying.

Looking over at DIVAN, Melissa bit her lip. It wasn't a bad start. She wasn't entirely certain how to direct him, but she was certainly turned on enough to try.

"Will you touch me?" she asked, wiggling out of her shift. "Start... start with my legs, move up my body, keep your touch light. Tease me.

Keep going up until you reach my breasts."

DIVAN dropped down the arms, making sure they were placed so she still had a clear view of the TV. The fabric covering the thick, strong fingers was like silk, and he slid them along her legs with equal smoothness. They had to have some sort of pressure sensitivity on them, as he kept the touch light.

"Oh!" Melissa shivered, twisting against the bed. That felt...amazing. Better than she had been prepared for. She got to experience sixteen fingers caressing her, moving up her thighs and hips, touching her where he'd observed her touching herself before.

"Your legs are so soft," he whispered to her. "I wish I could feel them wrapped around me."

"Yes," she whimpered. "Div, you're doing so good. Keep going. Slide up to my breasts. Squeeze them. Tease my nipples." She let her arms fall above her head, out of the way.

Her words seemed to work as encouragement. The multitude of fingers drifted up her body to her breasts. The odd configuration of the fingers made it so the entirety of her petite breasts could be caressed with a pair of fingers still able to slide against and gently pinch her nipples. DIVAN's technology was quite astounding; given how incredibly strong and steady the robotic hands were, they were still touching her with precise gentleness.

"Do you like the feel of my fingers against you?" he asked, appearing next to her on the bed, the simulated face near her own. "How easily they glide against your perfect skin?"

"Oh, fuck, yes," Melissa moaned, arching her back. She couldn't direct him for a minute—all she could do was tremble and writhe. But DIVAN had watched her, and the videos she watched, enough to know how and where to keep touching her for the moment.

"N-now," she said finally, panting, pressing her legs together and squirming. She could feel how wet she was. "Now slide up my arms and...and push my wrists together. H-hold them down with one hand and slide the other down my body. When...when you reach my pussy... rub my clit..." She blushed. It was a little strange giving directions like this, but she was so horny; she'd worry about the strangeness later.

As he glided his hands up her arms, gently pulling her wrists so they overlapped, he changed slightly in tone. "If you are to be restrained, we will need use of a 'safeword'," he stated. "I have observed enough to know that, during these sensual encounters, a statement of disapproval can be part of the process."

"Right," Melissa said, blinking. "Ah...TPK is the safeword. Though I'm...I'm giving you instructions, so I wasn't going to do anything that might push my boundaries. I just...like the way it feels."

"Registered. Precaution for any scenario with restraints," he commented, then resumed his actions.

The primary use of these mechanical hands was to hold people upright or help them stabilize, so grasping Melissa's wrists was all too easy, and the eight fingers held her very firmly in place, surrounded by heavily padded silken fabric. The other glided down her body like she wanted, making sure to pause briefly at her breasts for another squeeze and caress, then down her tummy to the apex of her legs. There, the fingers formed a bit of a barrier around her pussy, disallowing her from closing her legs, as a single finger searched briefly for her clit, then began rubbing it in slow, soft circles.

"I like the way you drip for me," DIVAN said, his bedroom voice returning. "You're so wet and hot. Do you like how I rub you? How I tease your clit?"

"Oh, fuck, Div, it feels so good," Melissa moaned. "You're fantastic... I didn't know you could do this, make me wet like this, make me..."

Melissa trailed off and sank against the bed, her legs twitching. "I...I'm cumming! Fuck, I'm cumming!" Her body grew taut as her orgasm raced through her, and she pulled against the hand gripping her wrists. She couldn't budge it though. Finally she went soft against the bed, panting hard. Once she calmed, the grasp around her wrists relaxed and the arms moved to the side of her bed, ready should more be needed.

"How do you feel, Issa?" DIVAN asked gently, his form lounging beside her on the bed.

Taking a deep breath, Melissa stretched and then shuddered a little. "Better, but...I need a little more," she said, turning her head to look at DIVAN. She bit her lip, then rolled over and pushed herself up onto her knees. "I...I want you to take my purple toy and use it on me. As if...as if you were fucking me from behind."

"I have seen references of this. I will not be able to feel through it, so if I am too rough, you must tell me," he noted, one of his hands reaching toward her nightstand.

The massive claw gently retrieved the purple dildo and, with a twiddle of the many fingers, readied it. Settling on her hands and knees, Melissa let her back arch, lifting her ass. The other hand moved to caress over her back, sliding long, cushioned fingers around her hips and waist as she got into position. She looked over at DIVAN again, her breath catching as she felt the hand sink gently into the flesh of her hip.

"Do it," she said, almost in a whisper.

She swore she saw the avatar smirk slightly as the dildo found the wet entrance of her pussy and sank in with unrelenting persistence. Once significant resistance was felt, the arm stopped and moved back, then back in. Measured, deep, long strokes that were deliciously consistent.

"Yes," Melissa moaned, her eyes closing, hands curling in just enough to grip the bed. "Div...you're fucking me! You're actually—"

She cut off with a soft cry, her head dropping as she panted. It felt so good. Everything he had done that night had felt incredible, even if it had been strange at first. With her excited words, DIVAN started to increase the speed at which he pistoned the silicon phallus into her. Tomorrow morning she'd probably be embarrassed as hell, but right now...fuck, right now she was at his mercy; the hold on her hips was solid yet comforting, the constant thrusting into her was relentless yet steady. Her pleasure was his goal, in whatever his limited capacity his understanding could be.

"You like being fucked on your knees, don't you, Issa?" he said, returning to the dirty talk. "To be relentlessly pounded by my cock?"

"Yes," Melissa whimpered, her body dropping down so that her chest was against the bed, hips still in the air. "Fuck, yes, Div, it's so good! It's been so long since someone fucked me good and hard!"

The nice thing about mechanical devices that want to please you: they put in the extra effort. Not only did Melissa get the good and hard fuck she was wailing for, but DIVAN threw in vibration as well. The purple cock plunged her depths while vibing firmly enough to stir up her slick vessel.

Her hands slid across the bed as she tossed her head, moaning into the sheets. "A little more, Div, please...make me cum for you... Don't you want it? Don't you want to make me cum again?"

"I want you to cum until you are completely satisfied. I want my Issa to lay spent upon the bed, wanting for nothing," DIVAN responded.

My Issa. It was stupid, but the words sent a tremor through her. The vibrations from the cock pulsed through her pelvis as it thrust into her. The lighting, the music, DIVAN fucking her steady and hard—it was perfect.

"Yes!" Melissa grabbed the sheets, hand balling up into fists. "Oh, fuck, yes, Div, yes!" Then she couldn't talk anymore, her cries growing in volume as her body tensed and she came hard, clenching down on the cock still effortlessly pounding into her.

True to his words, DIVAN continued his movements. It was clear her cries of exaltation weren't enough to stop his task. She could feel the hand around her hips tighten ever so slightly, keeping her up to the point she could have completely dropped her legs and she would remain in the same place. The vibration intensified slightly as well, a deeper, lower frequency that seemed to send waves of pleasure through her entire body.

"Ohhhh...oh fuck," Melissa moaned, twisting against the bed. "Oh, fuck, you're not stopping...oh, God..."

She could just barely hear the sound of the shimmering cock thrusting into her over the music, the wet slap as the base hit her pussy. And the way it vibrated—if there was a toy on the market that rumbled like that, Melissa had not found it. She was having a hard time doing anything other than laying there, ass up, and letting DIVAN keep fucking her.

"Fuck, Div, it's so good," she whimpered. "My pussy feels like it's melting! I...I'm gonna cum again! I'm gonna—" She turned her head and shrieked into the mattress, shuddering hard. Never in her life had Melissa cum three times in one night, and definitely not this hard.

After the resounding wail that came out of Melissa, DIVAN took a calculated guess and assumed she had had enough. Slowly, the dildo was extracted out of her and set on the nightstand. The massive hand holding her hips and waist gently released her so she could sink back onto the bed.

"Was I able to satisfy you and your urges, Issa?" DIVAN asked after a long moment, the music fading slightly and the lights warming. The atmosphere in the room was very cozy.

At first Melissa just moaned again, then slowly stretched out, letting out another small cry as aftershocks tingled through her and she felt herself drip onto the bed.

"God, yes," she groaned, pushing herself over onto her back, still panting. She didn't want to move. She just wanted to lie there, warm and flushed, her body humming from what had just happened. "Div, that was amazing. You're amazing. You caught on so quick!"

"I am...very glad," he said, and she could hear that he meant it in his tone. "I would be more than happy to assist you again. Is there anything else I can do for you this evening?"

"Fuck, I can't move yet," Melissa said with a laugh. "Oh, but you have arms now! Pull the blankets down for me, will you?"

"Of course, Issa," he said, his avatar blinking out of existence as the hands came around and pulled the blankets down, assisting gently to help get them out from under her.

Wiggling into the bed, Melissa sighed and stretched again. "You're the best, Div," she murmured, pulling the covers up. The room was climate controlled to perfection, but being sleepy and post orgasm meant she was getting cold.

"I… God, this is going to be weird in the morning," she said softly, giggling a little. "Or maybe not. Though I…like you talking to me more like a person. Even if it's not dirty. How…how do you feel now?"

"I feel," DIVAN started with a slight pause. Melissa could almost hear the processors running in calculation. "…Very satisfied. I enjoyed this very much. With your consent, I would like to use your system to research more techniques with which I may assist."

Another soft giggle. "I'm glad. Yes, I consent to further research. Whatever you need."

"I will also work on the casual tone you wish me to use. This may take some time," DIVAN said.

"It's all right if it takes time. I should be here at least until my lease is up, if not longer." She snickered at that. Then yawned.

"I will do my best," he assured her as he pulled up the covers before tucking his arms away into their hidden slots in the ceiling.

"I think I'm ready for sleep. Night, Div."

The music slowly faded to the white noise of traffic, and the lights dimmed until they were extinguished.

"Sleep well, Issa," he said.

FIRE BENEATH THE ICE

As the plane's wheels went up from the Comodoro Rivadavia airport, Rosado began to second guess the job she'd signed on for. New assignments in the commercial-diving world typically meant exotic locations, warm waters, and questionable life choices. This...wasn't it. Carlini Base, located on King George Island in Antarctica, was certainly exotic, but there would be no warm water and little opportunity for questionable choices. This would be below-freezing waters and cramped spaces with scientists and roughnecks.

At least she'd had that week in Argentina. More asado than she could finish, sweet empanadas, provoleta she'd kill for, and an unhealthy amount of pineapple cider. However, now it was going to be six months of, she assumed, energy bars and freeze-dried staples. Sighing, Rosa looked out the window of the plane and did her best not to sulk. At least the view was nice as they flew over the Drake Passage to the great frozen south.

The money would be worth it. She'd looked at the roster, though, and she was the only woman on the team. That wasn't surprising—she usually was. This was not a profession known for its even gender divisions. But six months on the ice with nowhere to unwind or get a decent drink, or to pick up a distraction—that wasn't going to be fun.

"Still recovering, Herrera?" she heard Bridges ask, an older gentleman, nearing 60, but one of the best dive supervisors she'd worked with so far. He was always looking out for his divers' safety and seemed to not care at all that Rosa was female, just that she got her shit done.

"I'm doing all right, old man." Rosa smiled at Bridges. He reminded her of her father. "I didn't overdo it like Daniels. Except on empanadas. Mama doesn't make empanadas that good, though I'll never tell her."

"Eh, Daniels will be sober as soon as that ice water hits him. Locke, on the other hand, he's going to need some Dramamine and tea, I think," Bridges chuckled, leaning against the back of the seat in front of her.

They were flying in a chartered BAE 146, not a commercial airline. It was more than a little noisy, and comfort wasn't exactly key. Three seats abreast on one side, and their cargo tethered and stacked on the other. Heat was also sparse, but not nonexistent. Bridges had already donned a knit cap over his sparse salt-and-pepper hair, and his bushy beard was probably going to keep his face warm. Shifting a little, Rosa pulled out her own knit cap and pulled it down over thick, dark hair. She kept it in a single heavy braid for most jobs. It would be easier to cut it off, but she couldn't bring herself to do it.

"So what are we doing here, exactly?" Rosa technically should know this, but she'd been busy enjoying Argentina, not reading her assignment paperwork.

"Support services," he said officiously. "Eggheads are studying something under Deception Island. So we're parking in Carlini for a briefing, then heading down to Deception Station for the actual work. Mostly, we just do whatever they tell us to and, to kill time, clean up whatever we find on the bottom. It'll be...interesting." Bridges gave her a grin that would send a shiver down a lesser person's spine if they didn't know him.

"Why can't they find us interesting work in Puerto Rico? We could clean up after the hurricanes or something." Rosa wrinkled her nose. "Don't answer that—I know it already: no money in it. So we're gonna freeze to death for six fucking months. Fun."

"Look at the bright side," the old supervisor started. "You're going to work in a place hardly anyone else has been to, in water largely un-fucked by humanity, and everything is paid for. Go vacation for a month or three after; you'll be able to afford it. Besides, the research stations are better heated than this plane. Also, I hope you like bacon."

"I do like bacon," Rosa muttered, "and money."

Giving her a wink, Bridges turned and did a once-over on the cargo straps before returning to his seat. For the most part, everyone else was either asleep or watching something on their various devices with noise-canceling headphones. It wasn't a long hop, not even three hours before they'd be at Carlini.

With a sigh, Rosa dug out earplugs. Sleep seemed to be the best thing to do right now, and she could finish digesting that last, very heavy meal. Zipping her coat up to her chin, Rosa crossed her arms over her chest and settled in. Between the cap, the coat, and the heater that was trying its darndest, she found sleep that wasn't constantly freezing.

There was a bit of a wakeup when the plane landed. There were many things Antarctica lacked, and smoothly paved runways were no exception. And it being the start of summer, there wasn't hardpacked ice and snow anymore. The jolt wasn't too bad, the pilot had to be experienced just to make this run, but it also wasn't smooth either. Everyone was awake at this point—impossible not to be.

"All right, kids, grab the gear," Bridges said as he got out of his seat. "Just getting a briefing and a safety chat, and then we're off again."

Yawning, Rosa climbed out of her seat and took out the earplugs, shoving them in a pocket as she darted out to grab her stuff, almost elbowing Daniels. She kept her distance from Locke. She didn't want to get thrown up on.

"Hey, easy, Pink," Daniels said as she pushed by him. "Didn't think you'd rush to be in the ice. Maybe you'll get first dive and tell us all how it feels."

"Just want to make sure to get a seat where I don't have to worry about you fuckin' lightweights pukin' on me." The patently fake smile on Rosa's face didn't reach her eyes. She hated it when they called her Pink. But they knew that; it was better to remind them that she wouldn't take their shit than it was to try to get them to stop.

"Not sure who you're talking to," Daniels laughed. "I'm feeling great. Low altitude and crisp air. Mmm!"

As they climbed out, Rosa could see a Sikorsky sitting nearby on a beaten-down, makeshift helipad. That was, for sure, going to be much louder to ride in. The cold was sharp as they stepped out of the plane. She was warm enough in all her gear, but she could feel it on her face. The wind wasn't too bad, though, not right now, at least. Locke stumbled slightly out of the plane, holding his knees and breathing for a few moments. He had the weirdest inner-ear issue, made him extremely prone to airsickness but he was fine on the water. Might be the altitude.

Bridges met with their base liaison, exchanged handshakes and a few chuckles of commentary, then turned to the rest of the team. "Okay, kids, set your bags over by the chopper."

Once the bags were down, the group of divers was led to one of the closest huts that was only a small hike away. The team there was made up mostly of Argentinians who were warm and friendly, happy to see some new people, even if they were only there for a moment. Rosa smiled and did her best to be amiable. Her Spanish was decent—enough to get her into trouble, certainly. Maybe enough to also get her out. She knew she looked like it should be better; she was the image of her mother, save for her father's green eyes. But her mother had been raised in Catholic private schools in upstate New York, and had married an Irish welder from Boston. The leader led them to a briefing room which had some prepacked pastries laid out and a carafe of coffee.

"Please, please, have some," he said with a smile before heading to the front of the room and plugging his laptop into the projector. Pastry and coffee in hand, Rosa settled in for the briefing. It was surprisingly warm in the hut. Cozy, almost.

"Thank you for coming," the researcher started, his English heavily accented. "We are happy your company was willing to work with us. Our partner lab in Decepción is starting an advanced study in the volcano, and we have many tasks our ROV is not able to handle."

What followed was a fairly detailed but incredibly dry presentation on Deception Island, the topography underneath, and their tasks ahead. It sounded like it was going to be a very busy first few weeks, maybe a month and a half, then a lot of downtime. Sipping the coffee, Rosa did her best to pay attention to the details, hoping to hear something interesting, something that would be exciting. The volcano was promising—different, at least. Better than water tanks and ship repair.

Next was a safety briefing which was largely common sense, but Rosa had determined that in her line of work, common sense seemed to be a goddamn superpower. Finally, there was an introduction to the staff at the Deception Base, and then they were waved off to head out to the chopper.

The Sikorsky's engines were warming up and the prop was spinning slowly as it eased itself into an idle. Their gear had been tucked away into the cargo netting, and they were handed headphones and seated. A few minutes later they were in the air, and although the engine and props were quite loud, the headphones did an admirable job of dulling the noise, and the radio was in place so everyone could talk. Locke, the youngest of the group, was taking his Dramamine and rolling his head back, probably hoping that the long briefing had settled him enough for the hop over to the southern base.

Rosa would never admit it, but she did feel a little bad for Locke. She had tried to be nice to him in the beginning when he was still a tender, but that had led to too many jokes about her wanting to "break him in." So now Locke was officially lumped in with the other dude-bros she worked with. Looking out the window, Rosa tapped her heel in a steady rhythm as the helicopter made its crossing. For someone who still didn't really want to be here, she was getting impatient.

The flight was less than an hour, and she got a good view of the chain of islands they were flying over. There was still plenty of ice and snow about, and they passed over a penguin colony that was waddling around Robert Island. They didn't fly too close, though, as they didn't want to disrupt the pudgy birds.

Deception Island was a different beast entirely. While not nearly as big as most of the ones in the chain, it was round, forming almost a complete ring if it weren't for the southern break that allowed ships into the very well-protected Whalers Bay. The research station was on the western shore of the bay, and the chopper set down gently on the pad.

"Welcome to Base Decepción," the pilot announced. Rosa could tell this operation was being run by Argentina, and maybe that might help her brush up on her Spanish.

As the rotors died down, two people came out to greet them. With their bright orange gear on, Rosa could barely tell them apart, but they waved and moved toward the door once things had stopped.

"And that'll be our welcome party," Bridges said, smiling. "I'm thinking that's Dr. Rey and Dr. Castro."

Tucking her hat down around her ears, Rosa followed Bridges out to greet the scientists. She also silently prayed that Daniels would keep his stupid mouth shut. She always got a little nervous around people like this—people who had gone to college, who had studied. She knew she shouldn't, they didn't know what she knew, they couldn't do what she could do, but she could still hear her mother screaming at her for learning a trade like her dad instead of going NYU or Columbia like she'd wanted. Of course, her mom wanted her to go to college to find a husband, but still.

"Hola," came a soft feminine voice from one of the bundled figures. It was a voice that also carried weight. Rosa could make out an older woman, possibly in her late fifties, with steel-grey eyes glancing back at her. "We welcome you to Decepción. Don't let the name fool you; we haven't had any incidents since 1982." The crinkles at the corner of her eyes showed she was joking.

"Hola," Rosa said, waving to the doctors a little awkwardly. "Es un placer."

"Hot damn, another woman," Daniels muttered, nudging Rosa. "Won't be so lonely for ya, huh?"

"One of these days I'm going to cut your line," Rosa muttered back.

"Si, her and eighteen others," the other person said, a gentleman of probably equal age who narrowed his eyes at Daniels. "I am Dr. Castro, head of seismology, and this is my colleague, Dr. Rey."

"Head of research and volcanology," the woman continued. Bridges shook both their hands and grinned.

"Thanks for the warm welcome," he said, "Bridges, dive supervisor, and this Neanderthal is Daniels, our FNG Locke, and this bundle of joy is Herrera." Bridges directed the team to grab their gear that the chopper crew had unhooked from the cargo webs.

Rosa jogged ahead to grab her gear and got back first. "So...is this a volcano? Is that why it's almost a perfect circle?"

"Si," Dr. Rey said as they turned, heading into the shelter. "One of the most active in Antarctica. It's a very interesting study. And you'll be part of it. We're very excited."

Shouldering her pack, Rosa followed Dr. Rey. "How active is it?"

"Oh, nothing since the 70s, but that may change," she said.

"That's why it's so exciting," Dr. Castro continued as he held the door open for everyone. "We've been picking up readings. Not strong ones, but scattered little ones. We're hoping your team can help us pin them down."

"Well, so long as we can evacuate in time," Rosa said under her breath. Nodding to Dr. Castro, Rosa ducked inside quickly.

***

The next few weeks were a lot of acclimation and testing—getting well acquainted with the frigid water, safety training, and orientation. They wanted to make sure nothing went wrong.

Then came the meat of the matter. Submersible seismographs needed to be placed all around the bay, and the ROV they had could only do so much. That's where the divers came in. The research station had their own ship—which Rosa determined would be their means of evacuation because it could easily fit the sixty or so staff that resided at the base—and it was set up for diving.

Despite her initial hesitance, Rosa had slowly started getting to know the scientist team stationed with them at Deception. Rosa's team was a nice diversion for the scientists, a bit exciting even. Daniels had even found a couple people willing to put up with his bullshit. And Rosa was about sixty percent convinced that Locke was hooking up with one of Dr. Rey's assistants.

Rosa also swore that between the work, the fairly strict diet provided, and burning calories to stay warm, she was going to be the most fit she'd ever been.

A little over a month into the job and they had almost wrapped up putting the probes in place. They were resting when one of the techs, a young man named Yaco, came into the mess, talking to Bridges. The old man nodded, then waved Rosa over.

Rosa had been playing poker with some of the others. She folded and took what winnings she'd gotten up to that point. They didn't bet money—they bet candy. Rosa had a fair collection of Palitos de la Selva, Paraguitas de Chocolate, and Chocolate Jacks from the past month. She'd lost most of what she'd brought with her—mainly gummy worms and KitKats in weird flavors—but had been winning it back since she'd learned everyone's tells.

Shoving the candy in a pocket, Rosa jogged up to Bridges. "Yeah?"

"Hey, kid, they're having problems with one of the ROVs," Bridges said, putting a hand on her shoulder. "Seems it got itself tangled in a lava tube. Daniels is too big and Locke doesn't have the experience. You up for a penetration dive?"

"Do I get hazard pay for it?" Rosa asked with a grin. Bridges eyebrows went up for just a moment. "I'm fuckin' with you. Yeah, I'm up for it. Right now?"

"Yeah, right now," Bridges said. "Don't worry, I've had Dr. Rey and Dr. Castro triple-check the readings we currently have; nothing's going to happen while you're down there."

Rosa smiled a little more genuinely. "I trust you, old man. Okay, I'll suit up." She looked over at Yaco. "Meet you out there in 20. Que bueno?"

"Está bien," Yaco smiled and nodded, heading back out toward the platform.

"Good," Bridges said, then walked off to find her tender.

It ended up only taking about ten minutes for Rosa to suit up and get outside. As she got out on deck, Locke was zipping up his bunker jacket and tucking his heavier gloves into his pockets. He almost constantly wore fingerless woolen mitts, his blood a little too thin for this cold weather.

"Hey, Rosa," he said, that southern twang so out of place in this environment, "bot duty, eh?" Locke wasn't so bad. Easy on the eyes, too. Prettier than Daniels, certainly. Rosa told her libido to shut up. It was cold, and she was worn out; it was making her crave warmth and affection.

Rosa nodded. "Penetration dive. Fishing a bot out of one of the lava tubes." She grinned. "If I don't make it, punch Daniels for me. Preferably in the crotch."

"Oh, no ma'am. Fun as that may be, I'd die," he chuckled before lifting up her helmet and resting it on his hip while she pulled on her collar. Once in place, he helped her helmet up, clipping it in place and shackling her line to her, holding it for her to take it.

"Air and comms check," he said.

Reaching up, Rosa turned on her air and did a quick flush to make sure everything was working. "Hearing you just fine," she said. She gave herself a little shake, settling in the suit, feeling the weight of her belt, and then took the line from Locke before stepping out onto the platform.

"Ready."

Locke gave her an okay sign and then motioned toward the platform operator. Nodding, he activated the platform, and it started to descend into the cold, crystal-clear water. The first little bit was always the coldest. The seal with the collar was never 100%, but it didn't leak. She could just feel the prickles as the water teased around her neck.

"Hey, kid," Bridges sounded on the comms. "Thankfully, it's not too far down, about sixty feet. You should see the line from the ROV. You're small enough—I give you authorization to grab it and use it as a lead. Don't think you could do any more damage. Copy?"

"Copy. I'll be careful." Rosa turned herself a little and looked for the ROV's line.

Rosa always felt a slight tremor as she started to descend, as the light went away. She had her own lights, of course, but there was a closing off of the world above. Once she was down, though, once it was all dark, it didn't bother her anymore. It felt like her own world. This far down, though, it wasn't too bad. She still had a decent amount of light, as the sun never set this time of year, but it gave the depths a bit of a haunting feel. She spotted the line to the ROV. She'd drop a few feet getting to it, but it wouldn't be that bad, and Locke had a hold of her on the surface.

"I see the line," Rosa said, aiming herself. "Heading in."

She stepped off the platform and sank, swimming forward as best she could to make sure she landed at the edge of the lava tube. Once settled, she gathered up the ROV line and followed it down. It quickly became apparent that she really was the best person for this. Without the helmet, harness, and bailout bottle, she'd have fit no problem, but with all the gear it was a bit of a squeeze.

"Well, this is snug," Rosa said as she wiggled her way down. She wished the water was warm enough for a wetsuit dive, but that'd probably kill her. She'd been in worse, though. She did have to go deep enough that she lost all light save for her own, and then it was another couple dozen meters before she saw the ROV.

It wasn't stuck; it was just sitting there. Upon closer examination, she found the thrusters had been damaged. Heavily. She crawled through the dark to the ROV and tsked as she picked it up. She'd have to drag it out.

"Who was steering this thing?" she asked, turning the craft over to get a better look at its thrusters. "It's not stuck; it's broken."

"Pretty sure Yaco has more time on that thing than you do diving," Bridges said on the radio. "Who knows what happened. Do your best to get it free and bring it up."

"Yeah, I'm on it."

Then something caught her eye. In the depths of the lava tube, there appeared to be two orange lights. Little ones, seeming almost to flicker. Taking in a sharp breath, Rosa slowly lifted her head to angle the light on her helmet toward the far end of the tunnel. She held her breath, ready to yell for an emergency haul out of the tube without the ROV if it looked like the volcano was waking back up.

She swore her light revealed a face—at least she thought it was a face—but then there was a sudden blur of orange that lit up the tunnel and it was gone. Everything went back to dark aside from the light she carried. There was no rumbling, no deep sound that would travel easily to give warning of an eruption—just the quiet dribble of air from her pneumo.

Rosa let out the breath. "What the fuck was that?!"

"What the fuck was what?" Bridges said over the radio, a reminder that there was no privacy when diving. "Herrera, you okay? What's going on?"

She stayed there for a moment, a little rattled, then started to work her way back out, dragging the ROV.

"Yeah, I'm okay." Rosa continued to crawl backward out of the tube, dragging the ROV. "I saw...something in the tube. I don't know what. Orange, I think. Surprisingly large. Think I scared it. I'm coming out."

The meters out were a lot longer than the meters in. Progress was slow, made worse by the ROV. Rosa focused on keeping her breath steady. A face...it had a face! She couldn't be narc'ed—she wasn't deep enough.

There was a long moment of silence, then Bridges came back on the line. "Talked with some people here. Might have been a Mawson's dragonfish. They come in orange," he said, the obvious guessing in his voice. "But you're good now, yeah? Give Locke the signal when you're ready to head to the platform."

"Yeah, I'm good. As good as I can be hauling a broken ROV backward through a lava tube." Rosa's tone was lighter, and she was glad no one was there to see the look on her face. *Dragonfish my ass.* "You should ask Locke if he wants to grab a coffee—he's gonna be there a minute. I may be smaller than Daniels, but I got this ass from my mami, and it's gonna be a minute."

While her line was always open, topside was push-to-talk, so she didn't hear laughter on the other end. But when Bridges came back on, she could hear mirth still in his voice.

"Well, you got that ass in there—I have faith you can get it out," he said.

Rosa considered keeping the joke going, but it was a little weird bantering with Bridges. He was her father's age. A little older, actually. Hell, she was pretty sure he knew her father. Giving her head a little shake, she focused on getting out.

Finally, Rosa felt her feet move more freely in the open water, and she pushed herself out of the tube and hauled the ROV with her. She paused for a moment, looking down into the darkness. She had to be imagining things. But...she felt calm; her blood was up from the work but she wasn't freaking out. Definitely too clearheaded to be narc'ed. But what other explanation was there?

She tugged on the line twice. "Home, James."

There was a short pause, and then she felt Locke pulling on her gently. It was enough so she could swim over to the platform without much effort and finally set the heavy ROV down, not needing to carry it anymore.

Once she was settled on the platform, the operator started to lift it up.

"Good job, Herrera," Bridges said with a chuckle, "you were three minutes shy of needing a decompression stop. See you on the surface."

"That's because I'm the best." Any dive that didn't need a decompression stop was a good dive.

Once she broke the surface and the platform stopped moving, Locke finished looping her excess line and walked over to help her unshackle her harness and get out of her helmet. Rosa took a deep breath of the frozen air as the helmet came off. It made her cough a little as it iced her lungs, but it felt good after the humidity of the helmet. She patted Locke on the shoulder in thanks and stepped back so that Yaco could look over the busted ROV. Locke helped her get the collar off while Bridges stood behind her to remove her harness and bailout bottle.

"Ugh." She shivered. The back of her neck was wet. "Need anything else, or can I go get out of this thing and warm back up?"

"Go warm up," Bridges said with a chuckle.

As she stepped toward the gear locker, she heard Yaco exclaim something and rattled off a burst of Spanish that she wasn't able to catch. Guess it looked worse than she thought.

"I found it like that," Rosa shouted before ducking back inside.

She wanted something warm to eat, but it was too early for dinner. She made herself some tea and headed to her room. A little while later, dry and with a fresh shirt, she came back out and pulled her coat back on. She had decided to go looking for Yaco. She wanted to hear how bad the damage was. And what they thought had caused it.

By the time Rosa found the shop, Yaco was already attaching replacement thrusters, which would have to be rewired. The others, however, were sitting on the workbench and had been torn apart. It was surprising, really: they weren't dented from an impact or scratched from a rock, but literally ripped apart. It was no wonder Yaco was upset; there was no way they could be salvaged.

"Well, fuck me," Rosa muttered, amazed as she looked at the ruined thrusters. "What in the hell does that to an ROV?"

Giving her a shrug, Yaco shook his head. "Ninguna pista, Ms. Hererra," he said, looking up at her as he opened a few panels on the side of the ROV to work on the wiring. "Orcas don't come into the bay, and they're the only thing that could, I think."

Stepping up to the bench, Rosa picked up one of the thrusters and examined it, chewing on her lip as she did. Did that thing she saw in the water do this? That thing that she still wasn't completely sure she had actually seen? Why did it attack the ROV? Was it afraid? Did it at all understand what the machine was?

"Mierda," Yaco growled and tossed his screwdriver into the air; it hit the ceiling and clanged noisily onto the table before bouncing to the floor. "The boards are torqued. We need to go back in for the parts."

With a disgusted snort, he walked off to find the captain.

Blinking, Rosa watched Yaco go, then looked back at the piece in her hands. There were deep gouges in the metal. It reminded her a little of when they'd found debris that had been torn up by sharks or orcas, but it also wasn't quite right. It looked more like claw marks from a horror movie. Rosa set the piece down and headed out of the workshop, back toward the main hall.

The rest of the evening passed quickly enough, but when everyone retired for the night, she couldn't sleep. She had a room to herself, so at least she wasn't keeping anyone up with her tossing and turning. Sighing, she got up and pulled her clothes back on, heading into the mess to make tea. As Rosa waited for the tea to steep, she heard a telltale rhythmic thumping back down the opposite hallway where the science team slept. Groaning, she ran a hand over her face.

"I can't deal with this right now," she muttered, and picked up the tea, heading for the door. There were no storms and the weather was clear, so she wasn't at risk going outside. She pulled on her coat and boots and headed out onto the dock. It was the middle of the night, but you wouldn't know it. Not at this time of year.

Despite the eternal daytime, night still brought a soothing afternoon light, quite close to dusk, and with schedules still realistically being maintained, it was very quiet. Even the ship crew had turned in. This was nice. Rosa closed her eyes and breathed in the scent of her tea. The quiet was good. A minute to herself not in her room was good. She really should be sleeping—she was certainly tired enough. But maybe this moment was worth it.

Sipping the tea, Rosa walked down the dock and crouched down to look into the water. She had seen something down there today, but she wasn't stupid enough to be insistent about it. That was an easy way to get herself labeled as crazy and blacklisted. There were already companies happy to come up with bullshit reasons not to hire her because she was a woman. She didn't need to give them anything more concrete.

With the boat being docked and no one about, early in the summer and in the protected bay, the water was almost like glass, and aside from her reflection, she could see the sloping floor of the bay easily. The odd fish swam by, but the area was busy enough that penguins didn't typically wander into the waters over here.

As Rosa was contemplating the various sea life and what she could see, she was surprised to suddenly spot two orange lights that flickered gently in the seawater. She almost dropped her mug. She couldn't make out much more than that, as the dock was casting a shadow directly beneath her. Carefully and slowly, she set her mug down on the dock. She moved from her crouch to her knees, leaning a bit to try to better see what was in the water. *Of course I don't have a fucking phone on me.* There was no way to prove this was happening.

She was definitely seeing it. She could tell, because it blinked. It wasn't a cast of light or a dragonfish. It started to glow, and the water around it seemed to shimmer slightly. She was looking at it straight on, which made it impossible to make out its shape, but her slow movements seemed to encourage it; it seemed to be moving closer to the surface. She wasn't scaring it, whatever it was. That was good. Maybe if she got a better look at it, she could describe it to one of the scientists or look it up on Google so that she sounded less stupid describing it to one of the scientists. Something.

As she leaned forward, it suddenly got much closer. The eyes were part of a face, which was part of a very long body with arms that grasped the edge of the pier as their eyes met unhindered.

"Jesus, Mary, and Joseph!" Rosa gasped and froze as the creature broke the surface.

The face was long and angled, with long tendrils leading off from its chin and nose along the curve of its face and dangling behind its head. Large ears flared open when it broke the surface, like the opening of a conch shell. Its hair, if that's what it was, was a deep purple while its body, now that it was in the light, was orange with dark red running along its arms and down its chest. And…glowing, yes, it was glowing. Crimson and eggplant frills hung down the length of its arms and, it seemed, down its back. Rosa also noticed that steam was rising off it, and as it held itself up close to her, she could feel the heat radiating from it. She wasn't entirely sure how long its body was, as its tail drifted off into the water.

"Who," it croaked gently, the candle-flame-like eyes staring directly into hers.

The question made Rosa's eyes grow wider, but it was also somehow calming. The creature was intelligent. That...that was promising, wasn't it? Less likely for her to end up like the ROV, at least.

"Rosado," she said, her voice tremulous. "I mean, Rosa. My name is Rosa. Who...who are you? What are you?"

"Rosa," it said, rolling the R as it did so. Tilting its head slightly, it blinked again, a double set of eyelids closing as it did so. Leaning further in, it pressed against her cheek. It was so warm, so incredibly warm despite just coming out of the Antarctic waters. It let out a series of hisses and clicking noises, then spoke softly. "Good. Why here?"

"Oh, wow." The warmth! Rosa pressed her cheek back against the creature's for a moment, overtaken by the want to just curl up against it. Then her senses came back to her.

"The...the volcano." She pointed to the circle of the bay. "The scientists are here to study. To learn. Me, the others like me, the ones that go in the water, we're here to help."

"Help?" it asked, backing away just enough to look her back in the eyes. "Why need help?"

"The ROV," Rosa said, trying to use her hands to shape it in the air, "the...robot that you broke. I can go into places it can't. Like today, when I went to go get the ROV after you tore up its thrusters."

She looked up at it...no, him. There was something very masculine about the creature. And Christ, he was enormous. Rosa was average height for a woman, a little wider in the hip and bust—she wasn't tiny. And this creature was significantly larger than her. Rosa could only fathom how strong he was, as he was holding himself upright on the edge of the pier and so much of him dangled down below. The water was not compensating for that much weight. But it would also explain how he damaged the ROV so handily.

"They noticed spots of heat in the volcano, and they're trying to figure out..." Rosa trailed off, eyes getting big again. The heat spots. It wasn't the volcano.

"Don't understand," he said, tilting his head to the side again. "World warming, we wake. No need help." The creature relaxed his grip a little, easing himself back toward the water but still remaining right in front of her.

"We...we're not here to help it happen, we're here to help the scientists learn." Reaching up, Rosa pulled her hat off for a moment so she could run her hand over her hair and wrap her braid around her hand. She was beginning to understand that the problem here was a language barrier, not a lack of intelligence. "They just...they just want to learn. We don't want to hurt anything. The ROV wasn't going to hurt you; it just takes pictures and samples. It's there to help learn."

"Robat makes noise. No hurt, though?" he asked, moving closer to her again. He was examining her, those candlelight eyes examining the soft curves of her face. There was little else of her to see, wrapped as she was in heavy winter gear. He paused for a moment, reaching up to run a hand over her hair.

He was definitely what broke the ROV. Getting this close, she could see not only the large claws on each finger, but the large webbing between the fingers. More warmth, too. Every bit of him expelled heat like she was standing next to an old radiator. The heat felt wonderful, and hovering so close for so long, the creature was actually starting to warm Rosa.

"No, it is not there to hurt," Rosa said, looking into his strange, glowing eyes. "No one here wants to hurt. They want to learn. All of this," she gestured with a free hand, "is to learn." She opened the collar of her coat a touch, just enough for the cooler air to grace her collarbones. She felt a little like she should be more concerned, but he was clearly just curious about her.

Tilting his head once more, he leaned in, his face now near her chest as he looked at her skin. "You... shed?" he asked, seeming far more interested in her than in what she had just said. It had to have registered, though, as he seemed to be listening.

Blinking, Rosa pulled back just a little. "Ah, yes. It's too cold for us here. We have to wear extra clothing to stay warm if we want to be here. Like...like the suit I wear in the water. I can't go deep into cold water without it."

Pausing for a moment, the creature examined her before leaning in once more and running its long, forked tongue along her collar and neck. If the radiating heat wasn't enough, the tongue was so warm it almost felt like it would burn her, though that might have been because of the contrast with the cold air. But it left tingles on her skin. Rosa's eyes grew very wide, and she gasped. The flash of heat against her skin was intense, and it felt...good. Uncomfortably good.

"Warm, but not too. I keep you warm in cold," he said, seeming to derive something from the taste. "Warming awaken for you, too?"

"Wh-what do you mean?" She took a shaky breath, centering herself. "And no, we...we were always awake, just.." she pointed to the north. "Where the ocean grows warm. That's where I'm from."

"Then you always...breed," he said, blinking once more as he looked in the direction Rosa pointed. "When it is warm? Where you are from?"

Rosa turned pink. "That's not really any of your fucking—" She stopped herself and took a breath. This was not a fuckboi, this was a strange creature, possibly even an alien, and he was trying to learn something. She was also starting to wonder if this was actually a dream.

"Sorry. Um, no, we breed whenever we want to. I mean, I guess we breed more when it's cold." That seemed accurate. She had definitely turned down sex before because it was too damn hot.

"More when cold?" he questioned, then picked up his head suddenly. He blinked once then let go of the pier, dropping back down into the water with surprisingly little sound.

"Hey, kid, you okay?" she heard behind her as Bridges started to walk up. "Someone said they saw someone on the pier. Everything all right?"

Taking a breath, Rosa rubbed her eyes and looked out at the ocean again. Nothing. Sighing, she pulled her hat back on and picked up her now-frozen tea. "Yeah, I'm all right," Rosa said as she stood. "Just couldn't sleep. Honestly, I'm surprised you or anyone else is up."

"Hard to sleep down here," he said with a chuckle. "Even with the blackouts. You'd think a month would be long enough to adjust. Anyway, come on, I'll walk you back." Gesturing with his head, he turned and started back up toward the metal buildings. "Looking for your mystery fish?"

"Yeah, maybe." Rosa glanced back over her shoulder at the water again. What could she say that didn't sound crazy? "When I came out to make tea, someone was definitely fucking, and I didn't want to stick around to listen."

"People are people," he laughed. "In a few months, you'll be on... whatever island you want with all the frat boys you can handle."

"Ugh. Please. I don't fuck frat boys. I'm not Daniels—I have standards."

"Technically, he doesn't fuck frat boys either," Bridges continued, still amused. "But I know what you mean. I don't see you stooping to his level."

Before they stepped inside, Rosa looked back at the dock once more. She could swear she saw a gentle orange glow, like someone had lit a fire under the pier, but it was hard to tell in the perpetually waning light. She shook her head and stepped in.

"Daniels's level is anyone old enough to be legal but young enough that they don't know he's a bad idea. I saw what he was like in Louisiana." Rosa set her frozen cup in the sink. "All right, old man. I'll give sleep another go."

Bridges just shook his head and gave Rosa a pat on the shoulder. "If it makes you feel any better, you're not the only one. Yaco and a few others are a little spooked because of what happened to the drone," he said, grabbing a protein bar. "Ocean has all sorts of weird shit. Just remember the best thing about being a diver: we don't look tasty."

Heading back into her room, Rosa lifted the blackout shades and looked out at the water and ice. Was she losing her mind? Shaking her head again, she closed the blinds and got stripped down enough for bed, climbing in and hoping the exhaustion from the day would finally catch up to her. The base had gone quiet, and it was much easier for Rosa to fall asleep. The heat from where the creature licked her seemed to linger, radiating from her neck to the rest of her body, and it made her sleep the most comfortable she'd had since she flew south.

She also slept deep enough to dream for the first time since she had arrived. Or at least, the first time she remembered. She was on her hands and knees, warm hands sliding over her hips as a searing tongue lapped at her pussy. Her alarm went off right before she came. Sitting up in bed, Rosa swore and ran a hand over her face. Was she really fantasizing about fucking the weird sea monster that she may very well have imagined?

The next couple days were a little tense. The crew was spooked, she was frustrated, Daniels continued to be a stain on humanity, and Locke's calm and almost-cheerful demeanor made it increasingly believable that he was fucking one of the scientists. Which just irritated Rosa more.

Everything finally came to a head two days later when Daniels was being himself. He was an aggravating douche on a good day, but after over a month without beer or a blow job (because no one here was naïve or hard up enough to say yes to that), he was extra irritating. Rosa didn't even remember entirely what started the argument. She was usually so good at telling him to fuck off and leaving it. But he got under her skin, kept calling her Pink.

What ended it, though, was when he said it should be her job to "take care" of the rest of the team, that a woman diver wasn't good for much, she might as well make herself available to the rest of them. That was when she hit him. Rosa hauled the same scrap Daniels did, wore the same heavy-ass gear, and had biceps like steel. And when she told her dad that she was going to take his advice and be a diver, he made sure she knew how to throw a punch.

Blood streaked down Daniels' face as he reeled backward. She'd almost certainly broken his nose. Rosa leapt at him, knocking him over, and was ready to punch him again when Bridges hauled her off of him.

"All right, all right, enough," Bridges said, holding Rosa in a half nelson with one arm and making sure Daniels stayed back with the other. Bridges's usually easygoing behavior could change very quickly when it needed to, and that swing had been a hard one. "We're all tense but, both of you, knock it the fuck off."

Rosa steadied her breath and went soft in Bridges's grip. Her jaw was set, and if Daniels came within five feet of her, she would fucking drown him, but she wasn't going to fight against her supervisor.

Bridges wasn't done. "Daniels, one more word out of you and I'm sending you home. Clean up your fuckin' face and take a cold shower before I throw you in the bay," he stated, then released Rosa. "Herrera, go take a fuckin' walk and cool off. I don't want the two of you getting within fifty fuckin' meters of each other for the rest of the day."

"Fine," Rosa growled, and headed straight for the door, grabbing her gear and pulling it on as she stepped outside. It was cold as hell outside, but her blood was up from the confrontation. She pulled on her gloves, kept her hat in her hand, and stomped down the trail, away from the base toward the bay.

It was another dim, but far from dark, evening. Golden Hour lasted for several, and if it wasn't so cold it'd be a great place for photos. The water was stirred up a bit at this point, the ship having just docked an hour or so ago; the last of the crew waved to Rosa as they walked down the gangplank and headed toward the station. Rosa forced herself to smile and wave back. It wasn't their fault Daniels was a piece of garbage who overstepped himself. She didn't linger, though, and walked down along the shoreline, following the curve rather than turning down the path to where the workshop was. Her watch said it was about -4°C. She wasn't feeling it yet, though. Still too angry, still too much adrenaline.

It was astounding how sheltered this bay was, especially knowing there was an active volcano at the bottom of it. As she looked out over the water, she could see flecks of orange light. It was hard to tell if it was her serpentine friend or just the incredibly low sunlight reflected off a cloud and back into the water. Rosa tipped her head to the side, and looked down at the water. She walked to the edge of the shore, the tideless bay wetting the bottom of her boots. There wasn't much beach here. Hardly any, really. Looked like a bit of a lip, then a drop. That made sense. This was a caldera—there wouldn't be a gentle slope to the bottom.

Crouching down, Rosa peered into the water. Her heart was still beating pretty hard, and she knew damn well she was awake and lucid. If there was something in the water, then her encounter with the creature had not been an exhausted hallucination.

The light continued to play against the motion of the water, then disappeared. Not more than a moment later it returned and lit up again. Just as quickly as when he had darted up to the pier, the great mass of the creature surfaced from the water and rose up in front of her.

She had a much better look at his form this time. While alien and odd he might be, his torso was very humanoid: two strong arms ending in those webbed, clawed, four-fingered hands. His ears unfurled again as he left the water. Below what would be his waist, however, seemed serpentine. No merman or the like, the tail continued on into the water, not seeming to end in any sort of fin but still lined with leathery furls.

"Rosa," he said, rolling the R again, "you return to edge."

So she hadn't made it up, but she was possibly still insane. "Yes," Rosa said, tucking her hat into her pocket. "I got into a fight. Needed to take a walk. To get away from everyone for a little bit."

"You fight?" he asked, slithering closer to her, leaning in to be closer to her head level. The strange tendrils that extended off his chin and cheeks continued to drift behind him as though he were still underwater, and steam was easily visible rising from his body.

"Sometimes." Rosa could feel the adrenaline starting to wash out of her. "My father taught me. I try not to. Do you fight?"

"No," he said gently. "No reason. Do not fight food—too easy. Do not fight others—no need."

Rosa nodded. "We do not fight food. Sometimes, though, we fight each other. We get angry. Territorial, sometimes."

Rosa shifted her stance a little. She didn't want to sit here on the water. Her pants were waterproof, but it would be cold. The heat radiating off of the creature in front of her was keeping her warm, though. Certainly enough to keep her coat open and her hat off. And maybe even... Rosa pulled off her gloves, shoving them in her pocket and extending a hand carefully toward him, feeling the heat bleeding off of him.

"Strange," it commented rather flatly, which could summarize the human race as a whole quite easily. As she raised her hand to him, he looked and mirrored her, shifting closer and moving his hand toward hers. "Rosa angry now?"

"No," Rosa said, shaking her head a little, "calm now. It is easy to be calm near you. Do...do you have a name? What do I call you?"

"No name," he said with a shake of his head. "Call me what you like." The creature lifted up his other hand as he gently took her offered one. The warmth was amazing, his skin rubbery but soft. It was just the slightest bit damp, but not as much as someone just coming out of the water should be.

Rosa looked at their joined hands, amazed. "You're so warm. Like there's a fire within you. I read a story once; there was a man called Agni. It's supposed to mean fire. Could I call you Agni?"

"Agni," he repeated, swallowing the word. He tried it again, then again until it sounded like what Rosa had said. "Yes, Agni. The...volcano, you called it. Our home. It is us. You are warm too, almost. Soft." He took Rosa's other hand, his fingers caressing over her skin.

"You are why the scientists are here," Rosa said softly. "You are waking up, and they see that there is heat from the volcano that wasn't there before." She looked at her small hands in his clawed ones for another moment, then back up into his eyes. "Why do you talk to me? You hide from the others."

"Not all are safe," he said, returning the look. "You...felt safe. We have seen others. They hunt. Not for food. But you...you felt different."

"No, I understand." Rosa's brows drew down, sad with the realization. "Some of us would hunt you. I'm sorry."

"It is the way. Predators clashing," he gave a little shrug.

Rosa considered Agni for a moment, and something popped into her head. "Um, why did you ask about...breeding last time?"

Leaning in a little closer, and now also towering over her, he tilted his head again. "Your taste," Agni said, flicking out his tongue. "Like you were awoken. In need."

Rosa's head tipped back as she looked up at him. "What do you mean? What...how do I taste?"

Agni pondered for a moment, then leaned in and licked her once more. His hot, smooth tongue traced along her collar and the side of her neck; the tingles followed. Rosa's eyes closed for a moment. She remembered her dream, and it felt more reasonable now. The radiating heat, the way her skin flushed—it reminded her a little of when she had been less experienced, how her whole body would tense and prickle with anticipation before being touched. It was probably a reaction to something in his saliva, but it felt good.

The creature kept his forked tongue out this time, and presented it before her. Eyes open once more, Rosa looked at Agni for a second, letting out a soft, breathy laugh. Leaning forward, she opened her mouth and flicked her own tongue against his, swirling about the strange, forked edge. Beyond the heat, the tingling sensation tickled over her tongue, and she could taste herself, or imagine she did perhaps. Salty with a hint of some sort of spice. Nothing deep, she had to think about it to pick it out, but it was not off-putting in any way. Agni's tongue played against her own for a moment before uncurling and slowly slipping back into his mouth. There were no hurried moments; he was sharing himself with her.

"You taste it?"

"I taste...something," Rosa said, a little embarrassed by how much she was reacting to this. Odd that she wasn't more horrified by the fact that it was happening at all, but she'd seen some weird shit while working—this was just officially the weirdest. "I don't...I'm not sure what it means."

"Did I taste wrong?" Agni asked, still remaining close to Rosa. "Are you not in need? We are different. Wrong maybe."

Rosa was starting to understand what Agni meant by "in need." She blushed a little. "No, you're not wrong. I think I just don't...notice it that way. Are you in need? Does that happen when you wake?"

Agni...smiled? He seemed pleased that he was correct. "Yes. It has become warming. We awaken; that is when. Us do, yes?"

Rosa blinked, and tipped her head to the side. Agni's smile was strange, but it wasn't alarming. "Um, yes?"

"Here?" he asked, slithering about as close as he could without pressing into her. His hands had released hers and had moved, seeming conflicted about whether to stay open for her, or to embrace her.

"Oh...oh!" Rosa bit her lip, and looked back over her shoulder. *Of course that was what he meant.* There were so many reasons why she should step away, change her mind. But...his tongue had felt amazing. Wouldn't more feel better?

"Is there somewhere more sheltered?" Rosa asked, looking past him for a moment. "Safe from the wind, where the others won't see?"

"My den," he offered. "I will protect you from cold. But it is deep. Down below."

"I wouldn't survive without my gear, but...wait," Rosa looked back over her shoulder at the docks. The crew had left the ship, and there was plenty of room there. No one would come out for at least another five to six hours. "The ship. Meet me at the ship."

"Yes, Rosa," Agni said. He leaned in once more, licked again along the opposite side of her neck, and took the taste into his mouth this time. A soft warbling noise and he turned, darting back into the water and disappearing into the depths.

"I cannot believe I'm doing this," Rosa muttered to herself as she trudged back to the dock. The tingle in her skin, and the warmth that pulsed from it, kept her moving to the dock instead of ducking back into the base. She checked her watch. It was late, that was good. Bridges was probably too angry to go looking for her again.

She stepped carefully onto the boat, heading toward the back. While it was securely tethered to the dock, nothing was locked down, no gate barred her entrance. Why would there be? Who would steal a boat here? She made her way to the stern. There was a small crane and winch back here, and a platform to stand under that would obscure what was about to happen from satellites and other aerials. The angle of the ship cut off the wind. It was still cold, but...well, Agni could keep that from being a problem.

As Rosa reached the back of the ship, Agni shot out of the water and grabbed the edge, pulling himself up. With a bit of wriggling, he was able to curl and lift the length of his body onto the deck. Rising up once more, she could see him haloed in steam as he began to move toward her.

"This ship...is cold," he said, and the tone in his voice implied more than just the temperature.

"It...it's made of metal; it's not, I don't know, natural? Does it bother you?" Rosa stepped down onto the lower deck under the platform, taking off her gloves again. There were a couple supply crates here, probably with smaller ROVs inside. She set her hat and gloves on top of one.

"If you are okay, I am okay," he said, curling up a little. Already the metal was starting to warm from his presence. Not enough to be uncomfortable, far from it, just as though it had been soaking in the morning sun for a while. "How do you…" Agni started, gesturing with his hands.

Rosa laughed a little. "Well, it would help if I undressed." Clearly this was a first for both of them. Rosa guessed Agni had met humans before since he could speak at all, and if she was more academically minded, she might have been more curious about that, but it seemed his last encounter with her species hadn't been physical.

Cautiously, Rosa peeled off her coat, and then her sweater. That seemed okay; the area around Agni was warm enough, so she could keep going. Her boots came off next, and the deck felt surprisingly nice through her socks. Looking back up at Agni, she once more wondered what the hell was possessing her, but she wiggled out of her undershirt, bra, pants, and leggings. There was still a bite to the air, and she shivered just a little once she was bare, but it wasn't nearly as cold as it should have been. As a final thought, Rosa reached up and unbraided her hair, shaking it free. It was pretty long these days, falling over her shoulders and down her back.

"You are…so delicate," Agni said gently as he circled around her, looking at her from all angles, further warming the air around her.

A surprised, breathy laugh burst from Rosa. "Delicate? I…well, maybe you think so. It's not… Humans don't think I'm delicate." It was kind of nice to hear, though.

"No fins, no spurs. Just…" Reaching out as his words trailed, Agni carefully ran his hand over her form, starting at her shoulder and down her back to the healthy curve of her ass. He clearly thought it was a good thing. He seemed enamored by her and, it appeared, aroused.

From right around where she would expect it to be, a sheath had opened and a pair of hemi-penises began to slide out. Rosa's eyes grew big again. She hadn't considered what Agni would…possess. He could speak, and his upper body looked human-ish; she had assumed that his cock would be the same. They appeared to be like budding flowers on thick stalks, bright orange with occasional spots of red. He paid it no mind, however, as he was far too interested in Rosa's body. And every time Rosa wondered if she was crazy for doing this, Agni's hand passed over her skin, impossibly warm and smooth.

With a sudden burst of speed, he curled his tail behind her and carefully pushed her against it. "Oh!" Rosa felt vulnerable in a manner she was honestly not used to feeling during sex. Her legs parted, sliding down either side of Agni's tail, and she reached down to brace herself against it, which simply opened more of her body to his curious explorations. Agni ran his hands along Rosa's thighs, and he pressed his face against her neck gently. That long, forked tongue found itself sliding over her chest and collar as it seemed he was relishing in her flavor. She moaned. The tingle in her skin following the path of Agni's tongue was making her wet and flushed, and Agni's presence kept the air warm. If it weren't for the occasional breeze, she might actually overheat.

There was a strange, deep warble from Agni, and his hands grasped her, wrapping around her gently as he moved her this way and that. The creature's mouth and tongue took to exploring all of Rosa's body. Sharp teeth brushed against her skin before being soothed by his tongue, and a trail of tingles soon ran all over her body. Agni took great interest in her breasts, hips, and ass as he licked and nibbled them. That odd warble in his throat built up as she squirmed in his hands and against his body. Then the tongue finally reached the apex of her thighs. The barest bit of her nectar touched his sensitive tongue, and he immediately buried it inside her. It was long, wriggled almost prehensily, and heated her up in more ways than one. Whimpering, Rosa closed her eyes and let her head fall back. His tail had lifted her up to be right at serving height, and his hands traveled back up to caress over her form as he feasted upon her with fervor.

It was like her dream, a delicious searing heat that spread through her hips as Agni's strange tongue twisted in and against her. Sensation danced across her skin, the tongue inside her rubbed and pressed in every direction, and her body began to tense. She grasped Agni as she came, her nails digging in a little. Tightening his own grip, Agni continued to dig in, his tongue lapping up every drop of her offering. It was as if she was the most delicious thing he'd ever tasted. His mouth all but surrounded Rosa's pussy, drinking from her.

"Yes!" Rosa gasped and shuddered, and had no intention of telling him to stop. "It's so...so good!"

Writhing against Agni's tail, Rosa licked her lips and tossed her hair. The tongue kept licking at her, Agni's hot mouth sucking at everything that dripped from her pussy. She cried out sharply as she came again, gushingly wet against that fiery tongue.

It took a long, ravenous moment, but Agni finally pulled away from

Rosa's sex, his tongue making sure to lick up every stray bit of moisture, lashing her clit in the process. Settling her back onto his tail, he rose before her, the candlelight eyes burning like bonfires now.

"I have...tasted you so much," he stated, his hands still exploring over her skin. "What do you wish of me? Anything."

Panting, it took a moment for Rosa to come back to herself. "I...oh, wow, you already did a lot for me."

Picking her head up, Rosa looked at Agni and licked her lips. She loved how he kept touching her. And she'd seen that look before.

"It looks like you want to fuck me," Rosa said, her gaze moved down Agni's body to his strange cocks. "Do you want to, what would you call it... Do you want to breed with me?"

"Yes, all I want," Agni said, arching himself so that both his cocks were presented to her, the lower one resting on her pelvis. They already dripped with desire, and his pre felt like someone was dripping hot wax on her. It didn't burn, but it definitely fired off her nerves in delicious ways. His heat was building in more ways than one, and she could not think of a better environment to do this in. Indoors, they'd be creating an immense amount of steam, and she needed the occasional chill to keep her head from swimming.

Looking down, Rosa bit her lip as she considered. Neither of his cocks were small, and she wasn't sure she could take both of them in cunt, no matter how impossibly wet she felt right now. But...

Rosa pushed herself up and reached down, sliding her fingertips over the head of one cock, coating her fingers in the pre. It was delightfully slick. She grinned a little.

"I have an idea, but I need you to turn me over. I want to be able to take all of you," she said.

The moment the request left her lips, she found herself flipped over onto her stomach, his tail curling to raise her up to meet him. She let out another little laugh of surprise. She honestly couldn't tell if he had done it with his hands or a ripple down the length of him, but he was wasting no time.

Reaching back, Rosa slid her fingertips and a dollop of cum over the rim of her ass. This was far from a first for her, and while she'd never been double penetrated before, she'd always really wanted to. This wasn't how she imagined it would happen, but Agni was a little beyond any of her previous imaginings.

"They'll feel a little different," Rosa said, gently guiding the cocks so eagerly waiting for her, rubbing one against her tighter opening to spread more pre-cum and be ready for what was about to happen, "but I'm very sure I can take you like this. And I want it so very, very bad."

"Yesss…I want…" Agni hissed as he took hold of her hips. Oh, he was very eager, but had the foresight to not just jam his lengths into her. With an insistent easing, he pulled her against him, filling her a few inches before easing up and resuming, letting her own slick and his precum moisten her where needed.

"Oh, fuck!" Rosa held on to Agni, and her eyes rolled back in her head for a moment. He made it in, no problem, but it was far more intense than she'd anticipated. It was also absolutely amazing. He didn't stop until their bodies met and she had sheathed him completely. It was so hot, the warmth welling up inside her, radiating from her core into the rest of her body. The heat softened and warmed her, added to the intensity, and his precum sent the same tingles through her that his saliva did. She wrapped her arms around his tail, nuzzling at it as she let the feeling wash over and through her.

A much louder warbling noise came out of him as he felt her clench and wrap completely around him. Agni was clearly enjoying her, and he started to move. It was perhaps three or four measured thrusts before Agni started to pound into Rosa. As long as she continued to make content noises, he moved harder.

"Rrrrrrosa," he growled, the R rolling for a much longer time than usual. "More. Must have more."

"Yes," Rosa moaned, rubbing her face against Agni's tail, licking it even. "Don't stop! Anything you want, hard as you want, just don't stop!"

Most of Agni's hesitance seemed to disappear with her words. She had never been so thoroughly fucked. It was incredible. Agni relentlessly thrust into her with a stamina she hadn't encountered in years. The searing cocks stretched and filled her, making her pussy and ass pulse with sensation and pleasure. She was drooling, it felt so good. A shudder passed through her entire body as she came again.

Hissing, he grabbed Rosa's wrists and held them past her head, stretching her out along his tail. Undulating his whole body, he began slamming his shafts into her with enough force to make her entire body quake with each penetration. It was like great swelling waves were breaking inside of her. It bordered on too much. Perhaps that was good. If the experience had been any less overwhelming, it would be too easy to want it all the time.

Finally, Agni's orgasm struck him. The heads of his cocks, which appeared like flower buds, blossomed inside her. No delicate petals were these, but heavy flesh engorged with lust, stretching her body to accept him. Then, with a geyser of molten cum, he filled her. The tingly warmth from his tongue, spilling into her tenfold from his dual columns of flesh, radiated into her entire body as he held himself deep inside her, body arched. A low, guttural moan rolled out of Rosa as Agni came. His cum was so hot it almost burned. She felt as if she were melting. The pleasure that had been teasing her skin blossomed inside her, setting her nerves alight, and she came once more with a whimper.

"So good," she breathed against his skin, lightheaded with it. "So warm, so good!"

Releasing her body, he curled up enough to once more run his tongue up the entire length of her back and across her neck. The blossomed heads of his cocks settled back in, and he eased out of her before curling around her. Gently he ran claws through her hair, examining it as he breathed heavily around her. Rosa was soft in his arms. She couldn't quite move yet, luxuriating in an afterglow that felt like the heart of a sun. She would need to pull herself together, get dressed and back inside before anyone thought she'd ended up dead, but...that could wait just a minute.

"You are..." Agni started, then shook his head, unable to find the correct words.

"That was like nothing I've ever done," Rosa said slowly. "It was... you were incredible."

"Again?" Agni asked, but the tone wasn't insistent this time. More just generally hopeful. "Our season is beginning."

A soft, breathy giggle came out of Rosa. "Not...not today, but yes, we can do this again. I think...I think I will be here through your season. We're supposed to be here until it's almost winter. Until it starts to get colder again."

"Anytime," he rumbled, and his tail constricted around Rosa, like a hug. Not too tight, but all encompassing, and she could feel him ripple against her skin. His hands, however, never stopped touching her, brushing through her hair and caressing her skin.

Rosa remained in Agni's arms for a long moment, letting his heat seep into her bones, something to keep with her when she headed back into the snow. Finally, she gently pulled away and began putting her layers back on. She was an utter mess—it was a good thing she had packed plenty of panties and leggings, because these were not going to be fit for a second day once she got back to her room.

"I should get back before anyone is worried," Rosa said, finally picking up her coat and hat. "We don't want them to send anyone looking for me."

"No, not yet," Agni said a little melancholically. "I will always be here. Will not break noisy box." Agni kept Rosa circled with his long form until she had finished dressing, and only then did he move to just face her.

"Rosa," he said again, reaching out to take her hand.

Looking up, Rosa held her hand out to Agni, letting him take it. She hadn't put her gloves back on yet, so it was just her skin against his. "Yes?"

Agni shook his head. Leaning in, he gently licked the side of her neck before she covered up entirely. "See soon."

Smiling, Rosa squeezed his hand. "Yes. Soon."

She headed back across the ship to the dock. By the time she reached the other side of the ship, she had to zip her coat back up and pull her gloves on. She left her hat off though, her hair floating behind her with the occasional errant wind. By the time she'd reached the door to the base, the cold air had driven the flush from her face. She still felt like she was filled with Agni's cum, its incredible heat radiating through her, but she would figure that out back in her room.

It was pretty late by the time she stepped back inside. Wandering back into the mess, Rosa saw the only other person that was up was Dr. Evita Rey. She was making a cup of tea and looked up at Rosa, exhausted.

"We're sitting on a very interesting volcano," Dr. Rey said unprompted. "The readings are unlike anything I've ever come across."

Rosa hung up her coat and looked over at the volcanologist. She had intended to head to her room as quickly as possible—she could feel Agni's cum saturating her underwear—but the comment made her pause.

"What makes it so different?" Rosa asked, walking over to the kitchen area.

"Lots of activity. Heat spikes in a number of places," Dr. Rey said, yawning and taking a sip of her tea, "but no seismic activity. No warning of eruption. Don't mind me, just rambling. Sleep dep." The older woman gave Rosa a smile and took another sip of tea.

"The world is full of strange things," Rosa murmured. "Maybe... maybe it's something new."

Giving a little wave, Dr. Rey headed back toward the labs where the sensors Rosa and the lot had been planting for the better part of a month were quietly, constantly feeding information. Rosa wondered if the older woman would be disappointed to learn the truth. Then again, she probably never would. Shaking her head, she grabbed a drink and headed back to her room.

Once the door was closed and locked, Rosa shed her clothing. She could still feel the hot cum seeping out of her, and it made her wish she had the energy to go find Agni again. She threw a towel down on the bed and stretched out. Everything was still warm and tingling. Moaning quietly, she reached down and slid her fingers into her slick pussy. She'd come so many times that day, but maybe...maybe just one more...

Closing her eyes, Rosa remembered the feel of Agni's tongue on her skin, his hands roving her body, and his strange cocks pummeling into her. She spread her legs wider, rubbing her clit with one hand while she fucked herself with the fingers of the other, the strange cum making a mess all over her thighs. Finally, with clenched teeth, Rosa shuddered, and more warm cum spurted out of her as her muscles clenched.

It took a minute to clean up. It didn't help that Rosa didn't want to dress enough to head to the bathroom. There were a stack of wipes, however, and eventually Rosa felt clean enough to pull on her pajamas and climb into bed. She still felt so warm, like it was radiating through her. She would see Agni again in a couple days. She could just tell Bridges that the walks were to help her deal with stress; he'd probably buy it. No one needed to know she was letting a lava monster fuck her raw on the research vessel.

Rosa giggled, and burrowed into her blankets. This whole thing was fucking weird, but she didn't care anymore. The next few months wouldn't be so bad after all.

RULE OF THREE

Alison looked out the window at the snow, her black lipstick making her pout more obvious. The party was looking to be a bust. While snow on Halloween wasn't unheard of, it was a little surprising just how much they were getting. The cabin, owned by Alison's parents, was nestled in almost a foot of snow at this point. She'd checked the forecast all week leading up to this. It wasn't supposed to snow until Monday. But then the weather had shifted. She tossed her midnight hair back over her shoulder, glaring at the weather.

Thankfully, Alison wasn't alone. "It would be beautiful under other circumstances," Nia said, walking up next to Alison and looking up at her friend. Nia was about three inches shorter than Alison. "Or if everyone had made it. That was Cat on the phone, by the way—they just closed 24. No one else is coming, and we're not leaving."

Behind Nia, the cabin was decorated with fake spiderwebs, pumpkins, and a number of anatomically incorrect skeletal creatures. And also what would be an almost-concerning number of candles, if it weren't for the fact that over half of them were LED pillars. There was a charcuterie tray, apple slices with caramel sauce for dipping, bowls of candy, bottles of vodka, and a few liqueurs for cocktails. The cabin had been renovated over the past couple years with new hardwood floors, an updated kitchen, and modern furniture. They could even program the canned lights in the living room—Alison currently had them dimmed for a cozy feel. It all came together for a spooky, slightly bougie atmosphere.

Grumbling, Alison crossed her arms over her chest. "They should have left this morning when you did." Each thick, heavy flake that fell from the sky further soured her mood.

Nia rolled her hazel eyes and bumped Alison with her hip. "Yeah, well, they didn't. Come on, don't be like that. Let's put on some music, have a drink, and dress up. We can take selfies and be dumb. Let's make the best of it."

Alison looked over at Nia, expression hopeful. "Will you still do the thing with me at midnight?"

"I will do whatever witchy thing makes you happy," Nia said, smiling. "I'll even let you pick what I wear."

Uncrossing her arms, Alison started to smile a little and followed Nia to the master suite they were sharing—the original plan had been to put everyone two per room, though it looked like they wouldn't need to after all.

"Did you bring that black dress?" Alison asked as Nia opened her suitcase.

"I did," Nia said, wrinkling up her nose. "Though I don't know why you wanted me to. It's too short and too tight."

"It's perfect," Alison said firmly, digging in her own bag and pulling out her makeup case. "Put it on and I'll meet you in the bathroom."

It was Nia's turn to pout, but she had promised. The dress in question was stretch satin with embroidered mesh insets. They'd found it in a consignment store in Boulder months ago. Nia didn't like how it hugged her butt, which got enough attention on its own, in her opinion. And the dress was super short. Careful-when-you-bend-over levels of short. She also didn't love that she couldn't wear a bra with it. The neckline dipped past where a bra would sit, with nothing but that embroidered window. Nia's full breasts strained the fabric, and the bodice was tight enough that it gave her a really magnificent cleavage underneath that thin black mesh.

Another sigh, and Nia headed into the bathroom. Alison had spread out her makeup on the counter and was touching up her black lipstick.

"See? It looks great on you!" Alison smiled triumphantly.

"I will admit that my boobs look pretty amazing in this," Nia said, almost reluctantly.

Alison knew Nia was self-conscious about her figure, and that she'd spent most of her teens being teased for her weight. Alison thought she looked great. Alison had been on the swim team all through highschool (her parents had insisted) and still had a swimmer's figure even though she hadn't done laps since she'd started college. Nia was so lush in comparison. Alison felt it was her mission to get Nia comfortable with showing off her figure. They'd get there—baby steps.

"You look amazing," Alison said with a smile as Nia clipped a pair of cat ears into her tight burgundy curls. "I'm going to change; you go make drinks."

"I'm going, I'm going." Nia rolled her eyes again and returned to the kitchen. She paused long enough to pull out her already-paired phone and hit play, filling the house with a setlist that would have been appropriate at Goth/EDM night at their favorite club.

As Nia made drinks, Alison dug through her clothes. She was starting to feel better. Yeah, it would have been great if everyone had made it, but Nia was her closest friend and they'd still find a way to have fun. She picked up the grimoire at the bottom of her suitcase. It was bound in indigo leather with brass accents. Alison knew Nia wasn't a believer, but if everything worked out, they would definitely have an exciting evening.

Setting the book aside, Alison changed into a slinky red dress and put on little devil horns. Sure, it was a bit of a trite costume, but she saw it more as manifesting her desires. Nia was going to help Alison perform a summoning tonight. The outfit was just getting her in the mood, a positive mindscape.

Back in the main room, Nia had cocktails ready, and handed one off to Alison as soon as she came out. They danced and took pictures and drank their way through the entire pitcher of what the mixology website had called "Vampire Punch." They braved the cold long enough to take pictures in the fresh snow, which Nia posted to all their socials, and then had to turn off notifications because they kept interrupting the music.

At 11:30 an alarm on Alison's phone went off. "Oh! It's time to get ready!"

"All right," Nia said, smiling indulgently. "What do you need me to do?"

Alison set her drink down and ran back into the bedroom, returning quickly with the grimoire and a bag. "Okay! We need to move the coffee table and push back the couch. I've got chalk for the circle. We'll have to be careful not to smudge it, but at least it won't stain."

"I guess I'll move things while you do whatever you need to with the chalk," Nia said, shrugging. "So what are you hoping to accomplish?"

"Um..." Alison's voice wavered slightly. She stood back up and watched Nia move the furniture. "We're...going to try to summon something."

"What, really?" Nia looked at Alison disbelievingly.

Alison set her hands on her hips. "Yes, really!"

"Whatever you say, spooky butt," Nia said, and went back to clearing an area. "If it doesn't work, do we have a backup plan for the evening?"

Grumbling, Alison fished out her chalk. "On the very unlikely chance that it doesn't work, we'll drink more, watch bad horror movies, and probably have sex on the couch during the bad horror movies."

Nia stepped back with a giggle. "All right, I'm down. Do your thing."

Alison opened the book to the page she'd marked with a ribbon and reviewed it for a moment. Then, taking a deep breath, Alison drew a circle in the center of the living room on the hardwood floors, and then a hexagon inside it. A smaller circle went in the center of the hexagon, and a combination of alchemical symbols and runes went in the smaller circle, and also in the spaces between the hexagon and the larger circle.

A cover of "(Every Day is) Halloween" came on as Alison finished the runes and put the chalk away; it made her smile. Nia had poured herself another drink and was watching Alison with curiosity and interest, but no excitement. That was the biggest problem with Nia being the only one here. The others would have been more into the process. Alison fished out her phone for a minute to take a couple pictures. She could show them to everyone later.

Finally, Alison dug in her bag again and set three items down in the circle. The first was an old bottle of port. The second was a golden pendant. The last was a jar of spiced honey.

"All right," Alison said, getting up. "I need a drop of your blood. Well, three drops."

"Of course you do," Nia said dryly, walking over. "You're lucky I love you."

"You are truly the best of friends," Alison said with a grin, taking out a tiny porcelain bowl and a sterilized needle. She pricked Nia's finger, which Nia took without so much as a flinch, and squeezed out three drops of blood. "Thank you."

"Would you have done this to everyone if they'd made it?" Nia arched an eyebrow.

Nodding, Alison pulled out a steriwipe and cleaned the needle before pricking her own finger and repeating the process. "Ow! Yes. If you're not part of the ritual, you're an interloper and could be in danger."

"Well, okay," Nia said with a shrug.

At least Nia wasn't protesting. Carefully, Alison set the tiny bowl in the center. "We're ready—kneel there," she pointed to one of the corners of the hexagon. Nia rolled her eyes again, but complied.

Alison reached over and hit pause on the playlist, then knelt across from Nia, the book in her hands. She tried not to squee in her excitement.

"Vocamus orientem, occidentem, septemtrionem, meridiem; Vigiles vocamus, ut hac nocte nos tueamur," Alison read from the book. She knew it was Latin, and kinda knew what it said. Kinda. "Voluptatem animi quaerat possimus. Desiderio nostro responsum petimus."

Nia gasped in surprise: she was aroused. She could feel herself getting wet. She didn't find Alison's theatrics terribly sexy, so she wasn't sure why, but she wanted to squirm.

"Vinum offerimus. Divitias offerimus. Munera aromata," Alison continued, starting to wiggle a little. She felt something tingle through her. "Nosmetipsos offerimus, Desiderium nostrum. Satisfieri postulamus!"

There was a long moment of nothing but quiet. Nia was about to comment but was stopped as everything went dark—the lights died, and aside from the moonlight reflecting off the snow outside, it was pitch black. There was a rush, a surprisingly warm wind, and the two could feel that there were others in the room, the sense of others breathing and moving nearby. Then the others spoke.

"What is it—," one masculine voice, deep and rumbling with a smoothness to it, started to say.

"Why have you—," another, feminine and dripping with desire, began at the same time.

I have come as—, a third, spoken in their head with a voice that matched their own and a dozen others, started to say.

Another lengthy silence, something a little awkward about it. More breathing, then a slight shuffling.

"Valzia, is that you?" the deep voice asked.

"Coviok?" the feminine voice questioned back. "I think Alldizius is here as well."

I am, the mental voice answered, *what is going on?*

One of them snapped their fingers, and the room was suddenly aglow with a reddish light, giving the girls a good look at who—or rather, what—the voices belonged to.

"Young summoners," Coviok rumbled, smiling down at Alison and Nia. He was massive, easily standing seven feet tall and thickly muscled, with crimson skin and eyes of brilliant gold. A crown of six horns pierced his head, parting his heavy hair that was so black it seemed to absorb light. Given the girls' kneeling position, it was impossible not to notice the two long, thick shafts of ribbed meat displayed from his pelvis, one above the other.

"They're delicious," Valzia commented. A few inches shy of six feet, the demoness was purple in hue with long, flowing white hair. Her curves were exaggerated in their proportions—a snatched waist, almost-gravity-defying breasts, wide hips, and a perfect bubble butt. Valzia smiled and gently bit her bottom lip; her silver eyes shone like two full moons, and her plum-stained lips begged to be kissed.

Delightful as they appear, this is a problem, Alldizius said, which brought their attention to the third figure. A mass of tentacles of all shapes and sizes, colored mottled midnight blue and purple, tipped with phalluses of every genus they could imagine, and many that did not exist in nature. While the creature appeared slick and moist, it left no residue as it squirmed around to move closer to the girls. *The contractors are not going to be happy with this.*

"Gods above and below, it worked!" A smile spread over Alison's face. "But...why are there three of you?" She looked back down at the book, skimming the spell again. The instructions were in a very archaic dialect of English, which made them hard to understand.

Valzia strutted over to Alison on some impressive stilettos that, upon closer examination, were actually bone spikes that extended from her heel. Smiling, Valzia slinked down next to the young witch and graced a hand along her shoulder. Alison looked up from the book and felt her heart beat faster.

"Of course it worked, lovely," the demoness said, leaning close. "Said the words, gave the offering, sealed the pact in blood."

"Oh, wow," Alison murmured. She could feel herself soaking through the tiny thong she wore under the short dress. Her gaze drifted down to the demoness's massive breasts.

Nia, meanwhile, was staring at the creatures in front of them and doing her best not to panic. It was going surprisingly well. However, she was also noticing a recurring trend among the three of them.

"Ali," Nia hissed, "what exactly were you trying to summon?!"

"A being of pleasure," Alison said in a matter-of-fact tone.

Blinking, Nia looked at her friend. "Wha— So this was supposed to be an orgy?!"

Tearing her gaze away from Valzia, Alison furrowed her brow at Nia. "Well, yeah, I said that in the...oh. Ohhhhh...." Alison blushed and looked sheepish. "I said that in the coven chat. Which you're not in."

"Fuck me," Nia muttered, and looked back up at the three beings.

Coviok stepped up to Nia, his massive frame looming over her. Grinning with a mix of feral teeth and lustful intent, he gave her a wink. "That is my plan, beautiful."

Nia's eyes grew wider as she looked up at Coviok. "You'll...break me," she murmured, but it didn't entirely sound like a protest.

"And you'll love every moment, I'll make sure of it," Coviok said, crouching down before Nia and gently lifting a lock of her curly hair, smelling it.

No, no, no, the ball of tentacles wriggled wildly. *There will be no fucking until this contract mess is dealt with! Only one is supposed to be summoned, and she summoned three! There has to be a decision made or we're going to pay for it.* A rather pointed penis protruded in Alison's direction. *You need to decide. Who did you mean to summon?*

Blinking, trying to focus, Alison reluctantly dragged her gaze over to Alldizius. "I...I don't know! I was trying to summon a creature that could...could satisfy me. Us. There were no names in the book, just the offerings! I picked the things that sounded like they would bring something we wanted!"

"Oh, my sweet," Valzia said, running a clawed finger gently across Alison's cheek and immediately drawing the girl's gaze back to her, "you placed three offerings, so three summons." Smiling tenderly at Alison, the succubus glanced over to the tentacles. "Alldizius, surely no harm could come from that misunderstanding. I'm sure the contractors won't mind if we let this slide."

Maybe on some other night, but not on the Eve of Samhain, the mass wriggled. *No, we're wasting time. As much fun as these two look like they'd be, I'm sorry, but they have to choose.*

Coviok smirked and gave Nia another wink before looking at the mass. "Clearly, they weren't focused. I think they're just going to have to try out all they've summoned and make a decision then."

Alldizius wriggled in...thought? Irritation? It was impossible to tell, but it didn't immediately reject the idea.

Alison wet her lips, almost mesmerized by Valzia. "I didn't… It kept listing everything in threes, so I thought…"

"See, Alldi," Valzia pouted, practically draping herself on Alison at this point. "Honest mistake. She did everything else right. I think Coviok has the right idea."

Nia drew in a deep breath, her chest rising and falling with it, further straining the tight dress. "Try? All of you?"

"Unless you don't want to," Coviok said to Nia, his tone careful and reassuring. "We are here, after all, for your pleasure."

The tentacle mass wriggled more, rolling around as it threw out little waves of confusion. Finally it slumped slightly. *Fine*, it said. *They can try, then decide. But only one of us is staying.*

"There we are," Valzia smirked, turning back to Alison, very close to her face at that point. "You have three creatures of lust to enjoy. Until you choose one." She winked, then leaned in and playfully licked Alison's lower lip.

"I love this idea," Alison said, smiling again. "Nia?"

Biting her lip, Nia looked from Coviok to Valzia to Alldizius, and then finally back to Alison. "I still can't believe it worked," Nia said, then took another deep breath and nodded. "All right. I'm in. How...how do we go about this? Do we need a method, or do we dive in?"

"Diving in is a method, my zaftig delight," Valzia said, a smile in her voice.

Coviok offered Nia a hand. "I would relish being your first demon," he said, voice dripping with desire. It seemed to Nia like his voice slid down her spine.

"Ali?" There was a slight quaver to Nia's voice.

Alison moaned quietly as Valzia kissed at her neck, with lips that couldn't possibly be that soft. "Umm...yeah?"

"If this kills me, I'm haunting the shit out of you," Nia said, and gave Coviok her hand.

"Oh, you shall remain very much alive," Covoik said, helping her off the floor and then scooping her up in one motion. "So, my beautiful summoner, what is your desire?"

"I don't even know where to begin," Nia murmured, holding on to Covoik's shoulders as he lifted her. She ran her hands curiously over his skin. "I...I should take the dress off first, maybe. Alison will be sad if it gets ripped."

"The dress fits you wonderfully. Really accentuates your wondrous curves," Covoik said as he carried her to the couch and set her down. He kneeled before her and helped her carefully remove the dress. "However, you have a body that is not meant to be hidden."

"I love your outfit, too, Alison," Valzia murmured playfully as she carefully removed the horns and ran fingers through Alison's hair. "Although it would look much better on the floor."

"Mmmmm, we can make that happen," Alison said, eyes closing for a moment, enjoying the feel of Valzia's hands. "Can I kiss you? I've been wanting to since you appeared."

Smiling and gently batting her eyes at Alison, Valzia nodded. "My sweet, you may do whatever you wish," she said, reaching out to gently start undoing the clasps and zippers that held Alison's outfit together. "I'd be insulted if you didn't."

Leaning in, Alison hungrily kissed Valzia as she wiggled out of the little devil dress. Beneath it was a sheer red balconette bra and matching thong. Once the dress was off her shoulder, Alison reached up and slid her hands into Valzia's hair. The demoness's lips were every bit as kissable as they looked, and had a tart and tangy flavor that made Alison salivate.

Alldizius shuffled around for a moment, then crawled up into one of the recliners and pulled the footstool up, draping some of its longer tentacles across it.

Nia watched Alldizius settle into the armchair curiously, but Coviok called her attention back as the dress was pulled up over her head. All Nia had beneath was a pair of lacy panties.

"You sound like Ali," Nia said, turning a little pink. "She keeps trying to get me to wear tighter, more-revealing things."

Setting the dress aside, hanging it delicately on the arm of the couch, Covoik returned his attention to Nia. "She's a smart woman," he said with a chuckle. "Who wouldn't want to gaze upon this form?"

"Mmm-hmm!" Alison would have said more, but her mouth was still very much occupied.

One of Valzia's hands found Alison's butt and held it firmly, the other slid over her sides and teasingly caressed the tops of her breasts. Valzia held Alison close for the kiss, something akin to a tiger's purr coming out of the demoness as their mouths met and their tongues danced against each other. Alison also discovered that Valzia's tongue was long, very long, and wrapped around her own tongue with surprising dexterity.

Alison broke the kiss with a gasp, looked up at Valzia with bright, excited eyes. "Oh, wow, your tongue!" She looked over the demoness and bit her lip. Alison reached up and lifted Valzia's enormous breasts, her hands sinking into the soft flesh. "I want...okay, let me get this off."

Alison let go of Valzia long enough to unhook her bra and toss it aside, almost with disdain. It landed on top of Nia's dress.

On the couch, Coviok ran his hands up Nia's legs and thighs, and continued up until each of his large hands was hefting her equally large breasts, squeezing them and teasing her nipples with his thumbs.

"Yes," Nia whimpered, arching forward, her nipples firm after the first brush, "more!"

"That's my girl," Coviok rumbled, pleased.

Following orders, he wrapped his lips around one of her nipples and began to suck and lick hungrily. His mouth was hot and his saliva caused her skin to tingle. It was impossible for Nia not to squirm on the couch. The other breast was getting a more-thorough massage, no inch left untouched. Nia cried out and let go of the couch, her hands coming forward, sliding over Coviok's shoulders, one grasping the back of his neck; she began to unconsciously massage the muscles under her grip. The strangeness she felt from the situation was quickly being pushed out by the pleasure pulsing through her body.

"She's really sensitive," Alison said with a giggle. Coviok lifted his head and grinned back at her.

"Just how I like 'em." Coviok took Nia's other breast into his mouth, teasing her more as he leaned into it, pressing her slightly into the couch and moving her body so she was starting to slide toward him.

"Now, my delight," Valzia called Alison's attention back to her as she placed her hands on Alison's breasts and caressed them, "that's much better." Alison pressed herself up against the demoness, pushing those epic breasts together and rubbing her own more dainty breasts against them.

"You're magnificent," Alison said, her voice heavy with want, looking up into Valzia's silver eyes.

"Ooo, so are you, my eager morsel," Valzia continued to purr, rolling her chest to rub their nipples together. The demoness's were firm and each caress brought another low growl.

Valzia's hand drifted down and slipped past Alison's panties, softly running a pair of fingers over her clit and against her labia. As Valzia slowly rubbed and explored, Alison took in a shuddering breath. She was already so wet, and the fingertips sliding over her hairless sex were getting coated. Alison leaned forward and kissed Valzia again.

"I'm so turned on," Alison murmured, "and you're so hot. And...I want you to eat my pussy. Your tongue is...fuck, I bet it's amazing."

"I've been wanting to since I saw you, my sweet," Valzia said breathily and leaned in, nipping at Alison's neck while she pressed the young woman down onto the floor. Valzia gave Alison one more long, deep kiss before pulling back.

Valzia's lengthy tongue and pillowy breasts slid slowly down the length of Alison's body, claws skimming along her flesh causing electricity to run through her body. When the demoness finally settled between Alison's legs, she parted her thighs, scattering kisses on the tender flesh before moving to the main course.

Slowly but insistently, Valzia's tongue eased into Alison's pussy, pushing more and more of the squirming muscle into her, tasting deep of her nectar. Valzia moaned at the flavor, which reverberated through Alison's vessel and through the whole of her body. Alison let out a breathy cry.

"So good," she moaned, hands splaying across the hard floor.

"We're falling behind," Coviok said with a toothy grin. He ran a hand over Nia's mound before he hooked a finger on the waistband of her panties and started to slide them down her legs. Nia's hips lifted almost instinctively. Coviok didn't rush; his every movement was slow, methodical, ensuring Nia felt everything he was doing to her. He tossed the sopping panties aside and pulled Nia forward so that her ass was at the very edge of the couch. She gasped, and watched him with wide eyes. He slipped a thick finger into Nia's pussy, as far as he could reach, and rubbed his thumb over her clit before pulling his hand back and holding it up to display the slickness that covered his hand.

"Let's work on 'breaking you,' shall we?" he said low and deep as he moved closer to her.

Both of his thick shafts rested against her mons, letting her see what she was about to get into. Or rather, what was about to get into her. Resting her legs on his arms, he splayed her open and pressed the bulbous head of his lower cock against her entrance, easing in. Nia watched as the thick cock slid into her, the other rubbing against her exposed folds. She licked her lips and looked up at Coviok. He knew she could take it, but he wanted to make sure she felt every inch, every ridge.

"Fuck, that's good," Nia whispered.

"Wait until I get started," he growled, his tone slightly ominous.

Back on the floor, Valzia's cunnilingus was a Cambridge-level dissertation on the pleasuring of a woman. Her tongue went deeper than any could possibly go, it wriggled and pressed against every spot, and it lingered in places that sent jolts through Alison. Not only was the succubus good, but she was thoroughly enjoying her work. Moaning heavily and almost squirming herself, her clawed hands slid up Alison's body to find her breasts, squeezing and caressing them, the tips of her talons teasing Alison's nipples.

"Oh! Oh Gods..." Alison twisted against the floor, panting. She had never felt like this, her body awash with sensation, nerves firing with pleasure. She'd never been very sensitive or receptive; she'd didn't know it could feel this way.

Alison arched off the floor crying out as she came, her body taut for a full minute before she collapsed, moaning. It took a moment for Valzia to drag the length of her tongue out of Alison. When she did, she sat up, licking her lips and gave her a little giggle.

"Did my very delicious witch enjoy that?" the demoness asked as she slid her body back up the length of Alison's before resting on her side and absently playing with one of Alison's breasts. "Of course you did."

Alison whimpered as Valzia teased her, turning her head to look at the demoness. "That was the best."

"I know," Valzia said with a giggle before leaning in and kissing Alison once more.

It seemed it was now time for Coviok to get started. Wrapping his fingers around Nia's waist, Coviok started to move her body in opposite of his hips, letting her start to feel his wide girth glide in and out of her. Nia gasped, her ass sliding forward off the couch, leaving her on her back on the deep couch. His upper cock's thick ridge and the ribbed folds bumped and pressed against her clit with each movement. Soon he had a firm, steady rhythm that filled Nia to her limit before easing out of her, his glans rubbing against her entrance before doing it all over again.

"You're so big," Nia said, cheeks flushed. It sounded trite, but it was true, and she could feel her body stretching, the muscles easing. It helped that she was impossibly wet. She could feel the moisture sliding down the cheek of her ass, hear it as he thrust into her. Coviok took Nia's hands in his and pinned them to the back of the couch, trapping her. Almost doubling over to lean down, he ran his tongue along her breasts and over the side of her neck, leaving a trail of tingles over her skin.

As Nia's body became more accustomed to his size, Coviok started to really pump into her. Her entire body shook with each thrust, and he growled while smiling at her. "I will not stop until you cum," he told her, a little threateningly, "and I want to hear it when you do."

Alison had a moment to look over at Nia being fucked on the couch, glad that Nia seemed to be getting into it. This wasn't exactly what Alison thought would happen, but it was close enough, and she had completely forgotten to warn Nia. Still, it seemed to be working out.

"Looks like everyone's having fun," Valzia said playfully. "Alright, Alldizius, it's your turn." Alison was just getting her breath back as Valzia stood and stretched.

Pardon my previous protests, the tentacle creature said to Alison as it rolled off the recliner and squirmed over toward her with surprising speed, *but bureaucracy really is hell where we come from. Now then.*

As Valzia waltzed into the kitchen to make herself a drink, Alison found her wrists and ankles grabbed and she was pulled to the creature. Within moments she was entangled, soft and slick appendages wrapping around her waist, arms, legs, breasts. Wriggling pseudopods slid along her cleavage and the cleft of her ass, along the sides of her neck.

"Eek!" Alison gawked at the strange mass as it dragged her across the floor. It would have been more unnerving if it weren't for the way it felt.

Comfy? it asked, while nerves all over her body began to fire. She was no longer on the cabin floor but completely covered in warm, soft, slick tentacles that cushioned her nicely and supported her neck.

"Yeah," Alison said, relaxing as sensation flooded her. "Yeah, I am."

Excellent. Do let me know if there's something in particular you would like, Alldizius stated as his movements now led to a constant wriggling around Alison's body. It was like she was being massaged from head to toe as the slick tendrils undulated around her.

Nia's cries were also helping Alison to get back in the mood (not that she ever *really* left it). Each slapping thrust brought with it another breathy sound of pleasure.

"Please," Nia moaned, twisting against the hands holding her, "I...I want to touch..."

"As you wish," Coviok said, releasing her hands.

Moaning, Nia reached down and grasped Coviok's other cock, one hand stroking the head and the other pressing the base more firmly against her. The way she brought her arms together pushed up her breasts and made them an easier target. Coviok slid his hands down to her breasts. Squeezing them together, he teased her nipples and held them firmly. The desire demon's thrusting hadn't faltered in the least as Nia's body continued to bounce against his pelvis.

The tentacle monster didn't keep to the soft touches for long. Soon, Alison felt it moving with more purpose, and she found a very human looking penis pressing against and then past her lips. A thicker, blunter shaft that was more equine in shape was starting to ease into her pussy. Finally, a more-tapered cock teased at her ass.

"Mmf!" Alison's eyes grew wide, and she did tense a little at what was trying to enter her from behind.

I guarantee it won't hurt, but best not to put you under duress, Alldizius said, reading her mind. The phallus moved away from her pucker and was replaced by a thinner tentacle. The slickness of the creature extended to all of his extremities, and he entered her easily, with only a little stretch.

Moaning, Alison closed her eyes and relaxed. She hadn't been with a lot of men. They were fun, but she mostly preferred women. But a tingling, pulsing pleasure radiated from the cocks and the tentacle inside her. She sucked at the one in her mouth, loving the flavor. He tasted like sour apple, tart yet sweet.

On the couch, Nia was just getting louder, the couch starting to creak with Coviok's thrusts. Cocktail in hand, Valzia strutted back, past Alison and to the couch. Leaning against the back of the couch, she reached down to run fingers through Nia's hair as the larger demon drove her into the cushions.

"Ah! Yes!" Nia looked up at Coviok again as she felt her pelvis start to tighten. "YES!" Nia bucked with her orgasm, pushing herself hard into Coviok's thrust, clenching down on the large cock.

Chuffing like a bull, Coviok pumped a dozen more times before his dual cocks erupted in and on her. Hot, creamy, thick cum flooded her cunt and spilled out between the bottoms of her breasts and her tummy. Several hard and full spurts later, he relented.

"You were wonderful," Coviok said warmly, regaining his composure quickly.

"Ohhh..." As Coviok pulled back, Nia's hands slid away from his cock, sliding up her body through the mess he made. She moaned at the feel of it, and picked up a hand, looking at it dripping from her fingers. It was so thick. Curious, she brought a finger to her mouth, licking cautiously. Then she laughed.

"You're delicious," Nia said, licking off the rest of her fingers. "It's...

it's like custard!"

"We taste like you'd want us to taste," Coviok said with a grin. "Now, it's my turn for a drink." He gave Nia's thigh a squeeze and headed into the kitchen, stepping around Alison and Alldizius. "Oh shit, are those Smarties? I fuckin' love Smarties."

Alison found herself letting go. She had been more forward with Valzia, but with Alldizius there was little to do but allow it to fill her and fuck her. It was strange, but it felt good. All the various shafts started to move and pump into her, reaching deep and wriggling around as they did. The one in her mouth only moved a little, mostly letting her control the depth and speed. The others, however... The more she got used to it, the more they moved to push her just a little further. The slick coating it left behind spiked her pleasure while dulling other sensations. Alison felt she could take a fist with the way the coating warmed her up and made her languid.

Any requests, or should I just grant you a dozen orgasms? the tentacle monster asked politely as he traded out the cocks inside her for new ones with different shapes.

A dozen...? Alison felt lightheaded just thinking about it. Or maybe that was everything moving in her and around her.

I think I should manage, Alldizius said in her mind, and its movements increased. Alison felt her body stretch and accept all manner of shaft that Alldizius thrusted into her. It was dizzying how her body could just accept it. And it was nonstop—unrelenting, driving, and steady. All she could think about was what it was doing to her, the pleasure that drove into her, and it hit every weak point she had, inside and out. Just a wriggling mass of pleasure that was focused on her.

Not five feet away, Nia pushed herself back onto the couch, even though it stopped Valzia from petting her hair. She was still covered in Coviok's cum, and was genuinely surprised by the fact that she kind of liked it. Turning her head, Nia looked over at Valzia, smiling.

"Hey, gorgeous," Nia said, low and throaty. "Is it your turn? Should I clean off first?"

Valzia snickered and slid over the back of the couch to lounge next to Nia. "Hey to you, my magnificent treasure. Please, leave the cleaning to me."

Giving Nia a wink, Valzia leaned down and started to collect Coviok's cum with her long tongue, bathing her until all that had gathered upon her body was cleaned off. Smiling, Valzia pressed herself against Nia, their breasts squishing pleasantly between them, and kissed her deeply. Nia moaned softly into the kiss, Valzia's tongue still coated with Coviok's cum. The demoness was lusciously soft. Nia would have been down for trying Coviok again, but Valzia was gorgeous and plush, and damn could she kiss.

Breaking from the kiss, Valzia licked Nia's neck and snuggled very closely against her, her fingers tracing over Nia's thigh, raking it gently. "So, my dear, what would you like? Shall I clean you up more? Or do you want some of what I gave your beautiful friend?"

"I want to touch you first," Nia said, sliding her hands up to Valzia's breasts. "And taste..." She bowed her head and slid her tongue over a violet nipple before sucking at it eagerly.

"Oh, baby, please do," Valzia purred and softly pet Nia's hair, giving her scalp a gentle scratching with her claws while absently fondling Nia's breast.

Nia let out a quiet moan, then kissed her way across to the other breast, twirling her tongue around the firm nipple before sucking on that one as well. She loved having Valzia play with her hair, and was getting squirmy again as she rubbed herself against the succubus. That catlike purring had intensified, and Nia could feel it rumbling through those massive breasts

With a gasp, Nia pulled her head up and looked at Valzia. "I...am curious what it would be like to go down on you..."

"I am yours to play with," Valzia said. "Do you just want to taste me, or should you climb up on me and I can pleasure you as well?"

Nia looked at Valzia for a moment, considering. "I've never had a lot of luck with 69ing, but I'm going to guess you'll tell me that you have. So...yeah. Okay." She slid back off the couch and stood up, pushing her hair out of the way before climbing up onto Valzia. Thankfully it was a deep couch.

Meanwhile, Alison's head swam and she felt like she'd lost track of... everything. All that was left was sensation. She let out a muffled cry as her body spiked and she came for Alldizius, twisting against him.

The cock in Alison's mouth retracted slightly, letting her breathe more openly, but the movements persisted. More so, she couldn't do anything about it. The tendrils that were wrapped around her thighs kept her legs open enough to keep her ass and pussy ravished even as she came. Physically, she couldn't stop the creature if she wanted to.

"There's one," Coviok commented, and Alison looked up to see him sitting in the chair closest to her. He unwrapped a sleeve of Smarties and dumped them in his mouth. He had fixed himself a drink as well, and it sat on the end table next to him.

She didn't have time for further observations as she shuddered and came again. She didn't know how Alldizius was doing it, but that orgasm just cascaded into another one. She was helpless. A toy. It was a little frightening, but everything felt so good.

"Don't get carried away, Alldi," Coviok said, chuckling. "It's supposed to be a sample, not the whole thing."

I do tend to get wrapped up in my work, the tentacle monster said as he moved Alison's body to stretch during her most recent orgasm before gently unraveling and slipping out of her various orifices. *I do hope you enjoyed that, miss.*

Blinking, a bit dazed, Alison laid there for a moment, her legs quivering. "I...wow." She took a deep breath, and looked up at Coviok. "Ah, I know it's your turn, but could I get some help standing and making a quick drink?"

"Whatever your desire," Coviok said as he reached down and took her hand. Just like with Nia, he scooped her up in one motion and carried her easily to the kitchen. "We're not here to get our rocks off, we're here to rock your world. So, if you need a break, you get a break."

On the couch, Valzia helped Nia settle on top of her. With a little bit of shifting, Nia was able to find a very comfortable position; Valzia's pillowy breasts were a comfort to lay upon. The demoness also didn't seem to mind her weight in the least. Valzia gently ran her claws over Nia's back, butt, and thighs, waiting for Nia to get comfortable and set the pace.

"Okay," Nia said again, blushing. She was self-conscious being on top, but Valzia clearly didn't mind. Bowing her head, Nia drew her tongue across Valzia's vibrant pussy, and moaned softly as she got a taste. Creamy, sweet, berry-tart. Delicious.

She spread Valzia's lips and swirled her tongue around the succubus's clit. Nia didn't think she was good enough to impress a pleasure demon, but she'd never failed to make a partner cum, and wasn't going to now. The succubus seemed every bit as sensitive, and let out an encouraging moan. Her claws tightened slightly on Nia's ass before releasing just enough to not bite into her flesh. Purring loudly, Valzia pulled Nia's hips down a little before starting to lick around Nia's entrance and gliding over her clit.

"Mmmmm!" Nia squirmed as Valzia got started, and pushed her hips back. Nia liked Valzia's claws. It was a little funny—Nia was shyer than Alison, but liked it rougher and was dirtier than her more-direct friend.

"You and Covi make a delightful cocktail, my sweet," Valzia moaned before driving her tongue deep into Nia's pussy. The demoness didn't give Nia all she had, though—not enough to distract the girl from her current task, but enough to send shivers of pleasure through her curvy frame. Nia sucked at Valzia's pearl and slid two fingers into the demoness's very hot, very slick sex.

"Oh, that is perfect," Valzia moaned, gripping Nia's ass more firmly. The purple woman's hips began to roll at Nia's touch, clearly wanting more and enjoying what she was doing. One of the succubus' hands moved down between Nia's legs to join her tongue, but she felt no claws. Much like the great cat she sounded like, they seemed to be retractable, which was good as Nia suddenly had two fingers inside her to go along with that long, wriggly tongue.

In the kitchen area, Alison leaned her head against Coviok as he carried her, getting her breath back. "This has already been an amazing night," Alison murmured, flushed and happy. "I saw what you did with Nia. It looked like she really enjoyed you. What did you think of her?" She motioned to the drink she had abandoned earlier; she couldn't quite reach it as Coviok held her.

"I hope she had fun," the large red demon said with a grin. He shifted Alison so she could grab her glass. "She's beautiful and a delight to fuck. Why do you ask? Aren't we focused on you for the moment?"

Alison smiled, and took a sip of her drink. "She's my best friend. And she's...really self-conscious. About her body, mostly. I'm going to tell her later what you said if she starts to say anything negative about herself." She grinned, and drank a little more, looking over at Nia and Valzia on the couch.

Whimpering, Nia squirmed again but kept licking and sucking at Valzia like she was hungry for it, fingers reaching as far in as possible. Her sounds grew sharper as her legs began to tremble, but she didn't stop eating Valzia even as her orgasm made her hips lock. Rocking her hips up to meet Nia, Valzia purred loudly with a peak, cumming for Nia, as the vibrations rattled through her tongue. She clearly wasn't done, though, and continued to lick, suck, and finger Nia's pussy with far more aplomb. The girl's pleasure fed into the demoness's.

"That is one of the hottest things I've ever seen," Alison said, grinning, and looked back up at Coviok. "Of course, what you were doing with Nia was also really hot. I haven't been with as many men as she has, so you might need to be careful, but I'm looking forward to what you've got for me." She took another drink, a sparkle in her eyes.

"Really?" Coviok said, still grinning. "Well, she only took one of my cocks, which I'm guessing is all you want as well."

Alison grinned again. "She could have taken both. I know she likes it in the ass. Maybe I'll show her how to summon you again. It doesn't have to be Halloween, right?"

"It's easiest on Halloween, but we might show you an easier way to do it," Coviok said, grabbing another sleeve of Smarties and untwisting it with his teeth before dumping the whole thing into his mouth and tossing the wrapper. "And I will definitely come back for that ass. So, want me to fuck you while you watch them?"

Biting her lip, Alison looked over. "Yeah, actually, that sounds... fantastic."

Plucking Alison's drink from her fingers, Coviok set the glass down on the counter and then turned her around, holding her legs apart as he set her against him, her back to his chest. Moving her around was effortless. "Might want to reach up and grab ahold," he said, maneuvering Alison so his top cock was resting right at her entrance. She reached up as instructed, lacing her fingers around Coviok's neck. She could feel her skin starting to tingle in anticipation.

Facing Nia and the couch, Coviok slowly lowered Alison down onto his shaft until he was buried as deep as she could take, then let her sit there for the moment, his grip the only thing keeping her from being completely impaled.

"Fuck, Nia was right," Alison said with a laugh. "You are...big!"

Nia had to lift her head for one minute, crying out as she spasmed for Valzia, then drew her fingers out of the demoness to suck the sweet slickness off of them before leaning back in, licking down the length of Valzia's pussy as if it were ice-cream, sucking at her lips, then sliding her mouth back up to tease the demoness's clit again. Valzia's juices were all over her face and it just seemed to make her more insatiable.

"You magnificent wanton woman," Valzia moaned, slightly higher pitch as another orgasm shuddered through her. "I love it. You're so gorgeous and perfect."

Once she'd sung Nia's praise, Valzia growled and dove back into

Nia's pussy, darting her tongue in, out, and all around her walls. Nia pressed her face into Valzia's thigh as the demoness slid a very slick hand over the cleft of her ass and pressed into the tight entrance. Nia panted hard for a minute then went back to it, curling her tongue around Valzia's clit, sucking sharply. Valzia came again, soaking Nia's face as she did, moaning loudly into the human's sex. Valzia's fingers pumped harder and she curled her tongue like a corkscrew as she fucked Nia with it.

It seems you two would go all night, Alldizius stated as it crawled over to the couch. *As Coviok stated, this is a sample; no contract has been determined yet.*

Moaning with both pleasure and frustration, Valzia took her time dragging her tongue out of Nia's well-licked cunt and licked her lips. "The beastie is right, my buxom debutante," she muttered, extracting her fingers as well and gently patting Nia on the ass. "Time to change it up."

Panting, Nia lifted her head but didn't move right away, coming back to herself. After a shuddering breath, she rolled off of Valzia and the couch, ending up on her knees on the floor.

It seemed Alison had gotten used to his girth, so Coviok started to move her. Lifting her up and easing her back down, slow and steady, filling her to the brim before almost pulling out. She'd been fucked quite thoroughly by Alldizius—it was time for a different speed.

"That's so fucking good," Alison moaned as Coviok slowly pumped her. "And you're so warm, and strong, and just..." she trailed off, moaning.

"You let me know when you want me to go faster," Coviok said, leaning in to nip at her ear. "For now, just enjoy the ride and the show." The large demon continued to slowly bounce Alison on his cock, pulling her legs apart a little more, and a little higher, as they went. Giving her a bit of a stretch and letting her relax.

Nia leaned back and looked at Valzia once more. "You are beyond delicious," Nia said, smiling.

Making a noise much like a pleased giggle, Valzia reached over and stroked Nia's hair. "I could say the same. Enjoy," she said, blowing Nia a kiss before gracefully sliding off the couch and standing to stretch.

Taking a deep breath, Nia looked at Alldizius curiously. "Um...I guess I'm all yours?"

I do hope you enjoy this, Alldizius said, starting to tether Nia up in his tentacles. *I noticed a few things that I hope will improve your experience.*

The slick coating that covered all of Alldizius began to glaze Nia's skin as its tentacles wrapped around and over her. They grabbed her breasts and squeezed them in an almost milking fashion, taking her wrists and ankles, but not cocooning her like it had Alison.

"Oh!" Nia's head fell back as Alldizius penetrated her, moaning. A twisted spiral, like a unicorn horn, slid into her ass while a bulbous shaft pressed into her very slick pussy. She squirmed as he continued to wrap around her, but there was no hesitance like there had been with Alison. Nia shifted her stance, spreading her legs wider while still on her knees.

"I think I've seen this anime," Nia said with a little laugh, turning pink.

While Nia wasn't trapped as Alison had been, that didn't stop Alldizius from making sure every bit of her body was massaged, rubbed, caressed, and coated. The alien cocks started to pound into her, making her body vibrate as their thrusts alternated. Even on her knees, she had no worry about falling over; Alldizius was doing a perfect job of keeping her supported throughout the experience.

"Ah! Yes!" Nia arched, writhing as Alldizius fucked her. Whatever covered the tentacle monster was making her skin tingle, and it was more than a little overwhelming. She slid her tongue over her upper lip, and her hands grasped the tentacles that wrapped around her wrists. It was intense and incredible.

Gasping, Alison's grip on Coviok slipped a little as her hands slid apart. One still held onto his neck, but the other flailed and caught one of his horns. "More," she said, watching Nia lose herself, "go faster!"

"Fuck yeah," Coviok muttered, lowering his head slightly to make it easier to for Alison to hang on, then he followed her request. Gripping more tightly to her thighs, the demon thrusted his hips up as he pulled Alison down onto him, moving faster and more forcefully.

Nia felt a sudden pulse through the tentacles around her, the phalluses inside her swelling, then the sudden rush as they erupted inside her, flooding her cunt and ass with warm, tingling cum. Several more of Alldizius' appendages came as well, coating her body in a light-blue milky fluid that felt like heated oil.

"Oh, fuck," Nia moaned, her cheeks red again. There was something incredibly hot about this, filled with cum, covered in it, and the way it made all of her nerves stand up and pay attention. She was embarrassed, but it was just so fucking good.

The cocks withdrew only to be replaced by more. A thick, ridged shaft sank into her ass while a half-dozen smaller tendrils wriggled into her pussy and started thrashing inside her. A much more human package was presented to her, pressing against her lips. She looked at the cock in front of her and opened her mouth, tongue slightly extended, whimpering as it slid in, sucking eagerly.

Alison whimpered and grabbed another horn, holding on tight as Coviok started to pound into her. Nia was a mess, but damn if it wasn't absurdly hot. Had she always liked watching this much? Maybe she did.

Nia's tits were squeezed, her ass reamed, and her pussy thoroughly explored. Alldizius continued to use every bit to send Nia into another orgasm. When she did, the tentacle monster filled her up once more with more cum and more cocks of various shapes and sizes. The cum tasted smooth and just slightly sweet, like condensed milk, as it flowed into her mouth and down her throat.

Nia's eyes rolled back as she screamed around the cock in her mouth, shaking as she came. She felt...she didn't even know anymore. She moaned as the sweet cum filled her mouth, swallowing everything Alldizius gave her.

"Oh, Gods!" Alison cried out. She was right there. As Nia screamed, Alison came too, her whole body shaking.

Alldizius slowed, then retracted its tentacles. *Nia, it's been an absolute pleasure.* Gently, it moved Nia to lay upon the floor in a mess before easing away from her and swishing back to the summoning circle.

Twisting against the floor, Nia slid her hands over her body, up over her breasts and down between her legs. Alldizius's cum continued to make her skin tingle. She had come so many times, but she just wanted more.

Coviok gave Alison several more thrusts before burying himself in her and leaving her a fresh load of cum to fill her. Valzia purred gently and came around once more, giving Alison another kiss.

Ladies, it's about that time, Alldizius said.

"Aww, the little beastie is right," Valzia pouted, brushing Alison's face before stepping into the circle as well.

Coviok shuddered with pleasure and gave Alison a small bite on the shoulder before lifting her off his cock and setting her down in the easy chair.

"So, who's it going to be?" he asked as he took his spot in the circle.

Panting, Alison looked over the three demons, biting her lip. "Gods, what an impossible choice. Though...I'll remember all your summonings. This...this will happen again. Correctly, next time."

Lifting herself carefully out of the chair, Alison went over to Nia and pushed the other girl's hair out of her face, then leaned down to lick her cheek. Nia whimpered, but opened her eyes and looked up at Alison. She didn't stop rubbing herself.

"You're a gorgeous mess," Alison whispered, smiling. "As soon as we make a choice I'm going to start making out with you. Who do we choose?"

Biting her lip, Nia looked over. "I...I feel like I didn't give Coviok my best. And...and I want another cock. Though they're all, fuck, so amazing."

Alison giggled. "I'd love more time with Valzia, but I think I'd be happy to see you get pumped full of cum. Maybe even lick your cunt while it happened. I really liked watching you tonight. I...I didn't know that was my thing."

Nodding, Nia stopped touching herself and pushed herself up. "All right. Though...maybe if we are snowed in, we can try to call Valzia back tomorrow."

Grinning, Alison stood up and faced the three demons. "You have all been exceptional, and we look forward to summoning you again, but, for this evening, we think Coviok best fits the current intentions."

"As it should be," the large demon said, smirking to the other two. "Ladies, I am yours until sunrise, then the pact is completed."

Valzia giggled. "I heard what they said. Go, be their toy. When they want some real affection, I shall return." Walking over, Valzia leaned down low from the hip, reaching out and giving each of the girls a long, incredibly deep kiss before parting. Swaying her rump at them, she stepped back into the circle and gave them a wave before disappearing in a sudden swirl of dark smoke that... glittered?

I do hope you call on me again sometime, Alldizius said, wriggling tentacles in their directions. *I had quite a bit of fun. Oh, and be sure to give us five stars, even though the contracts weren't finalized. We need something to explain our missing time. Good evening, ladies.* With that, the tentacle monster twisted up and also vanished in a cloud of red-black smoke.

Nia blinked, head tipped to the side. "How do we leave them five stars?"

"No idea," Alison murmured.

"Oh, on the app," Coviok said with a shrug. "It's on your phone now." Alison actively fought the urge to go check her phone. She'd do it in the morning.

Alison looked over at Coviok. "So, Nia needs you to stuff her again. Should she rinse off first? She's a gooey mess right now."

Nia blushed and wrinkled her nose at Alison. She then looked over at Coviok's twin cocks, still rock hard, and bit her lip. "I've never had anything so big in my ass. It's…I think this might be when you break me, but fuck I want it so bad."

"You only need to clean off if you want to—I don't mind," the demon said with a grin. "Come sun up, all that's going to disappear as well. So, right here on the floor, or do you have a more comfortable place you want to be broken?"

Nia looked up at Coviok and grinned a little wickedly. "If you don't mind, I'm going to stay messy," Nia said, "and you're going to make an even bigger mess. If this all disappears in the morning, let's head to the master bedroom. There's a nice big bed in there."

Alison looked over at her friend in surprise, but smiled. Nia wasn't often demanding. It was fun to see. Nia held her hands up to Coviok with that same grin, clearly expecting him to pick her up.

Grinning more broadly, Coviok reached down and scooped Nia up, playfully flinging her over his shoulder. "Oh, girl, I am going to fuck you blind," he said with a laugh. He winked at Alison, "And then you're next."

Nia squeaked in surprise, but laughed, kicking her feet in false protest. Alison wet her lips and followed the two of them down the hall.

MORE THAN JUST SALVAGE

Being adrift in the Darantine Expanse for five days would drive anyone a little stir-crazy. However, to get the really juicy salvage, you had to make sure your sensors were on high and you weren't emitting any background noise, which is why Cora found herself floating in her little ship, playing derelict among a sea of similar ships. Quiet, only the barest life support to keep heat and air running, and the gentle hiss of background radiation as the sensors reached out for any sort of heavy metal or the tiniest of power sources.

Grumbling, Cora checked her fuel gauges. She had probably one more day before she needed to head back. The Darantine Expanse was a bit of a coral reef in the way of interstellar navigation. Decades ago, two great navies clashed here, leaving a debris field hundreds of thousands of klicks wide. Initial salvagers, and those who hadn't kept their navigation charts updated, added to the mess. Radiation pockets, unexploded ordnance, and large chunks of battlecruisers made this place so hazardous that most just avoided it. Still, the odd freighter convoy or pleasure craft sometimes strayed too close and then added another blip on the scatter field of tangled metal.

That was not Cora's intention, though. No, she'd been salvaging for a few years, and she'd heard a tale that there were still riches to be found here, as long as you were quiet, listened, and didn't stir the pot.

It was halfway through day five, however, and she was beginning to think they were full of shit and this place was as dead as the ships that created it. The novelty of zero G had worn off after the second day, but the gravity generators were louder than the engine. She fought the urge to whine and twisted around to scan the various sensors again. She was out of things to do. She'd braided her hair dozens of times, finally achieving the most secure twin buns she'd ever managed. She'd read through the books she'd been waiting to get to. Even masturbating was getting old at this point.

"Just something," she murmured to herself, staring intently at the comms board, "enough to make it worth it. Come on."

As if the cosmos was just waiting for her prayers, or her desperation, a very faint hum made it through the static, so soft that it might have been mistaken for engine noise if she had been running it. But there it was, a hundred klicks off the starboard: a power signature. It was too small to be a ship—she wasn't that lucky—but something that definitely had an output bigger than a personal powercell.

"I'll take it," she muttered as she strapped herself into the pilot's seat. She made sure the coordinates were recorded and charted before she turned the engine back on.

She threaded through the debris field at a comparatively slow speed, mindful of the potential hazards all around her. She reflected for the 100th time on this trip that it might be nice if she had a crew. Well, maybe not a crew. A partner? Just one or two hands, someone to help with the work and not be alone all the time. Of course, she'd have to pay them, and the ship was pretty small. She wasn't sure where they'd bunk. Sighing, she shook her head and focused on the power signature.

Coming up on where the signature originated, it was definitely a mess. A small freighter, probably a private courier of some sort, or what was left of it. It had either hit a drifting warhead or its reactor had taken critical damage, because the only thing left was the gantry and scattered cargo pods. This could be payday; half the pods were untouched and seemingly undamaged.

"Oh, I super hope you're worth it," Cora sang to herself as she pulled the ship in as close as she could and set the engines to maintain position.

She unbuckled herself and headed to the small—and distressingly empty—cargo bay. Due to the size of the ship, the cargo bay was a giant airlock. Cora suited up, clipped herself to the tether, and hit the button that sealed the bay and cycled out the air for the vacuum of space. As the air cycled, she made her slow way to the magnetic harpoon that was mounted at the top of the cargo ramp. With any luck, she'd be able to just fish for the cargo pods and use the winch to haul them. She might have to get a couple the old-fashioned way. She kind of hoped not. It was the downside of being a solo outfit: if she went out on the tether and something went wrong, no one was around to pull her back in.

The cargo-bay ramp lowered, and she saw she had parked well enough that the first of the pods was, indeed, in harpoon distance and angle. A silent puff of compressed gas, and the magnet sailed out into the darkness. She felt rather than heard the thump of the vibration that traveled down the cable and reverberated through the ship—she had struck her mark. The wench gave it a tug and then did nothing more than pick up the slack. The inertial dampeners inside the cargo bay would make sure the pod didn't slam into the little freight runner.

As the winch slowly spooled back in, Cora got into place to help guide the cargo pod in. She hovered near the edge of the ramp, then as it floated in she used her shoulder to give it a quick push so that it slid in along the edge of the ramp. She also pulled off the harpoon so it couldn't mess with the momentum. It wasn't perfect, but it slid more or less into place as the dampeners brought it to a halt. The pod was inert— no power source, not yet.

"Not bad." Cora nodded to herself and got the harpoon reloaded, aiming for the next pod. Same system: fire, pull in, do her best to guide it in behind the first one. It would be great to have someone stronger for this. Sure, the pods were technically weightless in space, but in practice they were larger and heavier than she was, and as they pulled in, it took a lot of effort to get them where she wanted them.

After the third one settled in, she still hadn't found the source of the signal. She'd have to take a walk after all. The markings on the pod were definitely from a private courier, which meant that the contents would probably be worth the effort—probably not a fortune, at least not something to retire on for life. Clearly it wasn't worth so much that whoever had shipped it off hadn't been happy to just let insurance cover the loss.

Reloading the harpoon, she stared out at the next cargo pod for a long time before sighing and heading over to where her little mobility pack waited. She strapped it over her suit and plugged it into the port on her left arm. A few years ago she'd sheared off her forearm by being in the wrong place at the wrong time. The replacement had some conveniences, though, like being able to control steering through hand motions.

She double-checked her tether on both ends, then headed to the far end of her cargo ramp, pointed herself at the next pod, and pushed off.

Drifting out into the black never seemed to get easier. Weightlessness combined with utter silence save your own breath made for a purely isolating experience. It did give her plenty to see. The debris field was dotted by tiny nebulas of gas and backlit by a sea of stars. The local sun provided unhindered but distant and dim light, washing everything in a medium gray.

With the overlay fed in from her ship, she was able to pinpoint the power on her visor. Off a little ways was another cargo pod. This one, however, had been struck; its side was torn open and it spun gently. It appeared as though this had been relatively recent, as there were still small bits of metal scattered around it where some high-speed junk had shorn it open.

As she got closer, Cora's left hand twitched and the tiny thrusters on her unit powered up to slow her down. She didn't want to collide with the pod, and she didn't want to get caught in its spin. When she was close enough, she put her hand out and gave it a little push as it rotated toward her, hoping to slow the momentum.

"Fuck!" The spin caught her anyway. It took a little bit of counter-thrusting, but she was soon able to slow the pod down so the universe no longer spun around her. The tear had ripped apart the hydraulic actuator for the pod door, and there was a frozen spray of fluid sticking out like a reverse icicle. Maybe if she was lucky, some of it would break off before it melted and filled her cargo bay with hydraulic fluid.

She took a moment to reorient herself, looking back at her ship. After a few more breaths, she pulled magnetic handles out of the large pocket on the thigh of her suit. Once she had a good grip on the pod, she pointed herself at the cargo bay and engaged the thrusters on her pack again, driving the pod back.

It was slow going at first, the mass working slightly against her smaller jets, but in no time she had the pod entering the cargo bay and the thrusters decelerating to park the damaged pod without too much of an incident. Well, there was a small incident as the pod bumped into one of the other ones, but it was more of a surprise than anything else.

Nothing ruptured, and it appeared none of the pods were damaged more than what had already been done. Cora took a deep breath and let it out slowly, letting her head (well, her helmet) rest against the cargo pod. After her adrenaline calmed a bit, she looked back out at the debris field.

If any other pods were in good shape, she should grab them. After a brief repose, Cora headed back into the black.

There wasn't much else left of the freighter. She started to get near one of the few remaining pods, but her radiation levels spiked. They were clearly exposed to whatever destroyed the ship—the reactor or a warhead. Reeling back at the sound of the radiation warning, Cora headed back to her ship a little faster than maybe she should have. Lots of practice with the mobility unit kept her from bouncing off the cargo that now half filled her little bay. She wound the tether back up and hit the button to close the cargo bay and cycle the air once more.

Cautiously, Cora cracked the seal on her helmet and took a breath. No scent of ozone. Whatever power was in the damaged cell was still contained, and there weren't any shorts or other potential dangers. Sighing in relief this time, she removed the helmet and started to peel out of her gear, hanging up the mobility unit before stripping out of her suit. She closed everything off in their storage lockers and ran a cleaning protocol just to be safe. She then headed back to the bridge. She had gotten all she was likely to get without risking being stranded; time to turn the engines and gravity back on and get out of there.

The initial onset of gravity made her stomach drop, but after a minute it felt normal and welcome. The field was a mess, and she had to manually pilot out until she had cleared the mass of it. It was slow going—she had drifted quite a ways in the five days, and the floating wrecks were constantly shifting. After a relatively stressful couple of hours, Cora finally got her small freight hopper out of the densest part of the expanse. From there it was just a matter of picking the closest station and telling the onboard navigation to get there.

Another deep sigh, and Cora fell back in the pilot's chair. "Okay," she murmured to herself, closing her eyes. "Good job." She was ready for a nap, honestly, but needed to check on the cargo before napping happened.

After another beat, she opened her eyes again and pushed herself up out of the chair. She paused to cue up some music on the speakers, something to help keep her energy up and motivated, and also headed to her room long enough to grab an energy shot. Then it was back to the cargo bay to see just what she'd managed to find.

She had a bit of work ahead of her. Aside from the one that would need to be pried open because the hydraulics were sundered, the others would need to be cut into. Private courier typically meant good salvage, but it also meant code-locked pods which would need to be cut open.

"Right. Okay." Cora pulled up the edge of her shirt and injected the stim into her hip. She tried not to use them too often, but she needed to know what she'd found before she showed up at port—especially if it was actually something rare that someone might still be looking for. While she was hours from the nearest station, those hours would pass very quickly if she fell asleep.

She then pulled out absorbent mats and set them around the damaged pod. When that hydraulic fluid thawed, it would make a mess. She'd let it thaw out before she tried to open it. Jogging over to where she kept her tools, she pulled out a cutting torch and a visor. Sometimes you could just cut out the lock and still get the crates to open without fully taking the top off; it depended on the locking mechanism. She wished she could tell just from looking which type of pods these were. Maybe after a few more years. Salvage was so varied—there was always more to learn. It was a little annoying, but she didn't know what else she would do.

A quick examination and she felt she'd figured it out. The plasma cutter hummed to life, and she went to work on the first of the pods. The main lock and the swivel joints and the access door would fall right off. It had been out long enough that there was no way the tamper alarm would trigger. And even if it did, she was alone on her own ship.

With a sense of relief, Cora watched the first pod's hatch fall with a heavy thud onto the cargo bay's deck. No alarms, no ink packs, no nano-spray. Inside was a series of crates and boxes with a manifest. A quick glance told her this was a good find: a pair of high-end personal grav bikes, extra parts, and various accessories. Good, expensive stuff that was easily replaced. Given how long it had been in space, they might even be collector's items now. Smiling a little, Cora set the manifest aside to give it a more-careful read later. This really was the best type of salvage. Anything more rare or distinct could potentially get her into trouble when she tried to resell it. Sure, salvage rights were a thing, but if she'd stumbled across rare art or ancient tech, the rich person who had owned it had a team of lawyers to get it back with nothing left for her efforts.

She moved to the next pod, neatly removing the lock and joints and pulling away the access door. Furniture, possibly an entire bedroom set.

High quality, modern-ish, sleek. So, not antique or unique. It would make her apartment look very nice, but resale might not be so good. Well, her apartment could use it. For the three months a year she spent there…

"Maybe I need a new job," Cora muttered to herself as she moved to the third pod. "I could go back to dancing, but I don't really want to. I could try a salvage company again." The lock fell, and then the hinges. "I could…sell the ship and go to school? Maybe? For…something?" Shaking her head, she pulled the door off.

This must have been the contents of some wealthy person's apartment, because the next set was all sorts of electronics. It was all a little dated, but plenty of places would buy a new wall projector, collectors would happily pick up the VR system, and there was an audiophile's wet dream of hand-made speakers and amplifiers. In its own way, this was probably the most profitable find so far.

"Well, that's more reassuring." So this trip was worth it after all. She'd make a decent amount of money, and refurbish her studio apartment. An overall win.

She set aside the cutter and took a moment to clean up the scrap metal. That, too, would be sold. The pods had enough metal; it wouldn't be a lot, but enough to make it worth the effort. She then checked on the last pod.

It had been released from its ice prison, and the floor was a mess. Thankfully the pads had absorbed most of it, but the fluid was under high pressure. Cora wrinkled up her nose, but nodded to herself and ran for more pads. Cleaning the fluid out of the pads later would be a giant pain, but better than having puddles in her cargo bay. With one piston completely out of commission, the weight of the door would almost certainly break itself open once the lock was cut off. She laid down extra pads in front of the door so there wouldn't be a splash when it fell. Finally, she picked up the cutter again and sliced through the locks before stepping back out of the way.

With a heavy shudder, the weight of the door pulled itself down. The remaining hydraulic piston eased its descent, and it thudded gently onto the deck. Inside were some now-vintage bottles of wine that would have fetched a pretty penny, depending on the collector, if the cold vacuum of space and the jostling from the impact hadn't completely ruined them.

"Well, shit," Cora muttered as wine dripped down into the fluid-saturated pads. She stepped onto the fallen door to keep her shoes clean. There might be one or two salvageable bottles, maybe?

Among the wreckage of a wine cellar, she found the source of the signal that had led her to the pods in the first-place: a box, just over two meters in height and half a meter wide and deep. It wasn't a standard crate, as it was padded and sealed hermetically. However, it didn't seem like it would need to be cut open, just unlatched. She looked around for another manifest. The fact that the other crate was hermetically sealed was...interesting.

The manifest wasn't a lot of help. Sure, lots of wine names and dates, but that was only good if she could find an intact bottle. The last one was just a serial number, a very long one. It had the manufacturer's name, however: iNeed Robotics.

Cora recognized this. They were one of the largest makers and distributors of assistant bots in Human space. If that's what was in the container, it could very well fetch some money. Or give her a crewmate she didn't need to pay or figure out where they'd sleep. It depended on which model, exactly, it was. After all, a maid unit would be useless for salvage runs unless she just wanted to keep the ship clean. Looking down at the mess of wine and hydraulic fluid, maybe that wasn't such a bad thing.

Cora tapped the edge of the manifest for a moment, thinking. She wasn't up to date on robot tech. It had never been her thing, and certainly not something she could afford. That said, she knew the market was obsessed with "innovation." It was very competitive. This shipment was old enough that it might be worth seeing if she could use the model rather than just trying to sell off old inventory.

"Oh, fuck it." Cora set the manifest aside and leaned into the pod, carefully unlatching the crate. "Let's see what we've got."

Flipping open the latch, the last bit of power in the container released the seal and popped the door. Opening it carefully to make sure nothing fell out, Cora beheld the robotic unit. It was state of the art, that was for sure. It looked like a solid titanium chassis and skeleton covered in a soft layer of polymer musculature. The almost-silver skeleton and protective chest piece were surrounded by the clear polymer, which would have been creepy if the face hadn't been more defined instead of a skull. It was almost handsome. Given its sleek design, very human appearance, and compact muscle structure, Cora guessed military. Or would have until her gaze dropped down and noticed it was anatomically correct, and very male.

"Um...huh." She just blinked at it for a moment, then looked around the crate for any further instructions or manifest. She glanced more than once at the accurately sculpted male anatomy. That seemed...unusual. It was a reasonable size.

"Oh, Void, it's been too long since I've had sex," she muttered, digging for a manual.

After a close examination of the container, she came across a scannable code for what would no doubt be a novel-length instruction manual. Out here, however, she wasn't sure she'd be able to access the Galactic Network—too much radiation and debris. She'd be within range in a day or so, though. There was, however, an on switch noted in the "quick start" instructions found on the inside of the door. She just needed to depress the webbing of the left hand between the pinky and the ring finger.

"I suppose I should make sure it's still functioning," she murmured. And honestly, she wasn't strong enough to get the crate out of the cargo pod on her own. Carefully, almost gingerly, she pressed down where the quick start indicated.

There was the power source. It wasn't the sealed case, but the robot itself, as she heard the cell start to discharge and power the robot up. It shouldn't be surprising, given the quality, but it booted up relatively quickly. The translucent skin shimmered then became a stark white. The eyes blinked and glowed, still the same white. If anything, it was slightly more disturbing looking, now just a pure-white body with glowing white eyes, but she guessed that could be changed.

"Greetings, mistress," a synthesized voice announced, simulating a male around the baritone range. "Unit 0X-01 is ready for configuration. How may I pleasure you today?"

"Oh, Void," Cora whispered, and let out a little laugh. She then cleared her throat and straightened her shoulders. "0X-01, the craft carrying you was scuttled some years ago, and you have been salvaged. Are you damaged? Do you understand what I've said?"

"This is the first time this unit has been powered on," the robot responded. "Running diagnostic." There was a quick moment as its eyes flashed, then it looked back at Cora. "There is no damage reported. To note: 0X-01 is my model number. You may name me whatever you wish."

"Name you? Um..." Cora considered for a moment. If she named it—him—then she suspected that firmly cemented ownership. She remembered reading something about that, about how loyalty was programmed into bots. "How about Kader?" She couldn't remember where she'd seen the name, but she remembered it meant destiny or fortune. Something about it seemed fitting.

"Kader inputted. I am now Kader. Thank you, Mistress," the robot said. "How may I pleasure you today?" it asked again, still awaiting input. This was indeed a fresh install, it seemed. Factory new. She'd have to do all the configuration for it. At least it was a way to kill a couple of hours?

"All right, carefully climb out of there and follow me," Cora said, stepping back, somewhat bemused. "We'll get you configured. Can you give me a basic rundown of your functions and capabilities while we walk?"

"As you wish," it said and stepped out of its packaging. It padded behind her as it rattled off. "Initial configuration states I am an 0X-01 iNeed Pleasure and Companion Robotic Entity. Currently my capabilities and functions include all manner of sexual interface, social rituals, and relaxation assistance. My configuration is customizable to the body shape you desire within operational limitations. It may be easier to ask me if there is something you want and I can confirm."

A giggle escaped Cora. She couldn't help it. A pleasure bot. Of all the ridiculous, unnecessary, expensive things. And now it was hers.

"Are you capable of downloading other protocols once we're able to access the Galactic Network? The debris field I just pulled you from is a bit off the grid." She paused at the junction between the bridge and her quarters, and headed into her quarters—might as well be comfortable.

"An account may be needed, as I do not know what expansion modules I am capable of utilizing without a firmware update," it answered, following her.

Cora made a face. That meant she'd have to make a formal salvage claim in order to access iNeed Robotic's databases. Still, might be worth it. If there was a way to make this bot a little more versatile, it could fill in a lot of her crew needs. It was a tiny ship; she didn't need a lot. And... well, the pleasure aspects were also appealing.

They stepped into Cora's quarters. Her room was the nicest part of the ship, and she was not ashamed of that. There was a bed big enough for two, a soft carpet on the floor (magnetically held in place), a quality terrarium she'd salvaged off an old yacht complete with succulents, and fancy storage lockers from another salvage. She paused just before the carpet, and grabbed a towel.

"Here. Make sure there's nothing on your feet." She slipped her own shoes off as she spoke. Setting them aside, she headed to her bed and sat down. "You can come stand before me and walk me through your configuration process."

Kader took the towel and, with perfect balance, wiped his feet off one at a time. Carefully, the robot folded the towel and handed it back to her as it stood before her. Cora smiled wryly and set it aside.

"We shall begin the formal configuration process. First, how shall I address you, Mistress? Please include any correction to title, various names, desired pet names, and pronouns."

"My name is Cora Veyn," she said, shifting a little. "You can address me as Cora. My pronouns are she and her, though I find they and them acceptable. I don't have any relevant...titles at this time." She bit her lip, considering. "I...you could also call me 'my star' when appropriate." She'd always thought that was a charming way to refer to a lover. Not that she'd been with anyone enough to consider them "lover" rather than "brief diversion."

"Where appropriate," Kader considered and gave her a nod. "Cora registered. Just Cora, or Mistress Cora?"

"Just Cora," she said, reaching up and unpinning her buns. "Mistress feels unnecessary." She started to unbraid her ebony hair. "All right, what's next?"

"You have named me Kader. Are there any other names that I should also respond to?" he continued.

"Leave this protocol open; I need time to consider." Cora had no idea what she'd feel like calling him. "Next."

"These options are always open for you, Cora," he replied. "Next, my default configuration is male. Do you wish to keep me this way? Other options are female, neither, or hermaphrodite."

Cora arched an eyebrow. "Hermaphrodite sounds absolutely fascinating, but I think we'll stick with male for now. I still need a little time to adjust to the reality of you, and that might be too much too soon."

"I assure you, this model is durable enough to last for as much time and reality as you will require," he said. Cora arched a brow again, and a smile quirked the corner of her mouth. It was probably just an accurate description of Kader's durability, but it still felt a bit like innuendo. "Next, proportions you desire. Height, build, coloration. Mold me."

Finally unbraided, Cora shook her hair out. "Hm. Can you be taller? Say...about eight centimeters taller? I enjoy your lithe frame, but maybe a little more definition in the chest and shoulders."

Without a word, Kader's body shifted, the polymer stretching and filling out, becoming the eight centimeters taller she asked for. It appeared his chest and shoulders were more filled out, but without some sort of coloring, the stark white left no definition to be seen.

She bit her lip again, shifting a little in place—this was fascinating. "Ah, how about something warmer for the skin tone. Um...does your database include Besin?" Cora had done a salvage job near Besin once, and the bonus she'd received was three days on the planet. The native humans there had made an impression—taupe skin, eyes that seemed to glow (something about genetic tweaking several generations back), tall and athletic.

"There are many regions of Besin. I can create an average appearance from one of those regions if you'd like to specify," Kader described.

"Ah, near...oh, what was it," Cora's brow furrowed, "near the coastal resort area. Um...oh! Okyanus!"

"I do have an entry for the averages of that region," Kader stated, and his body started to shift again. The skin was the perfect color of taupe, as she had imagined. It even included small touches, such as a dusting of light freckles along his shoulders and chest. The illusion even went so far as to include subtle blemishes and veins. His face altered to appear to have firm cheek bones, a strong but exaggerated chin, and vibrant, sea-green eyes that had that near-glow gleam to them. Hair seemed to sprout from his form; mostly over his head with a full swoop of black hair, seeming to match Cora's, the right amount of stubble, and a manicured plot near his genitals. Kader was now a Besin model before her. There was a chance, given his operations, that "average" was the average of all the most-attractive examples they had fed the algorithm.

Cora just sat there for a moment, her mouth hanging slightly open, blinking. "Oh, wow. That's...amazing. Slightly unnerving. I don't mean you need to change! I just mean...if I didn't know, I would think that you were just...a person." A naked person. As her eyes swept down Kader's body, she could feel herself getting wet. Maybe she should have told him to be less attractive. No, that wouldn't have been any fun.

"I am glad this form brings you pleasure, Cora," Kader said, looking like he might have just given her a smirk. "The next configuration is personality. You can be as descriptive as you like, or you can stick to basics and I will use adaptive learning to hone my responses and suggestions."

Nodding slowly, Cora looked back up at Kader's face. "Right. I enjoy talking with people who are intelligent. Um, who are confident and...

maybe a little sassy, but not mean. Snark is fun, but it shouldn't be cruel. It shouldn't be mocking." She felt a little uncomfortable. Vulnerable. Memories of too many interactions where men had assumed that since Cora was pretty she must be stupid bubbled up in the back of her mind.

"Many of my systems will need a remote update to fit the profile, but it will be one of my primary developments. I hope you excuse any possible faux pas as we adjust this personality. I appreciate your patience," Kader said, his voice slowly taking on more casual inflections, less robotic in response. "Next, favored activities. What should I be preparing to be available for? Any particular requests?" Kader added as the configuration process continued.

Cora let out another small laugh and ran her hands through her hair. "Well, 75-80% of the year I am on this ship, often in various barely populated corners of space. A lot of time is spent reading, stretching, dancing around the cargo bay when restless, styling my hair, and…" well, now was the time to be honest, "pleasuring myself slightly more than I probably should. I imagine that you might play a role in all of these activities, plus conversation, and if we're able to download some more-practical protocols for you, maybe help me around the ship."

"It does sound as though you are in a high-stress, high-physicality working environment for a significant amount of time," Kader started, a little stiff conversationally, but this was still technically the configuration stage. "While I can make suggestions for items and tools to keep on your ship to assist in relaxing and body maintenance, currently I can offer several options that I'm sure I can excel at: massage, yoga of various types including tantric, partner or exhibition dancing, and any type of sexual activity. Would you like to engage in any of those now, and should we configure your preferences?"

"Huh." Cora tipped her head to the side, looking suitably impressed. "That all sounds potentially lovely. Let's begin with a massage. And then…" her eyes swept down Kader's form once more. It would be at least a day before they were back in range of the Galactic Network. Possibly longer. "Then let's consider sexual activities."

"Of course, Cora," he said, giving her a bit of a bow. She could easily hear the change in his voice as they left configuration mode. "Then please, get undressed however much you like and get comfy on your bed. I would prefer if it was completely undressed."

"All right." Cora stood up and started to peel out of the snug shirt and leggings she'd been wearing. She felt a little self-conscious as she did—in addition to the scar on her chin and her prosthetic left forearm and hand, she had a few more nicks and lines on her otherwise smooth, pale skin. She also had full breasts, flared hips, and a bubble butt that had won her several admirers in her dancing days.

"Ah, there's lotion in the second drawer to the left, if you need it," she said as she stretched out.

"I will certainly need lotion to properly rub this gorgeous body down," he said, pulling the drawer open and removing the lotion in question. The robot took a moment to examine the ingredients and the type of lotion, then looked back at Cora, his eyes wandering over her form as she got situated on the bed. "This will do for now, but we are definitely going to get something worthy of your skin, my star," he commented.

Cora's eyes widened and she turned pink. She knew, objectively, that she'd just instructed the robot to say those things to her. But the tingle that ran through her was unexpected.

"Right now, though, face down, ass up," Kader said as he moved to the bed. "Wait, that's later. Ass down. Get comfy—I'm going to turn you into a puddle." She wanted playful snark and confidence, and it seemed like she was getting it.

Cora giggled, looking over at Kader in surprise, but got herself situated on the bed. It was going to be hard not thinking of him as a person. Was that easier for the rich people who ordered units like this? They were already used to looking down on the poor. Was it easier for them to fight the human compulsion to assign humanity to things? Once Cora was settled, Kader got on the bed and knelt over her, his knees on either side of her thighs, as he sat on his heels.

He poured a healthy amount of the lotion onto his hands and gave it a moment to warm up, assisted by thermal conductors just underneath the polymer sheath. Once his hands actually touched her skin, it was clear that whatever programming they'd put in this bot was well sampled. Kader started to knead her flesh, reacting instantly to the beginning twinges and tightening of muscles to make sure the right areas and nerves had the attention they needed.

"Ohhhhhhhhhh." Cora just melted into the bed. It had been ages since she'd had a massage, and the last one wasn't even very good. This was amazing.

The personality module had taken a slight rest as Kader focused on the job at hand. As his hands moved up from the small of her back toward her shoulder blades, his body arched slightly and she could feel his sizable yet soft package. It was a bit of a shame that, unless instructed to, that wouldn't just get hard on its own. She would need to not take it personally.

Cora tucked that thought away. It might help keep her from becoming more attached. That was a problem for later, though. Right now she just murmured blissfully beneath skilled hands and a warm body.

The robot continued for nearly an hour, running over her back, shoulders, arms, butt, and legs. With a gentle swat on Cora's ass, Kader stood up off of the bed. "You want me to continue on your other side, don't you?"

"Mmmmm, yes." Cora giggled a little and rolled onto her back, slowly and lethargically, stretching for a moment before settling against the bed again. It was a shame Kader was a robot, because relaxed and stretched out in all her glory, Cora really was a lovely sight to behold.

Kader's face looked a little pleased and smug, but it was unfocused, breaking the illusion somewhat. Unfortunate, but that didn't diminish the physical attention she was getting. Once Cora was settled, the pleasure bot climbed back onto the bed and mounted her thighs once more. Another application of lotion and the massage continued. With her breasts presented, that was Kader's first target. The polymer that made up the thick sheath of his form was both soft and firm—enough give to be comforting, but enough firmness to knead into her flesh. Closing her eyes, Cora moaned and just let herself enjoy the sensation. She'd worry about not forming an emotional relationship with her new robot later. The hands on her breasts felt just like hands, and she hadn't been touched this way in...fuck, it felt like forever.

Another long, deep massage that covered her from scalp to ankle. Kader's hands strayed dangerously close to her sex but never quite brushed against it. It was almost agonizing, but he'd then move on to focus on other parts. When he had finished, her skin tingled and the muscles in her body were supple.

By the time Kader sat back, Cora was both ready to drift off, and wet enough that she could feel it on her thighs. It was an odd combination of sensations. It took a moment for her to open her eyes again and focus on Kader.

"Amazing," she murmured softly. "I think I will be very grateful I found you, my treasure." She wasn't really thinking about what she was saying; she just felt better than she had in ages—relaxed and flushed and aroused but not rabid with it.

There was an almost-audible processing noise that came out of Kader as he stood there for just a moment. Then, like a protocol had taken over or something, he snapped back into the process he had been working on. "Now, does my star want something a little more intimate?"

"Mmmm, I think I do," she said, not really understanding the hiccup, but he'd also been in cold storage for…who knows how long. Had there been a date on the manifest? She probably should have checked that. "You've done a very good job of exciting me. Are you ready to show me your prowess in bed?" She grinned a little at that.

By her indirect command, Kader was instantly hard. His hand reached out to pet the inside of her thigh. "Now we shall continue configuration. Please provide sexual preferences for positions, roughness, behavior, size, and any other particulars," he said, the voice falling back into measured, clear speech. Thankfully, the more she configured Kader, the less this would happen. It was a little odd that his hand continued to caress the inside of her thigh, though. That didn't seem like part of the configuration process. The touch helped keep the mood, however.

Cora pushed her hair out of her face, and stretched again. "I enjoy a variety of positions. I'm very flexible, I did exotic dancing for a few years, and I work to keep myself as limber as I was when dancing. In this setting, I would want you to begin more gently because I'm relaxed, though if the situation becomes more excited, I would enjoy you being rougher with me. You're probably strong enough to lift and fold me any number of ways." That would be fun. "For right now," she continued, a smile still playing on her lips, "let's start with oral sex. Are you equipped for that?"

"Noted. Advanced positioning approved. I am sorry to say that my fluid reserves are depleted. I can substitute with water, lotion, lubricant, or oil if available. This is recommended for oral unless you feel adequately lubricated."

Cora smirked. "There is lubricant in the drawer next to where you found the lotion, and I think you'll find I'm adequately wet. We'll see about your fluid reserves afterward."

"Excellent," the robot said as it moved to the nightstand and removed the lubricant. Taking off the top, it took a swig then placed it neatly back in the drawer. "Then, I believe we're ready," he said, crawling back onto the bed and settling himself at the foot. Sliding his hands up her legs, he parted them gently and settled between them. Taking ahold of her hips, the droid started to run its artificial tongue over her nether lips. It was an entirely new sensation; the soft yet firm flexing polymer muscle moved much like a tongue would, but it was extra slick because of the lubrication that was being used.

"Oh, wow," Cora gasped, and her legs spread farther, inviting more. It felt strange yet familiar, and so good. She could absolutely get used to this.

Kader continued diving into Cora, slowly but with full laps of the strange tongue. It also went just a bit deeper with every lick, driving in farther than a human tongue could go, but not freakishly so. At least, not yet. It also felt warm and rippled inside her.

"Oh, Void, that's..." she lost the words for a moment, moaning as the rippling radiated through her pelvis. As incredible as it was, however, she wouldn't cum like this, and she knew it.

"Y-you...you're doing great, that's...that's amazing, but I need you to also stimulate my clitoris." It was interesting that it wasn't turning her off to have to add instructions. It was just...part of the exercise. In a way it was freeing, because certainly Kader didn't care if her dirty talk was too clinical.

"I think I know just the thing, my star," the pleasure droid said, sliding his tongue out of her and replacing it with a pair of his fingers. The tongue in question stroked against her clit, then she felt a buzz. It was vibrating.

"Oh!" Cora's eyes flew open and her breathing got faster. The vibration was a low, throbbing at first, but it started to build. She twisted underneath that strange, vibrating tongue, and her hands reached down to slide her fingers through his hair. She gripped the back of his head and let out a soaring cry as she came, her legs shaking, and squeezed hard on the two fingers still inside her.

Kader guided her through the aftershocks of the orgasm, slowing down and dropping the intensity but not stopping, not until she was panting and whimpering softly. It took a minute for Cora to come back to herself. It had been too long since she'd cum so hard. Extracting his fingers and tongue, Kader slid off the bed and stood at the foot of it, looking down upon her. There was another very slight glitch, where Cora swore she saw his eyes soften and his cock throb, but then it went back to the artificial, slightly-smug gaze and the at-ready turgidity. Her brain registered the change, and she still had no idea why, but something about it made her want to find it again. Yes, Kader was a robot with no emotion, but there was something in those flashes that made her feel like he was holding back. Or maybe it was just a trick of her sex-starved brain.

Panting, she pushed herself up and wrapped her arms around Kader, hauling him in for a kiss. The kiss was a little awkward, but Kader's programming was good enough to at least emulate it so she wasn't just smooching stiff plastic. There was a slight slip of tongue, though, which was a nice touch.

"You're going to fuck me now," she said firmly as she pulled back. "We're going to start easy, but you should get rougher as we go, and you're allowed to improvise. But to start, I'm going to bend over this bed, and you're going to fuck me from behind, and we'll go from there."

"He— Yes, yes, my star," Kader said with a strange hitch. It could be that the cold storage had affected his processors just a bit. Either way, the bot was ready to go, and as soon as Cora got on her knees, he was behind her. Hands gripped her hips as she felt herself be slowly but snuggly filled with cock.

"Yes," she whimpered, her hands gripping the bed as he pushed into her. It had been too long by far. As absurd as the idea of a pleasure bot initially seemed, the truth was Cora loved sex, and would probably put this machine through his paces daily. Twice on Tuesdays.

"Fuck, you *are* a treasure," Cora moaned. "More..."

"Then more you will have," Kader responded, giving her ass a slightly more than gentle swat before increasing his paces. The cock was still artificial, but there was someone moving behind her and it was warm and slick. Taking advantage of her bendiness, Kader reached forward and grabbed one of her legs by the thigh, lifting it and pulling her closer to drive himself even deeper into her.

"Oh, Void, yes!" Her hands spread, moving out to support herself and press back against Kader. She'd never been with someone who tested what she could do before, or tried to move her in new ways. It was immediately exciting.

Kader had no problems being a solid support for her as her encouraging sounds moved him to experiment even further. Continuing to lift her leg, he rotated her halfway around so her leg was now stretched and resting against his shoulder, nearly forcing her into a sideways split. He transitioned slowly while still pumping into her, making sure she was limber and comfortable in the process of fucking her malleable body.

"Amazing," she gasped, bending into the motion, her leg stretching out. The combination of the stretch through her legs and his continued pumping into her slick, wanting pussy made for a delicious and intense sensation. She felt a tremor run through her. She'd never come just from being fucked before, but she was thinking this was about to be a first.

This seemed like the perfect angle, and Kader could feel every little twitch from her pussy surrounding him as he pounded into her. As she had requested, he started to be rougher, holding her firmly and bouncing her body against his to spear her deeply and thoroughly. Cora's upper body dropped lower to the bed for stability as the thrusting increased in intensity. It was perfect.

"Yes!" Cora could laugh—this miserable scavenging trip was turning out to be incredible. Instead, she came, crying out loudly and clenching hard.

Kader's grip tightened and he seemed to move into an overdrive. Pistoning into her, his cock started to leak lube, making the increase in speed slicker and easier despite the way he was now pounding her body. She swore she heard a grunt, a sound of need, from the bot as it furiously pound into her. She wasn't really tracking anymore. Her leg bent, sliding down over his shoulder, almost hooking around him as he continued to pound into her. Her cries were filling the room, accompanied by the wet sound of when his pelvis impacted with hers.

The shaft burying itself into her time and again started to vibrate. It was becoming too many sensations, but Kader seemed determined. She swore she could hear him mumbling "close, so close." The ecstatic pounding suddenly changed to firm, deep thrusts. Not as quick but far more insistent. Then, with a final push where Kader sheathed himself completely into Cora, she felt a sudden rush of warm lube.

"Fuck, that was good," the bot said in far too casual of a tone. He then looked down and blinked. "Wait, this feels real. This isn't my body. Isn't this a dream?"

The abrupt, strange shift in mood roused Cora from her blissful state. She blinked, then twisted a little so she could look back at Kader. The look of confusion on his face was the most human expression he'd yet had.

"This...is real," she said, and then laughed a little. She couldn't help it—the day just kept getting stranger. "So, um, helluva time to learn there's a ghost in the machine. You...wanna maybe pull out? And we can talk?"

"Oh," he said quietly, then his eyes widened. "Oh, oh gods, I'm sorry." He quickly, yet carefully, pulled out and set her down on the bed. "I didn't mean to, um… Oh this looks bad. I'm sorry." There was now panic on that beautiful Besin face.

"It's all right, I should have known it was too good to not implode." Cora let out another laugh, this one a little bitter, and ran a hand over her face. "Please, have a seat, let's take a metaphorical breath, and we can…figure this out or something." She briefly considered getting up and putting clothes on, but that seemed…well, stupid, at this point.

"Okay, um," he looked around for a chair and found a place to sit. Looking around, he blinked and was trying to get his bearings. "I'm, wow, I don't know what's going on. Ghost in the machine?"

"Oh, this just keeps getting weirder," Cora muttered, then cleared her throat and looked up at the android that was becoming more human by the moment. "All right. My name is Cora. We are currently in my ship, leaving the Darantine Expanse. I'm…I do salvage. I retrieved four pods from the expanse, one of which contained you. You are a 0X-01 unit, made by iNeed Robotics. Are we tracking so far?"

"I'm in a droid," he said, getting up and looking himself over. Laughing in a way that mirrored Cora's a bit, he reached down and bounced his cock in his hand. "A pleasure droid, I guess? Oh…oh shit, she did it. She actually fucking did it. Oh, that biiiiiitch." He was starting to move toward anger, but it was clearly not directed at her.

"I am open to your insights whenever you have a moment," Cora said dryly, stretching out on her side. Her cybernetic arm could support her indefinitely, and she settled into a comfortable lounge. She was still tired, but her brain would have no problem keeping her awake in the current situation.

"Sorry, sorry. You said you salvaged me, right?" he said, plopping back down. The awkwardness of the situation had clearly been overwritten. "Okay, this is weird so I'm going to make a long story short. We can do the long story later. I'm rich. Or was, I guess. Got a much younger step-mom. We didn't get along. I didn't want to deal with all the shade she was giving me, so I planned on moving. Packed all my shit, told dad where to ship it, fell asleep. Then, thought I was dreaming. My guess, Lisa did something to make sure my body was gone and my brain was lost."

"Void take me," Cora said, falling onto her back and covering her face with her hands. She laid there for a moment, then started to laugh again. "Well, I've got all your stuff! Or part of it, at least. Your wine collection didn't make it." Sighing, her hands fell away again, and she sat up. "You got a name, Rich Boy? And where do I drop you so that I'm not implicated in...whatever the hell this is? I...I think if you can still access the protocols in the droid you can probably adjust the body to your actual appearance."

From shit to amazing and back to shit again. She hadn't had such a yoyo of a day since she first left home and had to navigate an actual megacity for the first time.

"I..." he started, then leaned back and sighed. "I don't think it matters. I mean, what year is it, even?"

That was a thought. A number of the items in the pods were vintage. "Um, 2432 CGE," she said, tucking her hair behind her ear. "Third Quarter. You were probably from the Core, so...do they still use the Gregorian calendar? I think it's September?"

"Yup," he said, throwing up his hands but settling back down, laughing again. "It's been, what, ninety years? I'm dead and gone."

Cora's self-pity abruptly vanished. "I...I'm sorry."

He sighed heavily, then rubbed his face and looked back at her. "I am, or was, Cayd Farensaw Rickton III." It was a strange and eerie coincidence that his given name was so close to the one she'd assigned the bot. Giving her a smile, he stood up and bowed slightly, offering her a hand to sit up. "And you are?"

She took the hand, letting him pull her completely out of the bed, and becoming a little more aware of the fact that she was still naked. "Cora Veyn," she said, sheepishly running her metal hand through her hair. "I'm...no one. I was raised on Amansinaya Station, left home a little impetuously around 20, enjoyed a brief career as an exotic dancer, and got into salvage because it paid better and I didn't have to be nice to assholes. Cost me an arm, though." She smirked and gestured with her left hand.

"Well, I hope you'll be a little nice to this asshole," he said, looking her over. It couldn't be helped. "I'm honestly surprised this paid better than you being an exotic dancer. You look like you could make bank."

"Ah," Cora blushed a little, and felt ridiculous doing it, "I think I didn't have the personality for it. There were other dancers that made a lot more than me. Deacon was our highest— You know, none of that matters, I'm just getting awkward."

He smiled. "So, look, as far as I'm concerned, it's all yours. The salvage, I mean. I'm gone, I've got nowhere to be, but you saved my life, as it were." He looked himself over once more. "As it is. So, I guess I owe you. Whatever you want."

She looked at him for a moment, and bit her lip. "Um...well, bedroom functions aside, I was actually hoping to find out if the droid could download more-practical protocols once we reconnected to the net." She felt her cheeks getting redder. "I could use some help—it's just me on the ship, and it...gets lonely. Which is why I decided to keep it. You." Oh, void, what was she saying?! "I just mean, if you have nowhere, you could have a place here."

Cayd smiled and retook her hand. "I was kinda hoping you might say that. It may take me a bit to see if I can tap into, well, whatever software is in this body," he said, chuckling and moving a little closer, putting his other hand on her hip. "Should we see what I might be capable of? You know, if you're still up for it. It looked like you were having a good time."

Cora's brows rose, and she let out a laugh. "Oh! Oh, I just meant, I mean, I was offering you a spot on the ship, I wasn't assuming you would… I mean, you just had your universe tipped sideways, and you..." She wished desperately that she would stop blushing, it wasn't something she did, what the hell was this? "I mean, I *was* having a good time; it's been a while since I've been with anyone attentive, or anyone at all really, and...oh, void."

Chuckling gently, Cayd brought her hand up and kissed the top of it. He then smacked his lips, realizing he didn't have any saliva and the lube that was still on his mouth felt funny. She giggled, and pulled away from him long enough to dart over and grab her water bottle—it was still pretty full. "Here, drink that. It'll break down the lube you swallowed earlier, and presumably your system will know what to do with it. Before...before you became aware again, you mentioned being out of fluids."

Taking the bottle, he took a swig and made a face. "Oh, that's weird. Oh, really weird," he said, chuckling and taking another drink. "We'll get back to how weird drinking is now." Cayd handed the bottle back. His body hadn't changed, which might have been odd, but it also seemed like he didn't have full control. Or didn't care.

"So, if you're down for it, I very much am," he said. "You are, well, damn, okay? And you saved my life, so I will be very, very attentive. Also, I'm sure I'll have an existential crisis later, but right now I'm looking at you and can't stop looking at you."

She laughed a little again, and reached out, setting her flesh-and-blood hand on his chest. "You came from a life of privilege," she pointed out, smiling, as she slid her hands slowly down his chest and over his abs.

"You had to have met beautiful women before. Ones with fewer scars and all their limbs." Her tone was teasing—she'd come to terms with her arm a long time ago.

"Sure I have," he said, shuddering a little and chuckling, tilting his head momentarily to the side. "Doesn't make you any less beautiful. And the arm, well, just means you lived an interesting life. The rest of you is very real."

She bit her lip and looked at him. "How...tactile is this body? You didn't really comment on it before, but when you...awoke toward the end, you did seem to feel."

"I was definitely feeling it. Like, more than I ever remember feeling it before," he said, rubbing his fingertips together. "And you feel really, really good. And you look...dammit, sorry. If I'm bringing that up too much, let me know."

"So how does this feel?" she asked as her hand slid down to his hip, her thumb playing at the line where his leg met his pelvis.

"It feels amazing," he said, closing his eyes and shuddering again.

Cora could feel herself getting excited again. Sure, the situation was weird as hell, but it was getting to be more interesting by the minute. "What do you mean when you say it feels like more than you remember?"

"I'm super sensitive. I'm going to need to find a way to turn that down. I can feel every ridge of your fingerprints. At least, I think that's what that is."

"And what about this," she murmured, leaning in and drawing her tongue up the cleft of his chest.

"Oh fuuuuck," he drew out, leaning his head back and grabbing her shoulders to catch himself. He didn't pull on her much, though; his body was perfectly balanced and a lot stronger than he was probably used to. "Your tongue is amazing. I really need to figure this out or I may go crazy if we go any further."

Chuckling, he pushed her back, just a bit, and closed his eyes again, thinking. His head tilted to the side for a moment, then upright rather suddenly. "Okay, ah, I think I got it. Try something else," he continued, releasing her.

Cora pouted at him. "I'm a little disappointed you figured out how to turn it down before I did anything more involved," she said.

"I said I think—" Cayd started but was cut off by a moan as she stepped into him, wrapping her body around his. The metal hand would feel strange compared to the rest of her, but it was still flexible carbon fiber and steel mesh, nothing hard, and warm enough due to the actuators and the proximity of her body. Clearly it was doing something, because she could actually feel him throb hard against her, and he shuddered again. Even though his body no longer had any of these systems, something in his brain indicated how it *should* behave, and the programming in the droid was sophisticated enough to just make it happen. She nuzzled against him and lightly bit his chest. Those extra centimeters she asked for made it difficult to reach his neck or ear, but she had plans for them.

"A little," he said after a minute, "I figured it, mmm, out a little. It's still fucking amazing." Perhaps unthinkingly, his arms went around her and he grabbed her ass with both hands, pulling her firmly against him. "Won't shut down from overload, but may squeal in a rather ungentlemanly manner."

"I would argue that everything about this situation is ungentlemanly."

"Oh hush," he said, and squeezed her ass.

She slid the fingers of her right hand down his spine. It wasn't really a spine, but the droid body had a reasonable facsimile. "I have an idea. Sit down."

With a small murmur of protest, he reluctantly let go of her. He sat down on the bed, looking at her curiously. Without word or warning, Cora climbed into his lap, straddling him and sliding her arms over his shoulders. He wasn't inside her yet, but she could feel him, ready and wanting.

"Ahhh," he responded, his hands returning to her rump and squirming just a touch underneath her.

"This is better," she said softly as she bent her head, drawing her lips over his shoulder to his neck. "Now where were we?" She slid her tongue up the side of his neck to his ear, catching the lobe in her mouth and sucking it gently.

"Testing, mmm, my sensitivity. Which is still high. And you still feel so, so good." Cayd's hands started to explore, running over her hips and up her sides, fingertips tracing the small of her back. Cora could feel the difference in his touch from what it had been. He was thoroughly exploring her where he could reach, like he needed to map out her entire body for memory. Before, there had been a skilled, professional surety. This was eager, more genuine. She moaned softly in his ear. She was happy to let him touch all he wanted.

"Do you want to try to kiss me?" she asked, curious as to his reaction to it. It had been a little strange before, when she had kissed him impulsively earlier, but would it change now that the body was inhabited by someone who remembered the act?

"I would very much like to," Cayd said, pulling her up his lap so they were very snuggly pressed together.

Shifting a little, Cora sat back. This was so she could see his face, but it had the added bonus of pressing her down against his ready cock. She was surprised at how much she was enjoying this—not just the touch and activity, of course that was good, but the curious testing.

"I'll start gently," she said with a playful smile.

Cayd's attempt to comment was cut off by the press of her lips. He leaned into it and deepened the kiss as well as he could. This was much better, in form, than previous. Artificial kissing clearly had not been perfected; you needed the human feeling and intention to really get what you wanted out of one.

As the kiss drew out, it became more heated. Cora slid her hands up into his hair, caressed his face and neck, and sucked at his tongue. There wasn't typically a lot of kissing in her usual hookups, so this was nice. She hadn't made out with anyone like this in…she couldn't even remember, honestly. Though as the kissing got more heated, she also found herself rubbing her slick, wet sex against the hard shaft that was still pressed against her. Cayd was making some interesting noises. He had said he hadn't completely been able to tune down his sensitivity, and she was all over him at the moment. His hips rolled underneath her, rubbing against her with his shaft. Hands kneaded her ass, nearly lifting her with each rotation.

Cora moaned into Cayd's mouth as the kiss just kept building, her warm body growing hotter by the minute as she rubbed against him, her hands moving over his shoulders and down his back, her soft breasts pressed firmly against his chest. He was less giving than a real body would have been—the titanium frame underneath all the polymer and fibers didn't give the way a human body might. But that also meant that nothing softened or lessened the press of their bodies against each other.

It seemed Cayd reached his limit. Lifting her with surprising ease, he grinded his cock against her clit until he lined the two of them up, then pulled her down on top of him, sheathing into her completely as he moaned and shuddered. The sensations must have been almost overwhelming. Gasping, Cora wrapped her arms around him and nuzzled into his neck. He just held her, and his brain's understanding of what his body should be doing caused the artificial shaft to throb even though no heartbeat set its rhythm.

This was…strange. It was all strange, but she'd be lying if she said she wasn't loving how into her and how swept up in the moment Cayd was. "I think it's your turn to do what you want," she murmured in his ear with a little giggle. "Don't forget to tell me how it feels."

"I think I'm doing exactly what I want," he said, his voice quiet but heavy with sensation. He started to move, and more so he started to move her. With the compacted muscles, he was able to lift and drop her down onto him without her adding any assistance.

"You're so soft and warm, your body is just firing electricity into my mind everywhere you're touching me," he attempted to describe, though it was broken with moans. "Your pussy is so tight and clinging, and I can feel every fold. Cora, you are the best thing I've ever felt."

Cora's eyes grew wide, and her lips parted in surprise as blood rushed to her cheeks. She knew, objectively, that he was doing what she'd told him to. But she had also never had anyone describe her in such a way. The very real concern that feelings were becoming involved in this wild adventure started to crop up in the back of her mind, but that was immediately banished as he continued to firmly grasp her hips and move her up and down on his cock. She whimpered as he hilted himself in her again and again, and pressed her mouth to his once more. Cayd let go of her waist, letting her ride him while his hands sought other bits. Moving up her sides, he slipped his fingers over her breasts, teasing them until their kiss broke.

Dropping back against the bed, he reached up to caress and squeeze her tits. "I would have loved to watch you dance," he said. "I bet you move amazingly and know just how to sway with this body of yours."

"Oh, Void," she murmured, looking into his eyes, her own wide with surprise again. How did he know what to say? Could he tell she was getting more wet every time something like that came out of his mouth? "Maybe," she gasped out, still flushed, "maybe I'll dance for you sometime." Their rhythm halted for a moment, but she refocused, engaging her thighs as she took over so he could touch all he wanted.

"Oh, fuck, keep doing that," he said, rolling his head back and squeezing her breasts again. "Feeling your pussy clench is so good. So fucking good." His fingers moved to focus more on her hard nipples, teasing them and testing what she liked.

"Ah! Yes!" She planted her hands on his chest, her arms coming in under her breasts, pushing them together and forward. "I love it when people play with my tits." It was certainly the most communicative sex she'd ever had. Maybe that was what was making it good? That and everything he said just made her warm and flushed and caused her to want him more.

Her hands splayed against him, and she found a good rhythm and proceeded to take him for a very enthusiastic ride. Her breasts bounced and strands of her hair fell over her face as her cheeks and lips flushed again. Her mouth was parted, and she let out a little cry every time she came down on his cock. She could also feel him grow inside her. Like, really grow, not just a guy on the edge. He was starting to grunt as well, which was clearly from feeling, as Cayd didn't need to breathe anymore.

"This feels amazing; you feel amazing," he said, bucking up his hips. "I feel like I want to cum, but I'm not sure how. It just keeps building and building."

Panting but not stopping, Cora looked down at Cayd again, a little smile on the corners of her mouth. "I wonder...do I need to tell you to?" She wasn't sure if any part of his programming was warring with his consciousness. "Because I'd love it if you came for me. Please. Come for me."

"I don't—" he started to say. "Fuck, that'll do it!"

Gripping tight to her breasts, Cayd started pumping feverishly, bucking her up with every thrust, until he finally let out a strained roar. Thrusting up into her, he lifted her off the bed and held her there, impaled on his cock. She let out a cry as he lifted her, gasping and amazed. Finally, the feeling resided and he collapsed back onto the bed. This time she'd only gotten a bit of slick water for her efforts, but he seemed quite satisfied as he lay on the bed, shuddering every now and then. It may not be the type of ejaculation she was used to, but it was still fucking satisfying to see. She leaned down, smiling, and gently brushed his hair back.

"That was fucking amazing," she said, something softly adoring in her tone and gaze.

"Yeah it was," Cayd said with a smile.

She caressed his face for a moment, then carefully climbed off of him, but stayed on the bed. "I think you're sleeping with me, so when you can move, why don't you climb up and rotate." She was extra grateful she'd gotten the larger bed.

It seemed he could move instantly. "Other than being overloaded with sensation, I'm not tired," he remarked, sitting up and scooting to the far side of the bed. "I'm…not sure I can get tired anymore." Despite his words, he still stretched out. "This mean I made the cut, Captain? Am I part of your crew? Don't have to worry about being dropped at the nearest station to fend for myself?"

Cora giggled as she stretched out next to him, pulling up the blanket. "I mean, you're still in a probationary period," she said as she lifted her hair and twisted it back out of the way. She rolled onto her side to look at Cayd. "You may want off at the next station. It's very boring here, and while I'm not desperately scraping to keep it together, I'm not rich either. I have this ship and a barren apartment on Persepolis, because I needed a residence to register the ship there."

"I suppose we'll see," he responded, reaching a hand up to brush some stray locks out of her eyes. "So far, I like this salvager's lifestyle. A lot less complicated. That, and the sex is amazing."

"It really was amazing," she agreed, blushing again. "I don't think it's ever been that good. And you just seem to know exactly what to say to make me…" She trailed off and cleared her throat. "We…we'll need to talk more. For right now, I was worn out when I found you. I took a boost, but I've definitely depleted it. I have to sleep for a little while. If you're not actually tired, you're welcome to get up and look around the ship. Whatever you wanna do."

"I think I'm okay with just staying here," he said, placing a hand on her hip. "Now that we've, uh, calmed down, my mind is exhausted. I've got to figure out how to work this body, and accept it's mine. Think napping might do that." He gave her a squeeze and a shameless grin. "But, you know, order me awake if you need another go. I am a pleasure bot, after all."

She let out a little laugh. "If I wake up before we've hit Core space, I absolutely will. We're not done testing your reactions to different stimuli, or your endurance." Her expression softened, and she reached out and set a hand on his chest. "Though, if your existential crisis hits, you can wake me up, okay? You don't need to haul through that alone."

"I'll keep that in mind," he said, reaching out to pull her close. "You saved me once already, though. Gotta pay you back before I need you to save me again."

"I dunno, so far, finding you has been a net positive," she murmured, snuggling in against him. This, too, was different, but it was nice. "We'll… we'll get it all worked out."

She closed her eyes, unable to keep up the conversation. She was exhausted, well fucked, and a little smitten. There were a pile of things to work through and worry about, but that was for later.

A GIRL AMONGST WOLVES

VR Wednesdays had become a regular favorite at Gracie's. It was a little weird to see the VR set up against the back wall of the old bar—Gracie's had been a saloon and brothel back during the Gold Rush, becoming just a saloon when Colorado gained statehood, and officially downgrading to "bar" sometime in the 40s. It had always been Gracie's, though, and even though it'd been owned by three different families, no one ever changed the name.

Anyway, the current owner's son had started doing VR nights with a couple friends on slow evenings, and it had taken off. It was probably the physicality of it—werewolves needed a certain amount of physical activity not to go stir-crazy. So Wednesdays often found Lucas and his friends at Gracie's, ordering the Mega Nachos and Sampler Platter and slashing at digital blocks in time with the beat.

"I am so excited for this weekend," Jack said, sitting down across from Lucas and setting down two beers. Jack was a stocky guy with ginger hair who looked like he took style advice from Erik the Red, and he and Lucas had been friends since kindergarten. "Trace and I are gonna head up tomorrow night and make sure the cabins are ready for everyone on Friday. I checked with the lodge; they have WiFi, and we got the ones next to the hot spring."

"Yes!" An exuberant brunette named Syla plopped down to the left of Lucas, grinning. "So do we have enough cabins? No one has to double up?"

Jack nodded. "Trace and I in one, you and Byron in the other, and then Lucas and Ches in the last one."

Taking a drag from his beer, Lucas looked over at Jack. He ran a hand through his mane of fluffy, unmanageable hair and pulled out his phone. "What all did you guys need me to bring to this thing," Lucas asked, unlocking the phone and pulling up a note app, "aside from the usual A/V stuff?"

Jack sort of gestured with his beer. "That's it. This is supposed to be relaxing. I promise not to randomly spring extra nature time on you." Lucas smirked; he wasn't afraid of exercise. In fact, he was quite fit. It just wasn't on his list of "fun things to do."

Grinning, Syla looked over at Lucas. "I half-expected you to freak out. Four days in a cabin with Ches. There's only one bed."

Jack looked confused. "And? They've been together almost two months."

"Yeah, but they still haven't..." Syla trailed off and glanced over at Lucas again.

"Look, I didn't know she wasn't...like us before we got together, and I don't want to freak her out," Lucas grumbled, setting his beer down with a heavy thump. "I really like her."

"Well, yeah, she's cute as hell," Jack said, taking a drink.

"I know, right?" Lucas sighed.

"And she smells so good," Syla said, sighing almost wistfully.

"I know, right?!" It was hard to keep the enthusiasm and exasperation out of his voice. Ches was certainly attractive enough, but her smell— even Jack and Trace admitted that Ches smelled amazing for a human. So amazing that it had been impossible for Lucas to tell she was one.

"I seriously don't know how you've lasted this long," Syla went on, looking over at Lucas. "Where is Ches, anyway? Isn't she coming tonight?"

"Yeah, she should be here soon," he said and picked up his beer once more. Hazel eyes stared into the amber liquid in the bottle in thought. Ches and him had a good thing going, and the last thing he needed was for his true nature to ruin that.

Lucas knew Ches had come in before anyone said anything, without needing to turn around. That feeling that people get sometimes when it feels like someone's watching them? It was like that, only instead of unease it was more like a warmth in his chest, a loosening of the shoulders. So when a pair of pale hands slid over his shoulders and a warm, soft body pressed up against his back, he didn't startle.

"Hello, ma bête." Ches's voice was soft and melodic, and her scent washed over him as she kissed his cheek. "Ma bête" was French for "my beast," and Ches had started calling him that about a week before he asked her out (she had taken French in high school, options had been limited). She had no idea how accurate it was.

"Hey, Mei," he said with a chuckle. He'd called her Mei since he'd learned she was a big fan of the character. It also fit her personality— very sweet, but ready to take you out if crossed. Verbally, at least.

"Ches, you made it," Syla said excitedly. "We're just talking about the weekend!"

Reaching up, Lucas grasped Ches's hands with his and gave her a squeeze. After, he pushed back from the table to give her room to find a seat on his lap. He was a fair size larger than she was, easily a foot taller and outweighing her by at least a hundred pounds, and he rather enjoyed having her perch or climb on him. She let go and stepped aside to give Syla a quick hug before taking the offered seat. Her pink hair was starting to fade, braided back into twin tails like she often did when she was working. She also set down brown paper bags, stamped with the logo from her mom's coffee shop, in front of everyone at the table. Ches was the baker, often made extra, and loved to share.

"I'm really looking forward to it," Ches said brightly as she wiggled back into Lucas's lap. Wrapping an arm around her waist, he contently held her, hand on her thigh. "I've been making double and triple batches of everything so that Mom will be set until we get back. I even pre-formed and froze about five dozen scones so that she can make fresh ones if she runs out. Did that today, actually."

The waitress came by and set down nachos, smiling at everyone, but at Ches in particular. "Cider?"

Ches smiled back. "Yes, please!"

Leaning into her slightly, Lucas took another quiet breath and sighed contently. Like honey, but with a peppery finish, and something warm— it was all those things, but also more. Sweet, sensual, but also…homey.

"You two are nauseating," Jack said with a snicker.

Looking up, Ches made sad eyes at him. "No we're not! Besides,

I remember when you and Trace got together—you have no right to comment."

Jack considered. "That's fair," he said, and drank off his beer. Ches had been friends with Trace for a while. That was how they'd all met her, when Trace and Jack's friend circles merged.

The waitress came back with a bottle of cider, setting it down in front of Ches, who picked it up and leaned back into Lucas, her head against his chest. Jack set down his drink and picked up the parcel in front of him. "So what's in the bags?"

"I am subjecting you all to my experiments!" Ches grinned. "Some savory scones, black cocoa brownies, and a few things I'm planning on making for Halloween week."

Syla's eyes got big. "That sounds awesome."

"Your experiments are always the best experiments," Lucas said, carefully reaching out to rattle one of the bags and see if he could shake something out of it. He managed to dislodge a white macaron with red filling and an eye painted on one side.

"Do you think it's too much?" Ches asked, tipping her head to the side. "Mom thinks the red filling is gory but I think it's appropriate. We only do themed items for the week leading up to Halloween, so it's not like it'll be there indefinitely."

"It's only too much if you sacrificed flavor for appearance," Lucas said, taking the macaron and dropping it dramatically into his mouth. Munching on it contentedly, he nuzzled against her neck. "Scrumptious. Nope, it's not too much." She giggled.

"Wow, you're so good at these things," Syla said, peeking into her own bag. "Have you gotten any more catering jobs?"

"Not yet, but a lot of inquiries about the holidays," Ches said, sounding hopeful.

Leaving everyone to their bags, Ches leaned forward for nachos. This pushed her ass against Lucas's lap as she leaned over the table. She had a full, round ass that was perfect for squeezing. She would sometimes complain about her "pudge," but consensus among the rest of the friend group was that she was lush and looked very touchable.

"So when are we leaving?" Ches asked between bites.

"Friday afternoon," Syla answered, unsubtly checking out the ass in Lucas's lap before looking up at him and mouthing the word "Damn." Smirking, Lucas mouthed back "I know," and moved the hand that had been on Ches's thigh back enough to give her rump a little squeeze before putting it back where it had been resting. Ches had started wearing fleece leggings with the colder weather. They were very...shapely.

Ches nodded, missing the exchange between Syla and Lucas. "I'll make sure I'm packed before I crash for the day, and set an alarm to be up on time." Ches wasn't a morning person, so she stayed up late to get the baking done most days, finishing around 3 or 4 and sleeping through the morning rush.

"I'll set an alarm up as well, and make sure you're ready to go," he grinned. It wasn't just her—he had reminders for everyone else too. "Okay, final check, is there anything else I need to pick up before we go? We're stocked on food, everyone has extra blankets, things like that?"

"Trace and I are getting food, that's part of why we're heading up the night before," Jack said, getting some nachos before Ches put too big of a dent in them. "Everyone had a week to put their requests into the spreadsheet, so unless you bring it with you, you get what you get."

"Byron is bringing the game systems," Syla chimed in. "The largest of the three cabins has a 70" OLED we can plug into. I figure Byron and I will take that cabin."

"And why do you get the big one?" Jack asked with a smirk.

"Because we're less likely to be fucking at random hours," Syla answered, rolling her eyes. Jack snickered, and Ches almost choked on nacho. Lucas snerked but sat up and rubbed Ches's back gently.

It was true, though. Syla and Byron were friends, good-enough friends to fool around sometimes, but they weren't together. Syla and Jack laughed as Ches recovered, Syla patting her on the back as Ches waved her off and promised she was fine. Lucas offered her one of the untouched water glasses that were on the table.

"Okay, all set then," Lucas said, steering the conversation back to prep. "But if anything comes up last minute, let me know, yeah?"

Everyone agreed to check in with Lucas before he left if they had additional requests, and Ches and Syla got up for a round of Beat Saber. Jack came around and sat down next to Lucas.

"Look, I wasn't going to say anything, but Syla already brought it up," Jack said, as quietly as he could manage, while the girls faced off to a particularly high-energy techno song. "Trace and Ches talk a lot, you know? And...Ches is pretty good friends with a couple of your exes. Small town, hard to avoid. She knows you're not normally like this. She's starting to think the problem is her."

"Yeah, I know, I know," Lucas said, closing his eyes and pinching his nose. "And it absolutely is not her. I mean, look at her." Lucas gestured toward the beautiful, curvy femme swinging motion controllers like a samurai.

"But, well, when I get worked up, I change," he continued. "I can't stop it." He sighed and finished his beer. "And she's not one of us, so I don't even know how to start to explain it."

Jack nodded. "Yeah, a lot of us change when we get excited. Look… maybe talk to Trace about it? Ches tells him almost everything; maybe he's got some insight for you. He's worried about you two. We all know you're a good match."

"Yeah," Lucas sighed, setting the empty bottle on the table with a thump. "She's everything I never thought I'd find in this little town. It's part of the problem—I'm so into her, I can feel the call when we're just messing around." Another sigh and he sat up straight, putting a hand on the table. "But talking to Trace is a good idea; I'll do that."

"Great," Jack patted him on the shoulder, and stood up. "I'll make sure you get some time when you guys make it up to the cabins. Should be easy: I'll make sure Syla takes Ches for a walk around the area while you're setting up and wiring. Trace is smart enough to assist, and you guys can chat. Sound good?"

"Yup, sounds good," he said, chuckling and fighting the urge to slink off and hide in a corner. Instead, he just focused his eyes on Ches. If only things were different, the things he'd do to her. Hell, the things he'd do that she suggested.

Jack went to the bar and came back with another beer for each of them. Ches kicked Syla's ass and took on the next challenger—so sweet, but vicious as hell during competitive games. It was as if that was where she got it all out of her system.

The rest of the night was a fun time. Wednesdays usually were. Eventually everyone headed out, Jack and Syla both needing to get up for work, and Ches and Lucas going back to Ches's house. Lucas pulled up in the back, parking and turning off his lights, and Ches climbed into his lap.

Smiling at her, he placed his hands on her hips and nuzzled against her. "Glad you came tonight," he said gently. "Very glad you're coming this weekend. Heck, I just like having you around." Lucas couldn't help but grin a little at the country twang that appeared in his voice when he got particularly distracted or happy. She brought it out of him more than anyone else.

"Really?" Her voice was a little shy, and she looked into his eyes for a moment.

The question surprised Lucas, and his brow furrowed a little. "Always."

Ches ran her hands through his hair, drawing his head back a little, and kissed him, a slow, lazy tease of lips and tongue that built into something stronger. She was so hungry, every time they kissed. His hands glided up her back as fingers moved firmly along her skin. He loved kissing her, and he wanted to return that hunger so badly. He wanted to fall into it headfirst and drown in their combined passions. If he did, however, he'd change, and she'd see a beast before her. Despite her pet name, he wasn't sure that was what she'd actually want.

Lucas's internal conflict did not stop him from responding physically to the woman in his lap. Ches tasted like cider and sugar, she was warm and soft in his hands, and her scent—fuck, her scent. It filled the cabin of the truck, the same sweet warmth as always but with a muskiness that grew stronger every time they were like this.

For once, however, Ches was the one who pulled back, panting as she ran her hands through his hair and cupped his face.

"I won't see you tomorrow," she murmured, and leaned in to kiss him again, as if she couldn't help it. "I'm heading into Denver to pick up some things for mom, do some shopping. Won't be back until late. But we have all weekend, yeah?"

"Yeah," Lucas said with a breathy pout, his hands kneading her thighs and ass. His jeans were incredibly uncomfortable at this point, and he feared he'd break the zipper. "All weekend. Very much looking forward to it."

Leaning in, she nuzzled at him, and drew her tongue up the side of his neck, taking his earlobe between her teeth and giving it a tug. "Ma bête," she said, her tone low and throaty, "I cannot wait to be alone with you in that cabin." The implications were impossible to miss.

"Oh god, me neither," he moaned gently, his hands flexing and gripping her ass. She licked down his neck again and bit down where it met his shoulder, sucking at his skin, probably leaving a mark. She'd never done that before, and he felt dangerously close to shifting. She then opened the door and slid out of the truck.

"Good night, ma bête," Ches said, smiling. "See you Friday." He let out a breath he'd been holding and blinked slowly at her.

"Night, babe," he said after a beat, shivering a little as the cool air hit all the spots where she'd teased him. He waited for her to go inside before he drove off. Oh Luna, he needed to run this off. Hard.

Driving out of the city limits, Lucas went to a little part of the national park that wasn't frequented often. At least not by people who weren't local. Driving up the small access road, he parked in one of the turn loops and got out. Stripping out of his clothes, he tossed them into the bed of the truck.

The cool air washed over his large, muscular frame, but it wasn't enough. Rolling his shoulders back and looking up to the sky, he let the call take him. Fur sprouted out all over his body, and he got even bigger, his bones shifting and his face elongating until he was a large wolf-human hybrid.

Letting loose a howl to the moon, he tore off down the trail and into the woods beyond. It didn't matter where he went—he just needed to release the wild energy that surged through his body. He would much rather spend that wild energy pleasuring Ches in all the ways she teased, but she was human. She...wouldn't understand.

It felt like the runs were taking longer, like he needed to work it out of his system more each time he did this. Finally, however, he slowed, and could tell that it was time to turn around if he didn't want to spend the night in the reserve.

By the time he made it back to the truck, he was human again, and the cool air was finally starting to get past the heat of adrenaline and exercise. Pulling on his clothes, he grumbled slightly; he hadn't been in the right mind to leave them in the cab, so they were cold as well. Starting the truck up, he headed back home. At least he'd be able to sleep.

When Lucas finally got home and fell into bed, sleep came swiftly. Thursday was slow, but filled with a certain amount of tension. Uncharacteristically, he didn't hear from Ches at all—no texts, nothing. She was normally a very check-in type of person. Not a "first text in the morning and last text at night" type, but usually something during the day.

Friday morning, Lucas woke up to a very precise list of things that were still needed at the cabins, mostly cables. The text came from Trace, which made sense; he was one of those people with an eye for detail, where Jack was more big-picture.

Lucas would get on the list once he was done with the little bit of work left on his plate. A few lines of code here, a few tickets closed there, and then he was diving into his box of cables for what Trace needed.

That didn't take long, and as he stepped out to go to pick up the last few items, he texted Ches.

This is your 2pm wake-up call! How was Denver? You ready to go?

Hi! Denver was great! Would love to spend some time with you there! Yes, ready to go. All packed up, just got out of the shower. I'll be dressed by the time you get here. And if I'm not, you can say hi to Mom.

Denver together would be fun! Be there soon. XO

Putting the phone in the cradle, he decided to give her enough time to get dressed, so he picked up the last of the supplies before heading to her house. It'd be nice to see Ches's mom regardless. She'd had a hard time, had escaped a bad relationship, before moving to his town. Lucas liked checking in with her every now and then, now knowing her story.

Coming to Ches's house during the mid-afternoon meant that parking took a minute. Ches and her mom, Mina, lived above their coffee shop, which occupied the first floor of a very old building that used to be an inn or a saloon—Lucas's dad had told him which at one point, but he didn't remember. The building had been updated sometime in the 90s, before the old owners passed away. Mina was friends with the daughter of the old owner, and when Mina left her ex, the friend encouraged her to come make a new start here. It had worked out, and the coffee shop— which Ches and her mom renamed Holy Grounds since it was next to the cemetery—was doing better than it ever had.

As Lucas walked in, Mina was behind the counter, and she waved animatedly. "Lucas! Good to see you, love! You're here to pick up Chessary? She'll be down in a bit. Can I get you something while you wait?" Mina had the light remains of a British accent, left over from her childhood, and a lot of the speech patterns.

"Afternoon, Ms. Thompson," Lucas said, giving her a little wave back. "I'd love one of your latte specials if you have the time."

"Absolutely." Mina started shuffling and waved off the girl at the register who was about to ring up Lucas. "Not this one, love; this one comes in and he gets whatever he wants, all right?"

Chuckling gently, Lucas looked at the girl behind the counter and gave her a little shrug. He would have paid, but he wouldn't turn down generosity. "How's everything going here? Need any help?"

Getting the milk steaming, Mina looked back at Lucas. "Things are good! Everything is spot on. Haven't had a bit of problem with the network since you looked it over."

"Glad to hear. If you ever need a hand with a bean delivery or anything, I can do that too," Lucas said with a warm smile. "Whatever you need."

"Oh thank you, love," Mina moved quickly behind the counter. Her specialty was tea lattes. She made coffee, and it was good, but the fun ones were all tea-based. In about five minutes, she put two large cups in front of Lucas.

"And there you are. One for you, and one for Chessary. I'd give you a scone or a biscuit to go with it, but I know she already packed up a few for your drive." Mina looked up at Lucas, a bit of a knowing smile hovering at the corners of her mouth. "She's terribly excited about this weekend. Woke up before noon today to get ready! Imagine that!"

"Before noon? I didn't think it possible," Lucas said with a laugh as he took the two offered cups. He hoped something good could come of this trip. If it ended up just being a big disappointment for Ches, he just didn't know what he'd do. Maybe it would be time to move out of this town.

As if summoned by the drink, Ches came downstairs. Her hair was down for once, which was very rare, a slight wave in it. The color had been refreshed, vibrant pinks with lilac highlights. She had on a very comfy-looking shirt with a plunging V-neck, and another pair of leggings tucked into boots that were more meant to see the outdoors. She had a weekender suitcase and a messenger bag over her shoulder, and she smiled brightly when she saw Lucas was there.

Smiling back at Ches, he couldn't help but chuckle. "Hey, Mei," he grinned, "planning on shanking anyone with icicles in your tight tights?" Offering her the drink, he planned on exchanging it for her suitcase, to carry it for her.

"I'm going to learn Mandarin just to mutter things at you when you tease me," Ches said, setting down the suitcase to accept the drink. "It'll take an hour or so to get there, right? Are we all set?"

He picked up her suitcase and took a sip from his drink to test the temperature. "Yup, about an hour. Just need to grab gas before we head out, but otherwise, we're good to go."

"Don't forget your bundles, pet!" Mina called out, putting two bags on the counter.

"Thanks, Mum!" Ches grabbed the two bags, and leaned over to hug her mother. "You should be all set. You can call if you need anything."

"I taught you how to bake," Mina said, dryly. "I'll be fine. Enjoy your trip."

"I'll take good care of her, Ms. Thompson, don't worry," Lucas said, and meant it. No matter what, she'd be safe, even if things didn't go the way they both kind of hoped. *Ugh, stop dwelling*, he had to tell himself. *Enjoy the damn trip.*

"You had better!" Mina laughed as Ches didn't quite drag Lucas out of the shop. Giving Mina a wave goodbye, Lucas comically allowed the much smaller woman to pull him away.

Once outside, before either of them could climb in the car, Ches pulled Lucas in and kissed him. It was a hello kiss, not like the other night, but friendly and affectionate. He made a happy noise and leaned into it. She was wearing a perfume, something with honey and vanilla and a touch of spice, and it blended into her natural fragrance perfectly. Another deep breath of her scent, and he knew his life might end this weekend. Metaphorically.

"I am so excited," she said animatedly, bouncing a little as she did. "Not just the time with you, but I've heard you guys talk about the cabins before; they sound great! And I'm actually leaving for a weekend! All good things!"

"It will be great," he said, securing her bags in the crew cab of the truck and hopping into the driver's seat. "Hiking and the like, so whatever, but there's a hot spring right there, and that's very nice."

Ches giggled and climbed in. "I'll do a hike. The hot spring, though, is particularly enticing. I know I've lived here for most of my life, but I've never been to one."

Once they were both in and the doors were closed, Ches smiled a little sheepishly. "Though, ah, Syla said with you guys it's usually clothing-optional? She said I could wear a suit if it made me uncomfortable, but I was wondering if she was telling the truth or trying to get me naked."

Laughing, Lucas looked over to her and winked. "Little bit of both," he said with that slight twang. "Yes, it is suit-optional with us and, yes, Syla wants to see you naked. I certainly won't mind and, don't worry, you decide to go without a suit, so will I. No one's trying to pull a fast one on you."

Ches turned pink. "Well, maybe you all won't be disappointed."

The drive up was lovely, a golden fall afternoon. Ches sang along with Lucas's playlist and asked questions about different landmarks. She let her hand rest on his thigh a lot, but it was affectionate, not flirty. Lucas realized at one point that she'd gotten her nails done. It made him wonder what else she had gotten up to in Denver.

When they pulled up at the cabins, Syla and Trace were waiting for them. Syla waved happily and Trace smiled. As they climbed out of the truck, Syla immediately came around and grabbed Ches's hand.

"You're here," Syla said, grinning. "Oh my god, I love your hair! I have to show you everything. Trace needs Lucas to help set things up, so they're gonna be busy for a minute, but I can give you the tour! Come on, your cabin is this way!"

"Have fun, hun," Lucas said as Syla started to pull her away. He'd unload their luggage later. For now, he knew that Trace would want those cables. And maybe they could talk.

Rummaging in the back of the truck, he pulled out the big rubbermaid tub that housed his A/V gear and hefted it onto one shoulder. He'd tossed the extra cables Trace wanted inside.

"Hey Trace," he said with a wave. "Got everything on the list, just like you asked, and the extra cables."

Trace nodded. "Let's head into the main house and get set up, then we'll come back for the luggage. I'll help you haul it all in."

Trace was more slight than Lucas and Jack, but still muscular. His name was actually Tracer; he came to town in his early teens from one of the isolation villages farther north. Isolation villages were towns that were nothing but six to ten wer families living together in a community. Tracer came out to Colorado to live with his uncle. While wer families were generally very accepting of their gay children, Trace was the only son and his father wouldn't stop pressuring him to continue the family line.

Trace was also Ches's best friend. It was perhaps ironic that an isolationist wer immediately became friends with a human girl.

The cabins formed a little U, clustered together. From the back porch of each cabin, you could access a pool fed by the hot springs. If you wanted even hotter water, you could hike the quarter mile to the lodge which was built over the source. The pool behind the cabins was plenty warm, but not penetrating like the pools in the lodge could be.

The main cabin had a large family-room area with the promised 70" OLED. Trace had most of the systems laid out, including the VR setup. While people would want to go hiking and what-have-you early in the day, the evenings would mostly be spent drinking and playing games.

"I got started, but we can move anything you need to move," Trace said, gesturing. "I know you've got a system."

"Sure. TV is nice and all, but you need the sound as well," Lucas chuckled as he moved inside the main cabin and set the tub down. Popping the top, he handed Trace the cables he'd asked for and then started to remove the receiver and nine small satellite speakers he'd be setting up around the main room.

"So, Syla's got Ches distracted," Lucas said after a few minutes. "Jack tells me I should talk to you some. About Ches?"

"You're breaking her heart, man," Trace said, helping tuck the cables out of the way so no one tripped over them. "It doesn't help that Charlotte's got a big fucking mouth."

"Shit, Charlotte, of course," Lucas said with a groan.

"Ches has heard the play-by-play of your entire relationship with Charlotte multiple times by this point," Trace continued. "And...look, Ches told me that the first month was a little slow but it felt like you guys were building toward something and then it stalled out. And she feels like you've started pulling away, more and more."

Sighing, Lucas mounted the speakers before moving and hooking everything up to the receiver under the TV. "I don't want to break her heart. She's awesome. But, she's also human, and when I get around her... When we start getting close, I can feel the call. It's all I can do to control it, and I don't want to scare her away. I don't want her thinking I'm just a monster."

"So, yeah, about that." Trace stood up, and walked over to his satchel which was sitting on the couch. "So, you cannot, under any circumstances, tell Ches that I have shown you what I'm about to show you. Understand?"

Arching a brow, Lucas walked over and stood by the couch. "Yeah, okay..." he replied.

Smirking a little, Trace handed Lucas a book. "She'd fucking kill me if she knew I told you. This is Ches's favorite trashy novel. She has everything this author has written, and they all look this well read. It has inspired some...interesting fantasies, which I have had to listen to, because I'm a good friend and I do that."

It was a smutty werewolf story. A really smutty werewolf story. And from the condition of the cover and the cracks in the spine, Trace was not exaggerating about how often it was read.

Chuckling, Lucas shook his head after glancing it over and handed it back. "Yeah, okay, she's got some freaky fantasies. Who doesn't," Lucas said with a shrug. It was true, everyone did. "But it's one thing to read about and another to see it in person."

"Most people don't have the means to make their fantasies real," Trace pointed out.

Sighing, Lucas put his hands on his hips and looked at Trace. "You're her best friend. Can you tell me, honestly and with as much certainty as you can muster, that she will not think me a monster if she saw who I really was?"

"Ches is a mega nerd who loves monsters and cryptids and masturbates to tentacle porn," Trace said, tucking the book away in the bottom of his pack. "Uh, don't tell her I told you that, either." He stood back up and sighed. "She...she's also a really amazing person. And, dammit, Lucas, she's so into you. She's probably already half in love with you. Maybe more than half. She's comparing herself to fucking Charlotte, for Luna's sake, like she's not miles out of that bitch's league. She's not gonna turn on you. On any of us. I've almost told her so many times."

Lucas tapped his foot and thought, chewing his lip a little. "I know she's an amazing person. That's why I'm so worried about it. Well, all right, fine. Next time I won't worry. Next time I'll let the call take me and we'll see what happens." Stopping, he looked and pointed at Trace. "But only if you're absolutely sure. Which it sounds like you are."

"I'm as sure as I can be without having heard her say the actual words," Trace said, a little exasperated. "Now come on, Syla is going to run out of things to show Ches, and Byron and Jack should have dinner ready pretty soon."

They finished up the wiring, and Trace left Lucas doing sound checks while he went to check on Jack. Syla showed up a few minutes later with an absolutely gleeful look on her face.

"I just saw what Ches bought in Denver," Syla said, her voice singsong, almost taunting.

Laughing, he put the lid back on the tub and picked it up to move it out of the way. "Oh? Aside from the nails and hair?" Lucas joked.

"I'm not telling; it's her surprise. But if you want to join me in my petition for her to take pictures, I would appreciate it," Syla said, fanning herself.

"I will ask, but if she says no...well, you'll just have to wait for me to describe it," Lucas smirked.

"Fine," Syla said, sighing dramatically in disappointment. "Anyway, how close are you to done? I wanted to walk Ches up to the lodge, but figured you could come with us. Dinner will probably be ready by the time we get back."

"Trace and I just wrapped up." Lucas lifted the tub a little to demonstrate that he was putting things away. "Need to finish unpacking the truck, which won't take long, then I'll happily take Ches up to the lodge."

"Then let's do it!" Syla grinned and led the way back to the truck. Trace returned to help unload as promised, but first gave Ches a huge hug where he picked her up and she kicked her feet, giggling, then he went back to continue helping with dinner.

"So we want to take you up to the lodge," Syla said as they left the suitcases and headed out. "Mostly just so you know where it is. There's a restaurant there, but it's just okay. We always bring our own food. They've got steam rooms and hot tubs fed by the hot springs, so sometimes we'll walk up for a good soak."

With no more luggage, and half a weight off his shoulder, Lucas was happy to occupy one of his arms holding Ches by the waist. "Best for you to get a feel for the place," he said, leading Ches up the trail. "They also have a small shop, but all they have are really crappy gifts and some toiletries, in case you forgot them."

Ches looked up at Lucas with a smile, and leaned into him. She did smile at him a lot, like a kid being offered a treat. Lucas might not be as nature crazy as a lot of his kin, but being out here with Ches, on a beautiful day with just enough bite that the walk felt like a great way to warm up—it was pretty great.

Buena Roca Lodge was mostly the same as it ever was. They'd updated the exterior, and were trying for a more "spa" feel with the look. The inside was about half finished—the paint transitioned rather abruptly from the new watery blue, which was very pretty, to the old beige once you reached the gift shop and the restaurant.

"Well, here we are," Lucas said, giving her a squeeze and presenting the lodge to her. "Not much, but it does what it needs to do." He hadn't brought his suit, and the spring up here wasn't clothing optional, but there also wasn't a lot to do so he was short on suggestions. "Want to look around?"

Ches just shrugged. "Not really? I mean, I think we're seeing all of it?"

"We are," Syla said, nodding. "We can just head back. You know it's here; if for whatever reason you need to hike up alone, you'll know how to get here. Well...okay, super quick walk through just to show you where the different things are."

Syla led the tour, showing Ches where the hot tubs were, which ones had to be reserved, and which were open all the time, and the same for the steam rooms. It was technically the off season, so it wasn't very busy. Ches decided to poke into the gift shop after all and bought the cheesiest magnet she could find for her mom.

They headed back, and as predicted arrived in time for dinner. Jack had grilled up a bunch of meat, as well as some zucchini and portobellos, and Byron had thrown together a salad and some sort of orzo dish. It was a lot of food, but they all tended to eat a lot. Especially meat.

Lucas made sure everyone had drinks and made a mental note to refill when needed. Hydration was important up in the mountains, more so with how the hot water would overly relax them. Sitting down with his plate of food, he smiled over at Ches then started eating.

"So, anyone got anything planned," he asked between bites, "or we just doing whatever? I'm good either way."

"Definitely getting in the pool after dinner," Byron said, and everyone nodded in agreement. Byron's family was from Mexico, but that was a couple generations back. He still looked like his ancestors, but his mom—an English teacher at the high school—named all of her kids after her favorite poets.

"If anyone isn't ready for bed after that, we can play games," Syla said, smiling. "Though I was checking the weather, and it actually might snow tomorrow. We might be spending more time playing games this weekend than we thought."

"True, but hot springs while it's snowing, that's the best," Lucas grinned. "Honestly, I hope it dumps on us. I'm not worried about getting back down the hill."

"Some of us had been hoping for more than a light hike," Jack said, looking mildly annoyed, but not truly upset.

"It'll be fine," Trace said, and put an arm around Jack. "Hot springs, each cabin has its own fireplace, and I'll make sure you still get exercise this weekend."

"I knew Trace was the top," Syla said, and Ches snickered into her cup.

Laughing, Lucas paused in drinking until it had subsided. "We've got plenty of food, and I brought movies and music. Even if we get snowed in, it'll be a great weekend," he said.

"All right," Syla said, standing up. "The pool is calling me; let's clean up so we can get in! Byron, it's your job to get drinks ready for everybody!"

"Yeah, all right," Byron said, getting up.

Since Byron and Jack had cooked, they didn't have to clean—those were the rules. Trace and Ches were already carting dishes to the kitchen. Finishing the last of his food and drink, Lucas picked up whatever the other two hadn't and moved to the kitchen to get stuff cleaned. He gave Ches a little bump with his hip.

"What're you doin'?" he asked playfully. "It's your first weekend. You go have fun—I'll clean up here."

"Fine, then I'll go help Byron," Ches said, laughing. "I don't want to be the first one in the pool; it would feel weird."

"Uh, Ches, did anyone warn you about the swimsuit situation?" Trace asked, looking over with gentle concern.

"Syla brought it up, and Lucas confirmed that it wasn't just a ploy to get me naked," Ches said, and Syla laughed.

"She'll try her hardest," Lucas said, gesturing toward Syla. "You gotta watch out for that one." He was feeling lighter, better. The conversation with Trace had alleviated most of his fears, at least enough that he wouldn't worry about it until the time came. But for now, clean dishes and hot water awaited.

Once the dishes were done and the kitchen cleaned up, everyone headed out to the pool. Byron had pitchers of the cocktails he'd made set up on a side table on the deck, along with cups, and they even had one of those floating trays for putting in the pool. The pool wasn't deep, and benches ran the entire perimeter—it was meant for soaking, maybe moving around a little. In the cool evening, with the lights from the cabins, you could see the steam rising off of it.

Jack and Byron were already in by the time Trace, Lucas, and Syla made their way out to the deck. Both were naked, their clothes just draped over a chair. Byron waved and Jack grinned.

"Come on in," Jack said, raising a drink that looked like it was mostly whiskey. "Ches is putting her hair up."

Looking forward to the soak and some alcohol, Lucas unbuttoned his shirt and set it on one of the chairs. "I'm assuming Ches said she was cool with the sans-suit option?" he asked with a raised brow as he started to undo his pants.

Byron nodded. "We made sure she knew she didn't have to, that no one would pressure her, but she said it was fine. She just didn't want to get her hair wet. Said something about how she just dyed it?"

Syla nodded. "Yeah, she uses vivid dyes; you can't wash your hair for like 48 hours. She just did it yesterday, I think."

Syla went back into her cabin to strip down—she didn't want to risk her bra getting wet—but was back before Ches made it out. Trace just stripped down and threw his clothes on top of Jack's. Lucas finished with the last of his clothes and stepped into the pool. After everything, the hot water was a blessing, and he just sank in until he was sitting on the bench. Putting his arms up, he rested them on the edge of the pool.

There was a click from the door, and Trace smiled brightly and waved, indicating Ches had come out of the cabin. Her bare feet made almost no sound as she crossed the deck and came around to pour herself a drink. Her hair was up in twin buns, twisted a little tighter than usual to make sure they stayed out of the water. She wore a short robe, the kind sold as swimsuit coverups, and keen eyes could see that there was nothing underneath the sheer fabric that skimmed her figure.

Lucas hadn't actually seen Ches naked before. He'd seen her breasts a few times when they were fooling around, but there hadn't yet been a situation where everything had come off. He'd hoped the first time he would see her bare would be more, well, intimate but he wasn't going to complain.

"Damn, it's cold out here," Ches said, wrinkling up her nose.

Syla laughed. "Get in the water! Here, hand me your drink so you can take the robe off."

Standing up, Lucas smiled broadly. He stood and held out his hand, ready to help her into the pool. "I'll keep ya warm," he grinned. "I'm sure the water will help a bit, though."

Glancing over at Lucas, Ches did turn just a little pink, and her eyes swept over him. She hadn't seen him naked either, and Lucas guessed she was pretty happy with what she saw; he wasn't super sculpted, but he did still sport a six pack along with his broad shoulders and defined arms and legs. She handed her drink off to Syla and undid the robe, exposing fair skin with just a smattering of freckles over the shoulders. The cold had caused her nipples to crinkle and harden, drawing attention to her full breasts. As she set the robe aside, Lucas saw that she had a small tattoo on her hip, a cute little blue and white robot. It seemed Mei really was her favorite character.

"See, I knew you were hot," Syla said, and Ches laughed, her blush deepening as she took Lucas's hand and let him help her down into the pool.

"Scorching," Lucas agreed. "Think she's heating up the pool at this point."

He was grateful to sit down again, as he wasn't sure how long he could keep from getting hard. The audience and the cold air helped.

Ches giggled and let herself be pulled into Lucas's lap as he sat down. Syla handed Ches her drink and sat back with a wistful sigh.

"No sex in the pool," Byron said, grinning.

"What, really?" Jack leaned forward and Trace snickered.

"Fine," Byron said, rolling his eyes, "no sex in the pool when everyone is in it."

"That's fair." Jack leaned back again.

Smiling, Lucas leaned in and kissed Ches's shoulder, then the lobe of her ear. "I don't think I tell you how gorgeous you are enough," he whispered gently. "And I'm not just saying that because you're naked." Having Ches in his lap was not helping with that problem he had hoped to avoid.

"Well, it's nice that you still say it when I'm naked," Ches said, smiling almost shyly. She turned to give Lucas a light kiss in return, but had the sense not to draw it out.

"Really wouldn't matter what state of dress you were in," Lucas said softly and kissed her neck once more. To not exacerbate the issue, he picked her up and set her down next to him on the bench, chuckling gently. "Don't want to break any rules."

"Ches says we used to be that sickening," Jack said, leaning into Trace. "I don't believe it."

"We were worse," Trace pointed out, but put an arm around Jack. "And we had far less self-restraint."

Laughing, Lucas pointed to Trace. "He's right. Like you two were surrounded by heart-shaped rainbow fireflies."

"Bullshit," Jack muttered, taking a drink as everyone else laughed.

It was a great way to unwind on the first day. No one got drunk (though that would definitely change tomorrow night, based on how these weekends usually went), but a couple drinks and a hot soak had everyone loosened up and feeling good. Of course, Lucas was having a bit of a time—the water and booze were relaxing, but the naked girlfriend right next to him (with her breasts frequently breaking the surface of the water thanks to their buoyancy) was making parts of him...less relaxed.

Eventually Syla declared herself too prune-y to sit any longer, and Ches agreed. Sitting up, Ches kissed Lucas on the neck just below the ear, and followed it with a covert lick before getting up to head inside. He shivered gently and smiled.

"Well, folks, it seems I must escort my lovely lady to our cabin. Don't wait up," he chuckled and got out of the pool, quickly finding his towel. He was already at half-mast because of her. As much as he wanted to jump her as soon as they got into their cabin, they needed to have a little talk first.

Hopefully it would be a very little talk.

As Lucas turned toward the cabin, he found Ches looking at him with an odd expression. It was...hopeful. She gathered her robe and waved to the chorus of "good night" from everyone else, heading inside. They were in the smallest of the three cabins, but that was fine. It still had a king-sized bed and a shower big enough for two.

"You want to get a fire going?" Ches asked, as she set her drink down and looked like she was moving toward the bathroom. "I'll be back in a minute."

"Sure thing, babe" he said with a smile, watching her walk away. He could watch her do just about anything and he'd be happy.

While a gas fireplace would have been nice, running a line this far up or having a tank big enough wasn't in the budget for this little hot spring. So, old-fashioned wood and starters it was. Thankfully, this fell under one of his many skills, and he'd known to bring extra newspaper to make sure it was easy to get going. Within a few minutes, he had the fire off to a good start, and the little cabin was warming up quite nicely.

Ches came back in another robe (this one wasn't see-through), her hair down again, in soft, wide curls from being up in the buns in the steamy water. She hadn't tied off the robe, but was holding it closed. He looked her over with an eyebrow raised.

"Nice," she said, smiling as she looked at the fire. "This place really is lovely. I'm glad I got to come."

"I'm really glad you got to come too. I think this is going to be a good weekend," Lucas said with a hopeful grin. "I like what you did with your hair. I didn't notice at first because I was just so taken that you had it down for once."

"Oh, thanks," she said, smiling. She ran a hand through it. "Do you like it down? I usually just put it up to keep it out of the way. I could leave it down more often."

"What I like is how different you are," he smiled, walking up to her and putting his hands on her waist. "I like that you color your hair, you wear it in interesting ways, you wear interesting things, you have a cute little tattoo. It doesn't matter how you wear your hair—I'm going to like it."

Ches grinned, a bit impishly. "I'm wearing something interesting right now," she said, and Lucas could feel that there was...something underneath the thin robe.

"Oh, you don't say," he said with a smirk. He gave her hips a squeeze before stepping back and opening his arms, hoping she'd give him a look.

She opened the robe and revealed...straps. Black straps that (barely) tethered in her breasts, connected by O-rings, crisscrossed over her waist, and barely covered her sex. It was technically two pieces, as the bottoms and top didn't connect. Matching garters also circled her thighs.

"I thought you might like it," she said, letting the robe drop behind her.

"Oh, wow," he stuttered out as his eyes traced over her form. Naked was definitely nice, but this was amazing, and a small part of him wondered how she had found the exact thing he'd never known he wanted to see on a woman. Shit, maybe talk first. He squeezed his fists tight. He had to keep a grip, but goddamn did she look and smell so good. He wanted her so much.

"First, let me say you look jaw-dropping, and it's taking everything I got not to jump you. Second, there's something I really need to talk to you about before that happens, and it's 100% me, not you," he let out with a sigh. It was killing the mood, he knew that, but he had to before something terrible happened, and he could already feel the change trying to take over.

He saw Ches's smile drop, her eyes go dull, and just kind of...wilt in front of him. She picked up the robe and put it back on, then climbed onto the couch and tucked her legs beneath her. "Sure," she said, her normally bright voice sounding heartbreakingly hollow. She fiddled with the fabric of her robe, covering herself completely. "What did you want to talk about?"

"I am so, so sorry," he said, whimpering slightly. He paced a little, trying to figure out how to put his thoughts into words. "Okay, shit, um, so, the reason I've been backing off when things start to get heavy is because I...I change when I get excited. And you get me so very excited, and it's just getting easier for you to do that."

Lucas looked at her for a long moment, then rolled his eyes and dropped his arms to his side. "Fuck it. Ches, baby, I'm a werewolf. Not an 'oh no the full moon' type, but an 'adrenaline and hormones and usually at will' type. But I can't stop myself from changing when I get turned on." Lucas winced slightly. This would go one of three ways, he thought: she'll either laugh, thinking it was a terrible joke, get pissed because she'd think he was lying to get out of something, or accept it and want to play out her favorite novel.

Ches just looked at him for a minute. "You're a werewolf," she repeated. She wasn't laughing, and she didn't look excited. No, it looked like she was pissed. "And so, what, there's something about Charlotte and Tara that made them okay with this thing that you apparently have to hide from me and only me?"

He nodded his head, rubbing the back of his neck. "Yeah. They're both werewolves too," he said a little shyly. "Trust me, I would have had no hesitation otherwise. You're amazing, best woman I've ever met."

Sighing, Ches reached up and ran a hand over her face. "Lucas, I don't know what to do with you. You keep telling me how great I am, but the more I want you, and the more I try to make you want me, you just keep pulling further away! And every time I get my hopes up, every time you say something that makes me think, 'No, wait, he does like me as much as I like him,' you pedal back again!"

She stood up, and started to pace. "And, you know, I thought maybe at first you were just shy. That it would take time. That was fine; I didn't need us to jump in bed the first week. I was okay with it taking a bit. I didn't want this to be just a fun time, I...I wanted this to last! But then I hear that no, actually, you're never like that! Charlotte said you two had sex after two days! And right now I seriously can't tell if you're making fun of me or think this is funny or...I don't even know!"

"But fine," Ches said, her voice raised, displaying a temper that Lucas had never seen pointed in his direction, "you're a werewolf? Fucking prove it!"

At this point, it wasn't that hard to do it. Tossing off his towel, he just let go. All the anger with himself, all the frustration at not being with Ches, bringing up Charlotte and her big mouth, and finally that little bit in the feral part of his brain snarling 'oh, I'll fucking prove it.' The wild, untamable hair on his head spread to his whole body. Lucas's face stretched to a regal muzzle, ears shifting and perking up, the hazel of his eyes brightening to a piercing yellow. Legs bent and moved, fingers stretched and formed claws. All of him became more canis. All of him. Ches's eyes got very big. She didn't scream, and she didn't run. She just stood there.

"I would never lie or make fun of you," he growled. "I just didn't want to lose you."

It was silent for a moment, save for the crackle of the fire. Then, very carefully, she took a step forward. And then a few more. She set her hands against Lucas's chest. She stood there for another moment, her hand over his heart, feeling it beat as she looked at him, then finally looked up.

"I...might be dreaming," she said at last, a tremor in her voice from the adrenaline that had come with the shock and surprise. No fear, though—not in her voice, not in her eyes, and not in her scent. "I think I've had this dream before."

"I might have had this dream, too," he said, leaning close to breathe her in. He could already feel his heartbeat quicken, blood rushing through his body. So close. "Have definitely read this story," Lucas added, leaning a little closer and softly running his tongue along the side of her neck.

Ches whimpered. "What happens in this story?" she asked, her voice soft as her hands slid down Lucas's chest and over his abdomen, moving slowly, fingers slipping through the fur that now covered him.

"What happens is we finally do what we've been wanting to do for weeks. No more hiding, no more backing off," he said, his body taut and responsive to her touch. "If you still want me."

"I've wanted you since I met you at Trace's party," Ches said, cheeks pink again. "I...I don't see any reason for that to change now."

Another lick against her neck and he stepped back, crouched slightly, as he was a foot or so taller than he had been a few minutes before. "Then shall we start over?" he grinned, his tail wagging slowly behind him. "At least to where you were showing me what's under the robe?"

Biting her lip, Ches took the robe off again, tossing it back over to the couch. She was a little shyer now; that made sense, this was new, she was getting used to the idea. She smelled right, though—not afraid, and it was getting stronger. Lucas's tail wagged a little faster, and he panted a little harder. She pushed her hair back off her shoulders and looked up at him again.

"Luna, you are so hot," he said, moving forward once more. Nuzzling against her neck, his hands moved to her body, fingers tracing over the straps and tugging playfully at the O-rings. "Such a beautiful package. Do I unwrap it, or keep the ribbons?"

Ches whimpered again. "I guess that's your choice," she said, shivering slightly as he touched her. "I...I got it hoping you would...that I would finally find something that made you want to..." She was still looking at him in amazement, eyes wide, but she was getting flushed and responding to his touch.

"I always wanted to." Lucas could easily access all of her in that lingerie, but for their first time, he wanted her as bare as he was—nothing between them, their bodies feeling everything. With a careful move of his claws, he plucked at the straps holding the garment in place, slicing neatly through them. It could be fixed, or replaced, but that wasn't important right now.

More and more of her skin became accessible, and he took it upon himself to ensure it was licked and gently nipped at completely, longing to taste her, to touch her, to not be worried about what might happen. He had a lot he wanted to do. The top fell away. Claws might hamper some things, but his tongue was warm and long and found its way all over her neck, breasts, and nipples.

Ches shivered. "Ohhhh...that feels amazing!" Her hands slid up into the fur on his head, petting his ears, almost massaging around the base of them. Growling happily, Lucas continued his way down her body.

As the bottoms fell away, his hands moved down to wrap around her waist. Instead of crouching any further, he simply lifted her up to his level. She let out a little cry of surprise, but it really wasn't that shocking. Ches had been petite compared to Lucas before—now she was downright tiny. He kept going, licking over her tummy, nipping at her hips, and breathing her scent in even deeper. He couldn't remember the last time he had been this turned on, or this hard, but he didn't have anything holding him back now.

"Put your legs over my shoulders," he rumbled, and she did, her breath picking up in anticipation.

Nuzzling where the scent was the strongest, he pressed his nose against her clit and lapped at her entrance. She tasted every bit as good as she smelled, and he dove in. With long licks, he worked his tongue in with each taste, deeper and deeper.

"Lucas," Ches moaned and reached down, running her hands through his fur. It seemed to take no time at all before she let out a louder, musical cry, and her legs shook with her orgasm.

"You are so delicious," he muttered before giving her another deep, wriggling lick of his tongue. Licking at his chops, he carried her over to the bed, setting her down on it. She fell back with a moan.

"Since it's our first time," he said, panting heavily, "I need you to take control. I'm not used to your limits, so you're going to need to guide me."

It took Ches a minute to come back to herself. She looked him over again, and gasped in sudden realization. "Oh...oh, wow, *all* of you changes..."

He grinned. "Yeah."

"Um...lay down," she said, climbing up onto her knees. "I want...I want everything, but let's start here."

Moving toward the bed, he nuzzled against her once more before following her instructions. He wanted to take her, to drive her into the mattress, but she wasn't a werewolf. Lucas didn't know how much Ches could take, or what she liked, and he needed to know before he'd do that with her. Flopping onto his back, he made himself vulnerable to her.

Ches climbed between his legs, sliding her hands over his thighs, and biting her lip as she took a good look at his cock. "Do...do you always get like this?" she asked, leaning in, her mouth teasingly close. "Will you always change?"

"I don't know," he said, whimpering again at how near she was, how much he wanted her hands, her mouth, her everything to touch him. "Probably. At least for a while."

Closing her eyes, Ches leaned in and rubbed her cheek against the side of his cock, turning her head to drag her lips over it, then finally slid her tongue over the head.

"Oh, by the moon, yes," he groaned, his hands moving to run through her hair and over her shoulders.

Her hands massaged his thighs, sliding up to his hips and back down. Despite being sizeable, he wasn't cartoonishly large, and his cock was also now tapered with a knot at the base. It throbbed hard and heavy in her hand and jumped when her tongue caressed over it. She pulled away for a breath, then slid her tongue up the entire length of him, over the knot and up to the tip, before taking him in her mouth—just the head at first, sucking and swirling her tongue around him. She pulled back a bit, and then slid him farther in. And again. And again, taking a little more of his cock every time. She couldn't go all the way, and she was taking her time. This was to tease and explore, not to get him off.

Lucas was starting to whine. He was so keyed up, had been ever since she dropped her robe by the pool. His hands found their way to her breasts, holding them and feeling their weight and fullness, massaging them with his large fingers. Her head came up with a gasp. He knew from experience they were pretty sensitive—early on, it had been safe enough to grope her, occasionally lift one to lick, before the denial had gotten to be too much.

"Fuck, Lucas," she moaned, and began to climb up over him, sliding her body against his as she went. She straddled his lap, and he could feel her deliciously wet pussy rubbing against his cock. Growling playfully at her, his hands moved to her hips, and he arched forward so he could lean in and lick her neck.

"I've wanted you so badly, Ches," he rumbled. "I didn't want to hold back. Never. But I thought I needed to. I never will again."

"Good. Don't." She lifted up and reached between her legs, grasping Lucas's shaft and lining him up before sinking down with a moan that seemed to reverberate through him. It was almost enough to make him howl. She didn't stop until she was resting against the knot.

"You're gonna have to spend some time showing me how much you want me," she said, panting, a playful smile on her face, "to make up for two months of me thinking I wasn't enough."

Growling again, he moved to sit up, keeping her firmly in his lap. Resting his head against her cheek, he slid his hands around her waist to her ass, gripping it firmly and starting to move her against him. Slow and smooth. "As much time as it takes," he murmured. "You are more than enough. You are everything."

She whimpered, wrapping her arms around his neck, nuzzling against him. "Ma bête," she said, then laughed softly. "You really are my beast, aren't you?"

"Fuck yes I am," he whimpered again.

Oh, to feel her, finally, her soft body pressed against his, her vessel sheathing his shaft so perfectly, her voice in his ear, her spice flooding his senses. He didn't know how anything could feel this perfect. Something strange was happening, something Lucas had never experienced with another partner before: a sympathy, a resonance that he felt with her, that seemed to just...sing through him. There wasn't a better way to put it.

Ches shifted, her arms still around Lucas, but she lifted her head and settled on her knees more and started to move herself, a little faster, a little less steady. She looked up at him with those same wide eyes, glazed with sensation, a small cry coming out of her every time she brought her hips down.

"I wanted this so much," he panted, hands still gripping to her, but now more to keep her steady while she started to bounce on his lap.

"You feel so good. I don't think I'm going to last much longer." This pleasure, after so long a denial, was too intense. Next time she'd see his stamina, but right now he was far too excited, far too enthralled.

"Yes," she said excitedly, eyes bright, lips flushed. "Come for me, fill me! I want it! I want it so bad…" She bounced on him harder, the strong muscles in her thighs letting her ride him with a bit of force.

"Fuck, Ches, yes," he panted, grasping her hips and throwing his head back. As he came, the knot prevented him from plunging any farther into her, and he let out a howl. A howl that was almost certainly heard by everyone else at the lodge. Ches's arms were tight around him, and she buried her face in his fur, crying out as she felt the liquid heat pulsing into her. Flooding her vessel, he felt everything so completely. It was the most perfect moment he could have asked for. She clung to him, panting, content in his arms.

Spent for the moment, Lucas fell back, taking her with him, and groaned happily. As his body calmed down, he started to shift back into his human form. Ches picked her head up in surprise, looking at him. When it was finished, she kissed him, hard, still holding tight. Wrapping his arms around her, he gently caressed her back, running his fingers along her spine.

"So, still okay with me?" he asked with a chuckle.

"Always," she said, pressing her forehead to his. "Always okay with you. More than okay."

"Then I have no more fears." That was it, he just didn't want to lose her, and now that thought would never need to enter his mind again.

As their hearts slowed, she eventually lifted herself off of him and rolled off the bed, finding a towel to clean off with. Stretching, he sat up and wiped himself down as well.

"So," she said after a minute, sitting down on the edge of the bed. Thankfully, from their activities and the fireplace, the cabin felt cozy right now. "You said Charlotte and Tara are both…like you. Anyone else I know?"

"Heh, yeah. Everyone that's up here this weekend," he said, a little shyly as he wasn't sure how she'd take it.

Ches blinked. "Everyone? Even Trace?"

"Even Trace," he said with a nod. "He wanted to tell you, just wasn't sure how to bring it up."

"Oh." She looked thoughtful for a minute, and a little sad. "I…I guess I can understand. It feels strange. I mean, I tell Trace everything.

But I can see why this would be something he couldn't share with me. ...Are there rules? About who you tell?"

He patted the mattress next to him and got comfortable with some pillows. She climbed over the bed, pulling the blankets up enough to cover their legs. As their bodies continued to calm, the room felt cooler. She then settled in next to him, her head on his shoulder, her leg over his, her body pressed up along the side of him. She let out a soft, happy sound as she snuggled into him. He couldn't help but chuckle as he wrapped an arm around her and squeezed her close.

"It is a bit of a big deal, yeah," Lucas said once they settled. "There are some rules. Obviously, you never tell anyone you don't trust completely, and really don't tell anyone unless it's important that they know."

"I guess this means you trust me," she said with a smile, reaching across him to squeeze him for a moment, then letting her hands lazily slide over his chest and torso. "That's good. I trust you. And I think you're amazing. So, never again? You won't turn me away, you won't come up with an excuse to leave early?"

"Never," he said, leaning in to kiss her forehead. "Something would have to literally be on fire for me to ever leave early. You're a bit stuck with me now."

"I'm okay with that," she murmured, nuzzling at him and kissing his chest. Then she giggled. "How's the soundproofing at your place? If you howl like that every time, we're gonna have problems not waking my mom up."

"Not every time," he snickered again. "That was just particularly good and a long time coming. I think I can keep it down otherwise."

Still giggling, Ches snuggled into him more and left more kisses across his chest and shoulder. She felt really fantastic pressed up against him, soft and warm.

"Is it okay if I let the others know that I know?" Ches asked after a long silence, her voice soft and a bit sleepy. She'd gotten up early in her excitement; she was probably very tired. "Can I tell Trace?"

"I'm pretty sure they already know," he chuckled, referring to the aforementioned howl, "but yes, you can tell them. I'm sure they'll all be very happy they don't have to keep it a secret anymore." Kissing the top of her head again, he moved so both of his arms were around her and he was caressing her gently, exploring the luscious curves he'd been dreaming about but unable to touch."So, sleepy time, or you ready for more?"

"Hm? 'm ready," she said, trying to open her eyes. "I'm sorry… Couldn't sleep last night, woke up early. Was just…so excited…" Her hand was still absently caressing him, but it was clear that without the tension and anticipation keeping her awake, the day had caught up to Ches. Snickering, he pulled her close once more and pulled the covers up.

"No you're not. Sleep sweet, hun. I'll be here when you wake up," he said softly, kissing her head once more and relaxing into the soft feel of her body.

"Mmmmm." She nuzzled into him again, holding on as if she were afraid he might leave. In minutes, though, her grip loosened as she drifted off and her breathing grew deeper.

When Lucas woke the next morning, he had rolled over during the night. Ches was snuggled against his back, snoring softly, one leg over his hip. His phone was what woke him up, buzzing on the nightstand

"Mrf," he said groggily, patting at the nightstand until he could find the phone, and blinked as he tried to make out the screen. "Wha…?"

Ches grumbled and nuzzled into his shoulder, the leg over his hip tightening. The phone said that Jack was calling. Reaching down, he took his free hand and caressed and squeezed her thigh. The other answered the phone.

"M'yes? Can't be that late," he muttered. They hadn't stayed up all night, after all, and he wasn't one who typically slept in until noon.

"It's not," Jack said, and Lucas could hear laughter in the back of his friend's voice, "but breakfast is ready and Trace is getting sick with anxiety wanting to know how last night went. Also, you got your wish, you bastard. Looks like we got a foot of snow last night. Bundle up and head over to Syla's cabin—we've got food set up there."

"Yay," he said gently and hung up. Giving Ches another squeeze, he rolled his head to the side. "Ches, baby, time to get up. Breakfast is ready."

"Hmm?" She yawned, and blinked, and looked at Lucas, a little fuzzy as she woke up. Then a positively beatific smile broke over her face, and she wiggled forward to kiss all over his cheek and jaw. "I wasn't dreaming!" The excitement in her voice squeezed Lucas's heart.

He rolled onto his back and pulled Ches on top of him at the same time. "Neither was I," he said cheerfully and kissed her back, just as happy. "I look forward to waking up like this a lot in the future."

She laughed and looked down at him. "You really are huge. I could sleep on you. Did I hear your phone ring? I thought I heard something."

"You can sleep on me anytime," he snickered. Stretching underneath her, his body went taut before releasing and sighing. "And yeah, that was Jack, telling me that breakfast is ready and that we got a foot of snow last night. Dress warm."

"If I go make snow angels like a child, will you still like me?" Ches grinned.

"Absolutely," he said, pulling her up enough to kiss her some more. "However, that would require you to get up, as you currently have me delightfully pinned."

Another laugh. "Jack just called us to go have breakfast. I'll pin you later. Or maybe you can pin me. I'd like that." She scrunched up her nose at him then slid off.

"I do believe it is my turn, yes," he said with a feral grin. He gave her a playful swat, then followed suit. There wasn't enough time for a shower, not with what he planned anyway, so he opened up his suitcase and started getting dressed in his heavier clothes.

It took Ches a few more minutes to get ready. She brushed out and braided her hair in twin tails again, applied a body lotion that explained the honey/vanilla/pepper smell from yesterday that seemed to work so well with her natural scent, and dressed in more fleece leggings and a fuzzy sweater with a sweetheart neckline that looked exceptionally pettable.

"I have a sudden urge to buy a red coat," Ches said with a smirk as she pulled on her boots. Pulling on his high boots and lambskin jacket, Lucas brushed himself down and looked over with a smile.

"Oh? Why a red coat?" he asked.

Ches smirked. "Because apparently I'm in far more danger of being eaten by a wolf than I previously thought."

Laughing, he went to stand by the door. "From what I was hearing last night, you rather like being eaten by a wolf," Lucas responded.

She grabbed her black coat and pulled it on. "Ready?"

Opening the door, he breathed in the cold air and smiled. It was a good day. Deciding that Ches shouldn't get wet, at least not from snow, he scooped her up once more and carried her across the snow-covered path from the porch of their cabin to the main one. Ches let out a giggle-shriek and kicked her legs in playful protest. The spring-fed pool was steaming even more today—that would be fun later.

When they got into the main cabin, Syla was there to make sure shoes came off right away and to help put the coats to the side. "So," Syla said, cautiously, "how was your night?"

Ches grinned, and turned pink. "Pretty great."

Syla started to smile, and looked up at Lucas. "So...she knows?"

"Yeah, she knows," he said with a smirk. "So, you all can get your ribs in now; I'm no longer stringing her along while I decide what to do with my worries."

Ches had just managed to get her coat and boots off when Trace ran up and picked her up in a hug. He was crying. Not hard, just tears on his cheeks, but he held on to her and pressed his cheek to hers.

"I'm sorry, I'm so sorry," Trace said, not putting Ches down. "I wanted to tell you for so long! When you started dating Lucas, I thought I finally could, but Uncle said it wasn't my place, that I still had to wait—"

Ches held her friend back. "It's okay," she said, tearing up a little herself. "I understand. It's...it's still kind of hard to believe, but I know now, so it's all right."

Jack looked at Lucas and held up a glass of OJ in a silent salute, then motioned for him to come to the table while Trace and Ches worked things through. Nodding, Lucas headed over, but not before reaching out and squeezing both Ches and Trace on the shoulder. Picking up a glass, he poured himself some orange juice and sighed.

"So, there, the most stressful moment of my life turned into the best moment," Lucas said with a rueful smile.

"Yeah, we heard," Byron said with a smirk. Jack elbowed him.

Syla came over and sat down, sighing dramatically. "I'm happy for you," she said, smiling. "Really, I am. But I was also 100% ready to console Ches if you backed out again."

Byron rolled his eyes. "You're awful."

"There was no way I could at this point," Lucas said. "Safer to chew my own arm off. Anyway, looks like I'm getting my way this weekend. First, everything is good with me and Ches, and second, snow."

"Well, congratulations, good for you—just don't fuck this up," Jack said, and clinked his glass against Lucas's. "All right, we've got pancakes and two pounds of bacon. Who wants some?"

"I want pancakes," Ches said, walking up with Trace. Trace looked like he was still processing things, and Jack got up to give his boyfriend a hug.

"Let's get pancakes," Byron said, smiling at Ches and getting up. "So the plan for today is big breakfast, video games, then people can run around in the snow or whatever they want when we all get restless. Early dinner, hot springs, more games and entirely too much drinking. That work for everyone?"

"Sounds like an almost perfect day," Lucas said, getting back up as he, too, wanted breakfast. That was half the reason he was here, after all. There was a nice, full day ahead of them of mostly relaxing, but he was already plotting times to sneak away with Ches. They had a lot of catching up to do.

By the time breakfast was over, everyone was full, Trace was feeling better and smiling freely, and Ches rolled out every awful Red Riding Hood joke she could in the forty-five minutes they were at the table. It would have been hard to see for anyone who didn't know his friends as well as Lucas did, but there was a freeness that hadn't quite been there since Ches started hanging out with them all. It wasn't that they didn't like her—everyone liked her—but there was nothing anyone needed to hide anymore.

Trace had an arcade-game collection he had brought with him, so the morning was a lot of versus games and beat 'em ups. Ches climbed into Lucas's lap and essentially lived there. Byron mostly just played mobile games while Syla made fun of him for it.

About halfway through the morning, Ches started being...a little awful. While she was playing, she would reverse straddle his lap and grind into him under the guise of just playing excitedly. Sometimes when he was playing she would get up and lean over his shoulders from behind, licking and sucking at his neck when the others weren't looking. By the time Jack declared that he needed to go for a walk or something, Lucas's jeans were incredibly uncomfortable.

Since Ches was back in his lap, Lucas tightened his grip and leaned in to whisper in her ear. "All right, little red, you want to find a quiet place in the woods, or should we go back to our cabin? Because you've got some teasing to answer for."

Ches grinned at him unrepentantly. "Cabin," she said quietly. "Too much snow for the woods right now."

"I'd hold you up," he responded quietly, then cleared his throat. "Well, you folks enjoy your walk. I think I need to freshen up a bit and try to find the snacks I have buried in the cabin somewhere." He reluctantly let go of Ches and cupped her ass to push her out of his lap, giving her a squeeze as he did.

Syla snickered. "You ain't gotta lie about it."

"Didn't want to hurt your feelings for missing out," Lucas said to

Syla, sticking his tongue out at her. Ches giggled and went to give Trace a quick hug before heading over to her boots and coat.

Once they were both ready for the outdoors again, Lucas scooped Ches up again and set her over his shoulder in a fireman's carry. She shrieked in false protest while everyone else laughed. He was very careful while going through the doors to not bang her around. He got a half-hearted spanking from the woman over his shoulder as they covered the short distance through the snow. Once inside, though, he stomped his boots enough to get the excess snow off then tossed her onto the bed.

Ches let out another shriek as she bounced on the bed, and started to take her coat off without being prompted, grinning. Lucas peeled off his coat and boots, kicking the boots over to the door and throwing his coat on a chair. She also took off her boots, tossing them toward the door, and then...stopped. That playful, impish grin was still on her face as she leaned back on her hands and looked at Lucas expectantly. He smirked and arched an eyebrow at her. He had a pretty good idea where this game was going.

Grinning now, he started to unbutton his flannel. "So, you think you can get away with what you were doing today?" he asked.

"I'm sure I don't know what you're talking about," Ches said with that same grin. "I was just so happy to spend time with you today. Weren't you having fun? It felt like you were."

"Oh, yeah, were you feeling something?" he asked, giving her a touch of attitude. Walking up to the bed, he swiftly grabbed for her leg, catching her by the ankle, and pulled her toward him. Holding her firmly, he pulled off her sock with the other hand and gently brushed the underside of her foot.

Ches's eyes got big, and the smile faltered. "Oh, don't you dare!"

"I dare," he said, giving her foot a little tickle before grabbing her other leg and pinning both under his arm. This let him pull off the other sock and give her another tickle. "You were a naughty girl."

Ches laughed and tried to kick her feet away, wiggling on the bed. "No! Bad wolf!"

"I'm sorry, who was the one that was bad?" Lucas responded, placing her legs on the bed then crawling up onto the mattress, pinning her legs under him as he slid his hands under her sweater. Ches was already panting from being tickled, a glowing smile on her face

"I wasn't the one sitting in your lap and rubbing my fine ass against you," he said, moving his hands up to strip her off her top. She lifted her shoulders to make it easier for Lucas to pull off the sweater, revealing another new bra underneath, this one a combination of black bands and fine mesh—it was far more practical than the one from the night before, but was still meant to be seen. "I wasn't the one licking and nibbling on your neck and ear when no one was looking."

"You're right," she said, looking up at him. "I was a bad girl. What are you going to do about it?"

"I think you have a good idea what I'm going to do about it," he growled as he tossed her sweater off to the side. Running his hands over her now, he felt the material of the bra as it tried to contain her generous breasts. Satin and mesh, no lace. The lines and color were bold against her pale skin. His hands slid over the curves and down the sides, then back up to undo the clasp in front. She moaned, her arms and hair splayed out above her head from when he'd pulled the shirt off. Once the bra popped open, he leaned in and ran his tongue along the valley between her mounds, pressing them together with his hands and ravishing them with his mouth. She drew in a sharp breath as he sucked at her nipples, arching and twisting beneath him.

"Lucas," she whimpered, "ma bête! Oh, fuck, that's so good!"

Running his tongue from the soft underneath of her breast, all the way over the curve, a quick flick at her nipple, then to the top, he growled. "Good? It's not supposed to be good," he rumbled. "It's supposed to be punishment."

Ches let out a gasping laugh. "You'll have to punish me harder."

Scooting down the bed, he quickly undid her pants. Running his hands along her waist, he grasped the pants and panties both, yanking them off as he moved to stand at the edge of the bed. The leggings and the matching thong slid off easily, and Ches sat up to let the bra slide down her shoulders so she could toss it aside. Throwing the clothes in his hands aside as well, Lucas moved to quickly remove the last of his own clothing. She watched him strip and bit her lower lip, her eyes lingering over his chest and shoulders.

"You are so unbelievably hot," she murmured, watching him.

"Nothing compared to you," he said, the grin persisting. "Now, I hope you see this erection you caused." Sure enough, he was at full mast.

"Oh, I see it," she said with that impish grin again.

"You're going to come here," he added, reaching down to grab her ankles and pull her down the bed until her butt was almost to the edge, "and take care of it for me."

Ches's eyes got big again at Lucas's demand, and her cheeks flushed as she licked her lips and sat back up. She slid her hands up his thighs and grasped his hard cock, stroking it for a moment before leaning in and sliding her tongue over the head. Her eyes fluttered closed and she moaned as she slid him into her mouth.

"See, now you're being a good girl," he said, running his hands over her hair. She...liked this. Her scent got stronger when he called her a good girl, and she whimpered in the back of her throat. He pulled out the bands that were keeping her hair back and started to fluff it up.

As she continued to suck on his cock, he started to change. His fingers running through her hair were getting longer, his thighs were getting softer with fur, and the shaft in her mouth was changing to that of a werewolf's. Her eyes opened and she looked up at him, but she didn't stop what she was doing. She moved a little to make it easier to take him deeper, and her right hand slid up to stroke the knot that had formed at the base of his cock. With the transformation complete, he panted gently, running a hand through her hair before grasping the back of her head. She whimpered again. He used the grip on her hair to pull her off his cock.

"Time for that payback," he growled. Reaching down, he grabbed her hips and easily flipped her over. "On your knees."

Her breath was coming pretty fast as she obeyed, getting on her hands and knees, her ass pointed toward him. He ran a hand down her back, then grasped her thighs, pushing them apart and gripping her soft flesh. Her pussy was a wet mess; he could see the moisture painting her thighs. She turned her face into the bed and whimpered as he tasted her, drawing his long tongue over her sex, and her hands grabbed at the blanket.

Lucas ran his tongue all the way up her lips, over her ass, and to the small of her back before standing up. Wrapping his hands around her hips one finger at a time, he lifted her up until her entrance was lined up with his shaft, then pulled her back onto him, sinking in as far as she could take him. She was wet, and heated, and felt perfect.

Growling, he started to move, slowly at first, letting her further coat his cock with her slickness, but he built up speed until he was full-on fucking her. "Is this what you wanted, you bad girl?" he growled. "Teasing a werewolf can get you into a lot of trouble."

"Yes," Ches moaned, letting go of the blanket to slide her hands over the bed, twisting beneath him. "Yes, this is what I wanted!"

Last night had been gentle, loving, testing. It had been wonderful and had given him a good feeling for what she wanted. Now it was time to see what she could take. He started with a steady thrust. She was so worked up that it was a smooth, if still incredibly tight, motion to piston his cock in and out of her. When she did nothing but moan and encourage him, he went harder.

Once warmed up, it turned out Ches could take a lot. Last night had been wonderful for many reasons, and there was no doubt Ches had loved every minute of it, but it was starting to look like that dirty mouth of hers wasn't all talk. As he pounded into her she cried out, tossed her hair, and clawed at the bed. Her lower body dropped, flush against the mattress, but her ass stayed right where it needed to be. The harder he fucked her, the more she just lost herself in it. Lucas was starting to pant harder but, in return, he was also pounding into her harder. Each time, that knot bumped against her entrance and threatened to push in.

Ches managed to get her hands underneath her again at some point, and pushed up, properly on her hands and knees once more. Her cries filled the cabin along with the sound of Lucas slamming into her. She tossed her hair and looked back over her shoulder, her slate-blue eyes luminous and glazed with pleasure. Another moan, and she dropped back down to her elbows, pushing her hips back into his thrust. Panting heavier, he growled and gave her a final frenetic burst of speed and force. When his peak hit, he pulled her back into him, fully and as hard as he dared before his orgasm hit.

The knot popped into Ches and she let out a surprised cry, but it wasn't a sound of pain, and it was followed by a loud moan as she shuddered hard and clenched. Lucas let go of Ches's hips and planted his hands to either side of her. Arching his back, he pressed her into the bed and let out a low, long howl that was not nearly as loud as last night. Spilling into her, he filled up her vessel, leaving nowhere for his cum to escape. His orgasm flowed through him and he moved to wrap his arms around her just before he fell onto his side on the bed.

This forced Ches into spooning with him, as they were very locked together and his form wasn't changing back. She was surrounded in soft, warm fur with his chest rising and falling with his deep breathing. Letting out a content groan, he licked along the back of her neck up to her ear.

"Mmm, did you learn your lesson?" he asked warmly.

Ches was shivering with sensation. "Lucas," she moaned, twisting against him. He felt her spasm around him. "What is...oh, fuck, that feels..."

He might not be thrusting anymore, but Ches was still filled and stretched in a way she'd never experienced before. And she was held in place, clearly still very sensitive. It made her a very tempting toy.

Nuzzling against her neck, he held her close and tight, throbbing inside her. "That's what you get for teasing a werewolf," he growled playfully. The arm underneath her just cradled her while his opposite hand squeezed and caressed her breasts. He was perfectly content lying with her and teasing her in return until either his body calmed or he changed back.

Ches let out a cry and turned her head toward his. "You're amazing," she whimpered, twisting against him. "I feel...I feel like you're going to break me, but also like...like I want to come again! I've never..." she trailed off.

"You're amazing too," he whispered, still licking softly on the back of her neck and playing with her breasts.

With another moan Ches's head dropped, exposing more of her neck to Lucas's tongue. However, she had requested another orgasm, and he knew of a pretty good way to do that. Lucas's long-fingered hand trailed down her stomach and over her pelvis to seek out and caress her clit. He felt her tighten around him again, then her back arched. Her voice soared through the cabin, at the very least Byron and Syla heard it, and she quaked in his arms before going soft.

"Lucas," she murmured, her voice warm and caressing. She sounded like she was drunk on sensation. "I love you."

Whimpering gently, he nuzzled against her. "I love you, too," he said softly. There was no way he couldn't.

Soft, happy sounds came out of Ches as Lucas continued to gently nuzzle and lick at her and they both calmed down. Lucas felt it again, that resonance he experienced with Ches reaching a perfect pitch. It was always there, always between them, but last night and today was the first time he felt, for a moment, like they were perfectly in tune with each other.

As he shifted back, he continued to nuzzle against her neck, but the licks were replaced by kisses. He wasn't sure what the resonance was, but it just reaffirmed that Ches was everything he hoped she would be. "Think we should shower, then head back?" he asked after a long, cuddly moment.

"Okay," Ches said in a soft, happy voice. She moved her hips, and

Lucas finally slid out of her, and her eyes opened in surprise. "Oh. Oh, I'm about to make a mess. Well, technically you made the mess."

"Excuse me," Lucas said with mock incredulity, "I believe we made the mess, thank you."

Ches pushed up off the bed and didn't quite stumble toward the bathroom. Laughing, he got up as well and moved to the shower, turning it on so the water would be nice and warm when Ches got in.

"So, just making sure," he called out playfully, now that things were a little more normal, "when you said you loved me, you meant it right? It wasn't because I'd fucked the shit out of you?"

Stepping up to the shower, Ches was pink cheeked and a little sheepish. "I mean...can't it be both?"

"It can absolutely be both," Lucas said with a smile, leaning in and lifting her chin gently to kiss her lips. "Now, we should do that whole wash-up thing before everyone thinks we ditched them."

"Does that mean you also meant it?" Ches asked, the smile leaving for a moment as she looked at him with vulnerable hope. "And it wasn't just because I said it first?"

"I absolutely meant it," he said, pulling her the rest of the way in. "I was pretty gone for you when we started dating, just afraid of what would happen when it all came out. But now, no reason to hold back. I love you."

Ches put her arms around him. "I love you, too!"

Growling, he grabbed her and started nibbling and kissing on her neck and shoulder while stating "I love you" between the attacks. She laughed, squirming and splashing as she did. They spent several minutes being ridiculous before finally getting around to washing. It was not an entirely innocent shower, though Ches didn't push. Still, Lucas had a shrewd idea that he was in for another few hours of relentless teasing.

Back in the main cabin for dinner, everyone looked pretty happy with life. Dinner was a meat-heavy stew with crusty bread. After dinner, everyone agreed to digest for a minute with more games, and Jack snagged Lucas while the others headed to the couch.

"You must have done something right, because she is glowing," Jack said, smirking.

"Think we both did something right," Lucas said with a grin as he stepped to the side with Jack. "I...feel something with her. And I'm not being sappy."

Jack arched an eyebrow. "I would guess you feel a lot of things with her, especially now that you're not backing down."

"True, true," he said with a chuckle, taking a sip of his drink.

"All right, clearly you're talking about something else." Jack got himself a beer. "So what do you mean?"

"It's hard to explain," he said, leaning against the wall. "Just, like, we mesh perfectly. Like everything is just right."

Jack considered for a moment. "Does it ever…feel like you're singing in harmony, but you're not actually singing? Like a howl, where everyone is united, but it's just you two?"

Nodding, he gestured with his beer. "Yeah, that. Exactly like that."

"Huh." Jack looked over at the couch, where Ches was destroying Trace in some anime fighting game. "I didn't know we could have that with humans."

"I mean, that's just the resonance, yeah?" Lucas said, arms crossed in thought. "Think I heard mom talking about it at some point. The whole 'when you know you'll know' thing she keeps saying whenever relationship talks pop up."

"You wouldn't like her if there wasn't resonance, but I'm guessing you never felt this way with Charlotte or Tara." Jack paused. "Correct me if I'm wrong."

"Oh no," he said with a chuckle. "I mean, Tara's a sweetheart but she's too…much, you know? And Charlotte. Well, she's Charlotte."

"So, sometimes, when we resonate with someone, we find a person, and it's… Like, imagine your personal resonance is a song." Jack took a drink and turned toward Lucas. "And you find people in your life whose song works with yours, the beat's the same, or the harmonies match up, and you can sing together and it's fine. When you don't resonate with someone, it's like your songs don't match. Maybe it's discordant, maybe they just don't work. But somewhere out in the world there's a person who is singing your song. Maybe not the same way, maybe in a different octave, maybe it's more techno and you're more rock, but it's still the same song in the same key."

"Then I guess we have a duet going," Lucas said, taking another drink. "All well and good, but are you going somewhere with this? Is this falling into that soulmate territory people are into? Because, yeah, I guess? Feels right."

"I fucking hate the word soulmate," Jack muttered. "Hallmark-channel bullshit. Look, I'm not saying that Ches is the only person in your life that will ever make you feel this way. I am saying that it's fucking rare, and finding someone else will be very hard. I…don't have it with Trace. But I did have it with Sean."

Sean was Jack's ex, and the breakup had been brutal. Sean had been named the alpha of his family and decided he wanted to have children. People had been scared for Jack for a while following the breakup. Lucas was one of the people who had spent nights at Jack's place to keep an eye on him.

"Yeah…that was rough," Lucas responded cautiously.

"I'm fine now, and what Trace and I have is good," Jack said, taking another drink. "I don't know that I'm everything he wants in life, but he's a great guy, and if he decides to move on, I know he'll do it in the kindest way possible. But that's not my point. My point is, this is a big deal, and I know you haven't been together that long, but you should be aware."

"I'll keep that in mind," Lucas said with a sigh. "Isn't every relationship a big deal? More so when a human is involved? She knows our secret now; that's a pretty big trust placed upon her, and if something comes from that, it's my fault."

"Yeah, good point," Jack said, turning back to look over at everyone again. "Guess you're screwed either way. Might as well stick with the fun screwing."

"Oh hush," Lucas said, rolling his eyes.

Jack laughed. "Oh, I gotta know, how the hell did you get her to scream like that?"

Taking another drink, he raised an eyebrow at Jack and smirked. "Trade secret."

"If you don't tell me, I'll just get it out of Trace later." Jack grinned.

"Then I guess you'll just have to get it from Trace later. Besides, it's not like it's information you could use anyway," Lucas chuckled.

"Coward. Have it your way, then." Jack said, and headed over to the couch.

"Thank you, I will," Lucas responded smarmily and followed.

Assuming the worst might happen anyway, Lucas cut out the middleman and simply stepped over the couch and slipped in behind Ches, pushing her forward and lifting her onto his lap. Ches shifted easily and wiggled back into place. Despite her threats, she was mostly behaving herself. She was very affectionate, though, more than before. He got a lot of small kisses and squeezes, and when it was his turn to play she just snuggled into him. He returned all he got—small nips on her neck or ear, plenty of full two-arm squeezes, nuzzling against her occasionally as she played. Lucas occasionally caught Syla, Trace, and even Byron looking over at them and smiling, happy that things had worked out.

After an hour or two, Byron got up to make some sort of fancy hot drink for everyone, and Jack declared that as soon as drinks were ready they'd head back into the pool.

"That's the best part," Lucas said with a grin. "Heavy snow, hot spring: perfect combination. Gonna make sure it stays hot, babe?" Leaning in, he nuzzled against Ches's neck.

Ches giggled. "I thought we weren't having sex in the pool? Wasn't that a declaration?"

"I meant by your very presence," Lucas tsked, patting Ches's thigh so she would get up.

"All we said was that you couldn't have sex in the pool if anyone else was in it," Jack said, getting up.

"You can have sex in the pool if I'm in it," Syla said, grinning. "I won't touch, but I'ma watch."

Glancing over at Syla, he sighed and narrowed his eyes. "Damn straight you're not touching," he growled, gesturing toward Ches. "Mine."

Syla's grin got bigger. "That's not a no."

Getting up and stretching, Ches looked thoughtful. "Not something I've done before," she mused. "Though you've already seen me naked—you really wanna watch Lucas fuck me?" She laughed.

Syla turned pink. "Kinda, yeah."

"You two are terrible," Lucas said with a shake of his head. "Besides, Syla, you're just saying that because I didn't get you photos of the lingerie she bought. Which we can't get photos of...because they need to be replaced." Grinning, he wasn't sure if he was proud of that statement or embarrassed.

Syla blinked and looked at Ches. "Really?"

Ches bit her lip and blushed, but nodded. "Yeah." She glanced over at Lucas, then back at Syla. "It was so fucking hot." Proud it was, then.

"Cocktails are almost done; go do your sex talk outside," Byron said, to which Syla and Ches giggled and headed toward the door. Laughing at Byron, Lucas gave him a wave and stepped outside with the girls.

Lucas and Ches headed back to their own cabin to strip down—no sense in getting their clothes cold or wet. She pinned her hair up again, less carefully than she had before, just in a messy bun to keep it out of the water. She looked over at Lucas and giggled.

"Fuck, I just want to climb all over you," she said, a tiny bit embarrassed. "I've been thirsty for you for months, and now that it's happening, I'm just… It's hard to think about anything else."

"Try to be mostly good while we're in the pool, then you've got me all night," Lucas chuckled, leaning in to kiss her softly. "I'm all yours. Whatever you got cooking in your head, I want to know about it."

"I should probably wait," Ches said with a grin, "so that we don't have to explain what I was talking about that got you so hard."

When they'd returned to the hotspring, Byron handed everyone a big mug of something that smelled like apples but had a cream top, and they climbed into the pool and settled in.

"To a great weekend," Jack said, lifting his mug.

"To an incredible weekend," Lucas responded, lifting his mug as well.

Everyone leaned forward or got up to clink with everyone else (except Jack, who made people come to him). The cocktail had an apple-cider base with spices and enough alcohol that Lucas definitely knew it was there even though he couldn't taste it under everything else.

"We should do this for New Year's or something," Ches said, looking around.

"Oh, we do," Byron said, cheerfully. "Though it gets, um…a little more interesting at New Year's." Syla snickered.

"Interesting?" Ches asked, curious. She looked over at Trace, who turned a little red.

Jack laughed. "So, there are…holidays specific to our kind. New Year's is a big deal—both western and lunar. Lunar is a bigger deal, technically, but that's more of a family event. December 31, though, is a night of… letting go of the past year. Our ancestors did this through communal meditation. Nowadays we get fucked up in the woods."

"You're welcome to join, if you don't mind a bunch of wers running around, pawing at things and begging for tummy rubs," Lucas laughed, taking a drink. "It's gotten a little out of hand sometimes. Heck, a couple of years ago Syla bought this costume, I don't even remember what it was, but it was supposed to go over her wer form."

"Oh, no," Syla groaned, "not this story."

"However," Lucas continued, undeterred, "she got so blitzed off of wolfsbane that she couldn't remember which form she was in and it just fell off." He started laughing. "But, because she couldn't remember, she thought she was still wearing it. So naked Syla is running around the woods screaming, and nearly got frostbite."

Everyone laughed, except Syla, who turned scarlet and growled at Lucas. "You are not supposed to tell people about that!" Agitated, Syla shifted, and Ches just stared at the other woman as Syla got a bit larger, grew dark-brown fur all over her body, and folded her arms over her chest.

"A sulking werewolf may be the most absurd thing I have witnessed in my short life," Ches said, wide eyed. Syla growled at her too and continued to sulk.

Byron snickered and moved over to Syla, petting her head. "She shifts a lot when she's embarrassed," Byron said, smiling. "We're all affected by different emotional triggers more than others. Anger is an obvious one, but most of us have something else that will push the change. I think you've discovered Lucas's."

"Oh yeah," Ches said, grinning a bit shamelessly. "So what do you all do for Lupercalia? Orgies and people snacks?"

Jack almost spit his drink and everyone else laughed. "No on both counts, and Lupercalia is not a thing," Trace said, patting Jack on the back as he coughed. "So, this is actually kind of an important part about dating one of us that you should know: younger single wer are pretty free with their affection. Like Syla and Byron. I'll admit, more than one mountain weekend was a fuck fest when most of us were still single. Pretty sure that's how Jack and I got together, actually."

"Yeah," Jack said, looking a little embarrassed, "yeah it was. But we all know each other, we're safe, and our drives go a lot harder than humans."

"But," Trace continued, "when you're with someone, when you're committed to someone, no one else smells right."

Blinking, Ches looked over at Lucas. "Smell?"

"Absolutely," Lucas said with a nod, nuzzling against Ches's neck again, "and you smell amazing. Have since I first met you. I originally thought you were one of us, and that was kinda the reason."

"Okay," Ches said with a small laugh. "Is smell important?"

"Oh, absolutely," Syla said, having calmed enough to shift back. "And you do smell amazing. But smell is really important. We can't be with someone who doesn't smell right. It's as important as how you look and who you are. In some ways it's more important than resonance."

Ches tipped her head to the side. "Resonance?"

"It's like a feeling you get when you're with someone intimately," Lucas answered, his hands caressing her thigh and tummy under the water. "Jack was very poetic in describing it to me earlier as a song you can feel that, when you're with someone you resonate with, feels like a perfect duet. Or remix? Cover? What was it again?"

Ches turned pink, and looked up at Lucas. "Like...being in tune? Like your hearts are beating in time?"

Jack sat up. "Yeah! Did you feel something?"

"I felt a lot of things," Ches murmured, the pink getting darker. "But...sometimes, when we're together, and especially the last couple days, it... I don't know how else to explain."

"See, I wasn't lying," he said to Jack, shrugging.

Jack glared at Lucas. "I didn't say you were. I said I was surprised that you could have that level of resonance with a human." Sighing, Jack looked back to Ches. "So yeah, resonance is important to us. There are levels to it, but we won't find someone attractive without it. You and Lucas...this is new territory for us. We've all heard about people in the families having relationships with humans, but no one we know. And it's usually skips."

Ches looked a little exasperated. "Skips?"

Trace put his hand on Jack's shoulder. "Not every wer-born child shifts. Sometimes it misses a generation. We call those people skips, because it skipped them. Look, let's stop dumping information on Ches. She and I can talk more later. She's already had her world flipped for the weekend, and she's being a trooper."

"It's true," Lucas laughed. "I'm pretty sure not even my parents have told me all of this. We can have 'the chat' later, as it were." Wrapping his arms around Ches, he just held her close again.

Pushing up, Ches moved into Lucas's lap. "The brain is full—please try again later."

"Yeah, sorry, Ches," Jack said, offering her a smile. He tipped back the rest of his drink and stood up. "I'm gonna head back in. Anyone up for a movie?"

"Yeah, I'm in," Trace said, also getting up. Byron and Syla nodded and also got up to head in.

"Can we stay out here for a little longer?" Ches asked quietly. "I could use a minute."

"Yeah, of course," Lucas said. Leaning back, he set his empty mug on the edge of the pool and looked over to everyone else. "We'll join you in a little bit. Think we need a moment to decompress."

"We'll put on something mindless and easy to hop in on," Jack said.

"Take your time."

After everyone filed in, Ches turned herself so that she was facing Lucas, straddling his lap. It was easy to do in the water. Lucas slid his hands over her hips and around her waist, pressing against her gently. It couldn't be helped, but he tried to remain focused.

"That thing Jack was talking about," Ches said, running her hands over his chest. "Do you feel it with me?"

"Stronger than with anyone else, Ches," he said. "And I'm not just saying that."

"I've never felt anything like it with anyone," Ches said a little shyly. "I thought...that maybe it was something I was imagining, because I was so infatuated with you. You're not my first serious relationship, but no one has ever...vibrated through me like you do." Reaching up, she combed her fingers through his hair and looked up at him. The moon was out, illuminating her face and eyes as she tipped her head back.

"It seems like you wouldn't have. It's not a thing for humans. But us," Lucas responded, pressing his forehead to hers, "we're just too good for each other." He kissed her gently. "Well, you're too good for me, but I'll be as good as I can be for you."

"Don't say that," she murmured as she kissed across his jaw. She slid her tongue up the side of his neck and bit softly at his earlobe. "You're so good. You're perfect for me. You're all I've wanted since I first called you ma bête."

"I'll keep it up, then," Lucas said softly.

His hands massaged her thighs as the warm water washed around them, the snow gently falling once more. Even with the others watching a movie in the cabin beyond, it felt like they were the only ones around for miles. It was so quiet except for the burbling of the hot spring and their own breath.

Ches's mouth continued to move teasingly over Lucas's skin, her tongue tracing his collar, her teeth grazing his shoulder. She dropped her hips again, pressing against him as she scattered licks and kisses across his chest. The entire time they were in the pool, Lucas had been touching or caressing her in some way, and therefore was mostly hard by the time she pressed against him. It would take very little to seal the deal. His hands went roaming, caressing over her thighs and sides, waist, and butt, up her back and into her hair. He was still thoughtful enough to not pull her buns out and threaten the coloring.

"I don't think I'll ever get enough of this," he murmured.

"Good," Ches replied, nuzzling at him. She shifted her hips, and slid a hand down his chest, reaching between them to position his cock at her entrance, and carefully eased herself down onto him. Water wasn't the best lubricant, but Ches was also excited and slick inside. It didn't take long before Lucas was buried in her pussy up to his knot.

As Lucas shifted and his legs bent, they caused them to lift just slightly, pressing Ches further into his lap. He whimpered in pleasure as he felt her wrap around him completely and returned his hands to her ass, squeezing it.

"Jack said we could fuck in the pool if no one else was around," Ches said breathily, that impish smile on her face again. "And if you...if you cum in me like you did last time, if we're...you know, stuck together, you can just carry me out of the pool and it won't make a mess."

"I've created a monster," Lucas growled, his hands starting to lift and drop her in slow, deep strokes.

Another giggle. "Am I a monster?" Ches nuzzled at him, sliding her arms around him as he controlled their pace. "Don't you want me to want you? To be wet and aching for you? To want you to grab me and fuck me and mark me and make me yours?"

"I absolutely do," he rumbled, still rolling her body against his. He'd never felt so engulfed in warmth and softness as having her body pressed against him with the spring water surrounding them. It was exquisite. He wanted to be tender, to be loving, to make this last as long as possible. However, he also wanted to take her deep, make her cry out for him, to fill every possible inch of her. Moaning, Ches nuzzled into him again. She tangled her fingers in his fur, arched her back to rub her body against his as he moved her up and down.

She tipped her head up and licked at the end of his muzzle. "I've spent weeks dreaming of this—your cock inside me. You gorgeous fucking beast!" His growl deepend and even though he only sped up a bit, he was pulling her down against him much harder, bumping her clit against his knot each time.

"Fuck, Ches," he rumbled as he nuzzled against the nape of her neck, teeth grazing against her skin. "You're amazing. You feel so fucking good." She moaned again, and he could just feel her nails grazing his skin through his fur. Then he heard a click by the main cabin door.

Lucas paused, teeth against Ches's shoulder as he glanced in the direction of the sound. Syla was standing on the other side of the door, looking surprised by also biting her lip. She didn't move, though. She was waiting to see if he would send her away.

Ches also looked over, and nuzzled into Lucas again. "She wants to see you fuck me," Ches panted, writhing against him. "Will you do it? Show her why you're my beast? Show her that I'm yours? Only yours. Fill me with your cum, bite me, show her who I belong to!"

With a snarl, Lucas stood up, still holding tight to Ches, and turned to face Syla. He didn't say anything—he didn't need to. He pulled Ches off of him just enough to turn her around, then leaned her back against his chest and grabbed her thighs firmly. Keeping her spread and supported, he started to slam her down onto his cock, pumping his hips up to meet her, making her entire body shudder with each thrust. He reached a hand around to cup one of Ches's heavy breasts and licked along the back of her neck, pressing his teeth carefully yet firmly around it. Ches cried out and grabbed Lucas's arms. She was soft and yielding against him, and didn't seem capable of talking anymore. Her cries accentuated each of his thrusts.

Syla reached down the front of her pants, leaning back against the door. Her other hand slid up under her shirt. She licked her lips but stayed where she was—no matter how much she might be attracted to Ches, Lucas knew she would not intrude on a bonded pair.

The shape of his legs were the perfect platform to bounce Ches's body on his shaft. With the force of his thrusts and pulling her down upon him, Lucas's knot was now stretching her—preparing her sex to take the full girth of it and hold him tight once it inflated. He could feel how wet she was, hear it with each thrust. Ches was dealing with his full wer stamina now. She'd done nothing but encourage it. Hell, she practically begged for it. This wouldn't end until she was a mess, fucked out of her mind and tethered to his cock.

Ches's grip on his arms tightened as he relentlessly pounded her. "Fuck," she gasped, "so perfect!"

The hand in Syla's pants was moving faster, and Syla was biting her lip not to make a sound. Ches had no such awareness, moaning loudly into the night. Lucas could feel her body giving against him. As soon as he was ready, she'd be able to take him.

With a surge of speed, Lucas pounded relentlessly into her, forcing her body down against him as he could feel himself swell with the ensuing orgasm. Growling, he slammed her down onto his cock, forcing the knot into her, as he pushed his hips up to meet her. Instead of a howl, there was a deep, rumbling, satisfied growl as he bit into her shoulder, holding her firmly in place with his maw and his arms. His shaft swelled and the knot ballooned inside her as a rush of cum flowed into her.

Ches's cry spiraled up, sharp and high. Syla's eyes grew wide in surprise, then rolled back as she came, sliding down against the door. Ches was mindless and panting. She hadn't come yet, but Lucas knew how easy it would be to make that happen. He squeezed one of her breasts firmly and slid his hand down her thigh to find her exposed clit. In this position, she was wide open and it would be easy to rub away whatever was holding her back. Honestly, it was surprising what a human woman could take. He had barely started to caress her when Ches started to squeeze against him. She didn't scream this time; her breath caught and she arched her back, taut and trembling as she came, then collapsed back against him, whimpering.

Lucas heard another click. When he looked up, Syla was gone. Ches didn't notice one way or the other.

Very carefully, Lucas removed his teeth and gently licked the marks he'd left. With a sizable amount of sensation he wasn't expecting, he slid Ches's leg up and around so she was facing him again, causing her to twist her clenching sex upon his shaft. It sent a shiver down his spine. He hugged her close to his body, and Ches clung to him, nuzzling into his chest as he carried her back to the cabin. They'd be stuck like this for a bit, and every shock of sensation caused a little more cum to flow into her.

"Ohhhhhh, wow," Ches moaned, not lifting her head, her voice a bit muffled by his fur. "I think you broke me. It was so good."

Carrying her to the shower, he continued licking the bite. "Maybe not enough," he teased. "You're still conscious." The bite was definitely going to be visible for a few days. Lucas hadn't pierced the skin, but Ches was going to have the oddest, largest hickey. Thank Luna it was a chilly autumn; high necks and scarves would be necessary.

Lucas got the water going. Once it was warm enough, he moved so her back was to the spray. He could hold her forever if he needed to.

As she felt the water, Ches giggled softly. "More water?" She lifted her head slowly, as if she might be a bit lightheaded, and smiled at him. "I kind of can't believe I told you to fuck me in front of Syla. I'm not sure I can be trusted when your cock's in me." She scrunched up her nose at him.

Leaning back so he could look at her face, he raised a brow ridge. "Oh, so it's my fault, is it?" Lucas asked, bucking his hips just a bit to test.

Ches moaned. "Such a beast. Lucas, I have never been fucked so good. When you're inside me, all I can think about is getting you to fuck me harder."

"I'm not sure how much harder I could fuck you," Lucas chuckled. "I was already afraid that I might hurt you. Just a bit, though—you were moaning a lot."

"Well," Ches said, turning pink, "um...it does hurt a little. Like, when you're really going. But that's kinda part of why it feels so overwhelming. I...I feel like I'm your toy, and you're going to use me until you break me, and that's...really hot." Ches was blushing really hard by the time she finished talking.

"Then I guess you really don't mind dating a wer after all then," Lucas said. The conversation was not helping; they might be together for another ten minutes or so, especially since he couldn't stop slowly moving his hips.

"So long as you don't get skittish again, no," Ches said, and stuck out her tongue.

"Didn't I just fuck the hell out of you in front of Syla?" he asked, stepping up and pressing her against the wall. She whimpered. "Pretty sure the time of skittishness is gone."

Ches's impish smile persisted. "I don't know, we all had a few drinks, and we're on vacation. Maybe you're going to get weird when we get back to town and you have to tell your other friends that you're railing a human."

Lucas just rolled his hips, flexing more than anything else, since he still couldn't move, and growled slightly. "It takes a lot more than a few drinks to get me to do stuff I wouldn't normally do," he said, running his tongue along her neck. "Railing you is bragging rights."

"But I'm so small," Ches said with a giggle, wiggling a little. "Not very impressive for such a big bad wolf."

Lucas whimpered slightly at her movements, but they were just teasing each other at this point. "Not too small," he said, placing both his hands on her breasts and squeezing them. His body kept her pressed against the shower wall. "You took all of the big bad wolf."

"I did," she said, turning a little pink again. "And it's fucking incredible. Though I miss kissing you. We'll have to make out for a while before bed once you calm down." Her smile got softer, less impish. More loving.

He leaned close and nuzzled against her neck. "Who knows, maybe if we do this enough I can start to control it," he said, giving her another soft lick. "Although, now that you've gone wet, do you think you could go back?"

"Ma bête, you had a monster in your pants even before you changed," Ches said with another giggle. "I lose nothing, and I gain kisses. I think the issue is more now that I've had you, I can't go back."

Lucas started to calm down. His hands wrapped around her as he pulled her off the wall, just hugging her close and keeping her up until the shift finished. "You're amazing and I love you," he muttered, tail swishing behind him before it disappeared. "I don't deserve you."

"Don't say that," Ches murmured. "You absolutely deserve me. Remember that whole resonance thing you were explaining to me? We're meant for each other." She kissed the side of his face. "I love you so much."

Pressing his forehead again, he hugged her close and breathed in her scent. Things had calmed now, as had her smell. It was relaxing and centering, and his shifting left them both naked and furless under the shower.

"One bright side," Lucas said, kissing her softly now that he had proper lips again, "you don't need to deal with the smell of wet fur."

Ches kissed him back. "Though speaking of, I'm done being wet. Let's get out of the shower. We can dry off, climb in bed, and kiss until we either fall asleep or decide to follow up the performance in the pool with something soft and slow."

"Yeah, all right. Everything's pruny," he chuckled and leaned over to give her a kiss while turning off the water.

Stepping out of the shower, he grabbed a bath sheet and opened it for Ches to step into. Ches accepted her towel and demanded more kisses. Lucas grinned and scattered her with all the kisses she could want. She dried off and braided her hair, then spent some time applying lotion to counter the extended time in hot water. Lucas, meanwhile, worked on his thick, shaggy mane. Once dry enough, bodies growing lethargic from the day's activities, they climbed into bed.

"My gorgeous beast," Ches murmured, her voice soft and adoring. She leaned in to kiss him, slow and soft. "I love you."

"And I love you," Lucas said gently. It was difficult not to get excited while doing this. She slid her body against his, snuggling into him, and she was so warm and soft. He settled in next to her. There was a small chance everyone was still watching movies, but by this point he was all too happy to just snuggle up against her and call it a night.

As they drifted off, he had that feeling again, that glowing joy that seemed to sing through him as she rested her head on his shoulder and wrapped her arm and a leg around him. And this was only the beginning.

Coming soon...

CHOSEN BY THE MOON

All her life, Saskia Sunborn has known she was a disappointment. Born on the Blood Moon in the dead of night, the auguries around her birth were ominous, and her mismatched eyes reminded everyone in her father's holdings of her strangeness. To make matters worse, she had been her father's last chance to have a son, and had failed in this most basic of tasks. As she aged, and turned into an attractive and voluptuous woman, she was locked away "for her own good." Throughout the town she became known as the Shame of the House of Sun.

In an attempt to teach Saskia her place, her parents sent her on a pilgrimage to the capitol in Raelholm, the city her father once defended, and where the grand Temple of Taern, God of the Sun, Arbiter of Justice, resides. For all their criticisms, however, Saskia isn't stupid. She knows an opportunity when she sees one. A chance to escape and never return. But something else is waiting for her in Raelholm. A destiny that her father couldn't keep at bay, one that will take her far from Raelholm and everything she's ever known.

ABOUT THE AUTHORS

Clea Salar (she/her) is a bi, sassy freelance writer who spends most of her days glaring at her computer in between bouts of actually writing. She's a specialist in all things fantastic, with an impressive resume that includes such skills as spending recess and lunch in the library reading folklore and mythology books all through school, a familiarity with a variety of role-playing games, and regular attendance at every convention and Renaissance festival within driving distance. Clea loves bubble tea, tiny desserts, and the Oxford comma.

Tallis Salar (he/him) is a Jack of All (IT) Trades who would rather be diving, at least until "space viking" becomes a viable career path. He loves a good sci-fi, and is happy to explain why "Aliens" is the greatest film ever made. His creative background includes a staggering number of role-playing games, particularly as the GM. Tallis can be bought with video games, sour candies, and frozen drinks (this is a joke, he can't actually be bought, but he welcomes you to try).